PERFECT FLING

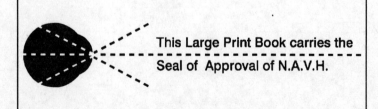

This Large Print Book carries the
Seal of Approval of N.A.V.H.

PERFECT FLING

CARLY PHILLIPS

WHEELER PUBLISHING
A part of Gale, Cengage Learning

GALE
CENGAGE Learning®

Detroit • New York • San Francisco • New Haven, Conn • Waterville, Maine • London

 GALE
CENGAGE Learning®

LIBRARY OF CONGRESS CATALOGING-IN-PUBLICATION DATA

Phillips, Carly.
    Perfect Fling / By Carly Phillips. — Large Print edition.
        pages cm. — (Serendipity's Finest Series) (Wheeler Publishing, a part of Gale, Cengage Learning.)
        ISBN 978-1-4104-6377-7 (hardcover) — ISBN 1-4104-6377-X (hardcover) 1. Large type books. I. Title.
    PS3616.H454 P465
    813'.6—dc23   2013031370

Published in 2013 by arrangement with The Berkley Publishing Group, a member of Penguin Group (USA) LLC, a Penguin Random House Company

Printed in the United States of America
1 2 3 4 5 6 7 17 16 15 14 13

In loving memory of my father, Leonard Weinberg (August 6, 1941–October 10, 2012), the best man I — or anyone who met him — ever knew. Daddy, I hope I appreciated you while you were here. I know you are with me now that you are gone. I just need time to feel you. This book is dedicated to you — for believing in me, for loving me, for somehow convincing me I can do anything I set my mind to. At some point I began to believe you . . . And look at me now. It's all because of you. I love you and I miss you more than words can say.

ONE

Erin Marsden had always been Serendipity's good girl. As assistant district attorney in the small upstate New York town, only daughter of the ex–police chief, youngest sibling of two overprotective brothers (both cops, one of whom was the current police chief), Erin always lived up to expectations. She'd never made a misstep, more afraid of disappointing her family than of stepping out of the stereotypical role she'd always, always fulfilled.

Until last night.

She blinked and took stock of her surroundings: a strange bed, walls she didn't recognize, and a warm, nude male body beside her very naked one.

Cole Sanders.

She stared at his too-long mess of dark hair and the muscles in his upper back and thought about the way her body ached in all the right places, and she shivered. No doubt about it, when she finally stepped out of the mold she'd created, she'd not only done a one-eighty but made the most un-good-girl move she could think of. A one-night stand.

A *one-night stand.*

The thought made her giddy and also slightly nauseous as she silently traced the path that had led her here. She'd started yesterday at her brother Mike's wedding to one of Erin's closest friends, Cara Hartley, now Marsden. Erin had been surrounded by friends, family, and happy, loving couples everywhere she looked, making her the odd woman out. Not wanting to go home alone just yet, she'd stopped by Joe's Bar. *Misstep number one.*

She'd let Cole Sanders, the man for whom she'd had an unrequited crush as a young teenage girl, interrupt her dance with an old friend. *Misstep number two.*

He'd pulled her close against his hard body. She'd looked into his dark, almost navy eyes and seen a world-weariness that tore at her heart, then acknowledged the sexual tension they'd both ignored since his return. *Misstep number three.*

And then she'd gone for the gold, agreeing to join him upstairs in his room over the bar for an all-night session of marathon sex.

But she couldn't label that *misstep number four,* because sex with Cole had been phenomenal. She didn't know two people could generate such heat. It had been that fantastic. In fact, Erin thought, she'd stretch and purr in contentment right now if she weren't afraid of waking the man snoring lightly beside her.

Although their parents were good friends, Erin didn't know Cole well. Nobody did, not anymore. Not even her brother Mike, who had been one of his closest pals, though Mike seemed concerned since Cole's return. Cole's father had been her dad's deputy chief of police until last year when Jed retired, but Jed Sanders never spoke of his son.

According to Mike, Cole had dropped out of the police academy mere days before his graduation. What Cole did after that was anybody's guess, but rumors ran crazy in their small town. Some said Cole had gotten involved in organized crime in Manhattan, others claimed he ran drug and prostitution rings. Having grown up around Cole, even if she had kept her distance from the rough-and-tumble bad boy he'd been, Erin couldn't bring herself to believe he'd gone so wrong.

Call her naive, but she'd always seen

something deeper in Cole, something good, even when he'd clashed with his tough-as-nails father. Which didn't mean she wouldn't make her escape as cleanly as possible.

What Erin didn't know about awkward morning-afters could fill a book. The quiet, tepid affairs in her past always ended the same way, with a polite *It's not you, it's me* before she walked away. She'd never had to slip out of a man's bed undetected before.

She snuck one last glance at his broad shoulders, rising and falling with every breath he took. His arm muscles, sculpted from hard work and marked by ink, caused her to shiver anew.

Breathe, she silently ordered herself.

Think, she commanded next. Her clothes were scattered around the bedroom, if she called her bridesmaid's dress clothing to sneak out in. With a last look at the man who'd made the earth move for her last night, Erin eased out from beneath the warm comforter and rose, searching for her dress. She bent over, stark naked, mortified that her butt was in the air as she grabbed for her clothes.

"I didn't peg you as the type to sneak out," Cole said in a lazy, masculine drawl.

She snagged her dress from the floor and

turned to face him, hugging the light lavender fabric against herself for protection, suddenly feeling every bit the good girl she'd been a mere twenty-four hours ago.

"I've already seen every inch," he reminded her, his heavy-lidded gaze never leaving hers.

She flushed. "What type did you peg me for?" she asked, ignoring the humiliating part of his comment.

He eased up against the headboard, sexy, tousled, and too handsome. One look had her wanting to crawl back into bed with him. That wasn't happening for a number of reasons, the first being that a one-night stand had a shelf life, and she'd used up hers. Second, to her extreme disappointment, he wasn't asking. And third, bad-girl Erin was an aberration. This morning, with no champagne in her system, respectable Erin had returned, more's the pity.

He stretched his hands behind his head and leaned back, studying her. The sheet slipped below his navel and it took all her strength not to stare at his flat abdomen and the tented sheet.

"You were pretty gutsy last night, so I wouldn't have figured you'd take the coward's way out." He cocked an eyebrow, his expression serious.

Did the man never smile? "And I wouldn't have thought you were the type who'd want a woman to stick around . . . *after.*"

Which made her wonder why he hadn't let her check out unnoticed, even if he had been awake. It would have spared them both the awkwardness of . . . this. Then again, they'd have to play this conversation out sometime. *Might as well get it over with,* she thought.

Then his words came back to her. "I was gutsy?" She straightened her shoulders a bit at that.

Erin was tough with her brothers and at work, where she had to be in order to keep up with her boss and hold her own against defense attorneys and their clients. But gutsy with men? That was a first, and she kind of liked hearing it.

"I left the bar with you. That took nerve," she said, almost pleased with herself.

He eyed her without cracking a grin, but she'd swear she saw a hint of amusement in his eyes. Before he banked it, that is.

"I meant you were gutsy in bed."

His words, along with the deep rumble of approval in his tone, warmed her inside and out, and the heat of a blush rose to her cheeks.

"Thank you," she said, immediately horrified. Had she really just said that?

That earned her a sexy grin she'd never forget.

"Back to my original point. We go way back. So no, I didn't expect you to sneak out," he said. "Regrets?" he asked, surprising her with both the question and the suddenly defensive edge to his voice.

She immediately shook her head. "None." It saddened her that he'd think she'd have them.

Not that it surprised her. No one in town had welcomed him with open arms, and if anyone found out about last night, they'd think she'd lost her mind. And if her brothers discovered her secret . . . She refused to go there. If regret hadn't kicked in yet, she doubted it would. And she wouldn't want him to think she was embarrassed that she'd slept with him.

"You surprise me," he admitted, studying her intently. "And I didn't think there was much left in this world that could."

He sounded as if he'd seen and done too much in his lifetime. A part of her wanted to reach out and soothe his hidden pain. But before she could dissect her thoughts or, heaven forbid, act on them, he spoke.

"But your instincts about me were right on. I'm not much for long, drawn-out

13

morning-afters."

Disappointment stabbed her in the heart, and *that* was too dangerous to even contemplate for long. "Glad to know I'm still on my game," she said, forcing flippancy when she felt anything but.

Now that it was time to say good-bye, it wasn't just awkward; it hurt a little more than she'd imagined it would. Which was what she got for thinking she could handle a one-night stand with a guy she'd always had somewhat of a thing for. No matter how young she'd been at the time.

"Since it was just a one-night stand, you won't have to worry about a repeat performance." She tossed the words as flippantly as she could manage.

"Pity," he murmured.

She jerked in surprise.

Just as she was wondering if she had the nerve to ask him to turn around so she could get dressed, he flipped the covers off himself and rose from the bed — stark, gloriously naked.

All thoughts fled from her brain. She tried to swallow and choked instead, ending up with another blush as she continued to cough until the spasm passed.

"And that just confirms why it has to be one night only," he muttered low, obviously more to himself than to her.

Erin hated puzzles and enigmas. "What does that mean?" she asked.

"Erin, honey, in a world where nothing and no one is what they seem, you're real. And that makes you dangerous."

"More riddles," she told him.

He ignored her. Strolling over to the dresser, he opened a drawer and tossed her a pair of drawstring sweats and a faded gray T-shirt. "Here. You'll be more comfortable — not to mention less conspicuous — leaving in these."

She swallowed hard. "Thank you."

He gestured to the open door in the corner. "Bathroom's there. Towels for the shower are in one of the drawers. Take your time," he said, and padded toward the small kitchen not far away in this small apartment. Nude. Clearly he was a man comfortable in his own skin.

She shook her head, pushing away all thoughts unconnected to the rush to shower, dress, and leave. Any emotions or lingering feelings could wait until she was alone. At which point she'd do her customary internal summarizing of events and tuck this episode away in her memory banks for safekeeping, never to be revisited again — except on long, lonely nights when it was just her and her vibrator. Because everything inside her knew, despite his brush-off and surly attitude this morning, Cole had set the bar way too high for any man who came after him.

And Erin had already set it pretty damned high on her own.

Three Months Later . . .

If this case didn't end soon, Erin would either pass out on the desk in front of the judge, the jury, and the entire courtroom or she'd throw up on her brand-new shoes. It was a toss-up which would happen first. Judge White, whose hair matched his name, droned on with jury instructions, while for Erin, the next twenty minutes passed in a blur of nausea and exhaustion. Finally she heard the blessed sound of the gavel adjourning them for the day and she dropped her head to the table with a thud.

"Don't worry, I took notes on everything the judge said and there wasn't anything we didn't anticipate or I'd have objected," Trina Lewis, Erin's second chair for this trial, assured her.

"Thanks," Erin mumbled into the desk.

"Come on. Let's get you out of here. Bathroom before we go home?"

Erin forced her head up. "Yeah. Please."

Trina had already gathered Erin's things and put them into her bag and together they walked out of the courtroom. To her relief, most everyone had already left, so she didn't need to deal with people.

"Erin, umm, can I talk to you?" Trina asked as she pushed open the door to the ladies' room and they stepped inside.

"Of course."

Trina had been working in the D.A.'s office for the last two years and she was close to Erin's age, and as the only two female lawyers, she and Erin had become friends. There was no professional jealousy between them — Trina was Erin's escape from the male posturing when she needed one, and vice versa. Along with Macy Donovan, she made up the threesome for their nights at Joe's, trips to the movies, and girls' nights at home, which had also included Alexa Collins prior to the other woman's move to Texas.

Before speaking, Trina checked underneath the stall doors to make sure they were empty. Ever since Lyle Gordon, the lazy bastard who just happened to be the defense attorney on their current case, had posted his paralegal in here to overhear anything that could help him win, Erin and Trina were extra careful about where they spoke and in front of whom.

"All clear," Trina said.

"What's up?" Erin turned on the faucet and splashed cold water on her face.

"Don't you think this is the longest stomach virus in the history of the world?" Trina ripped a paper towel from the dispenser and handed it to Erin.

"It's getting better," Erin lied.

"No, it's not. You've been sick for weeks."

Erin didn't argue. She'd run the gamut, from thinking she had food poisoning, to the flu, to a long-lasting virus.

"You've missed more mornings of work and left early more times than in all the years I've known you."

Erin shot Trina a wry glance. "That's a whole two years." But she got the point. Even her boss, Evan Carmichael, had begun to question her absences and illness with concern, and Evan rarely noticed anything . . . except Evan.

"Anyway, while you were sipping tea in the hallway during lunch, I ran out to the pharmacy and bought you this." Trina held out a brown paper bag.

Erin narrowed her gaze, cautiously accepting the bag. "What's in it?" She didn't wait for Trina to answer, peeking instead. "A pregnancy test?" Erin shrieked before slapping her hand over her own mouth.

True, she hadn't had her period, but she'd attributed the lack thereof to work-related stress. Not once had she connected her illness to being pregnant.

"Hey, it's possible," Trina said.

"Are you kidding me? We've been working twenty-four seven for I don't know how long. I can't remember the last time I used my battery-operated friend, never mind had a real man."

"Liar," Trina said for the second time.

Erin scowled at her friend. They both knew she remembered the exact last time she'd had sex, and Erin recalled every perfect, muscular inch of Cole Sanders and their night together.

Their *safe* night. He'd used protection each time, and there'd been many. Besides, what were the chances the one and only time she'd stepped outside her comfort zone, something life-altering had actually happened? Fate wouldn't do that to her after all her well-behaved years. Would it?

Erin regretted having shared vague details with her two friends, because one of them now stood next to her, pointing to the offending test box that every woman on the planet recognized.

"Take it," Trina ordered.

"I can't be pregnant." Erin's stomach revolted at the very thought, and every nerve in her body shouted in denial.

"Good. Then prove me wrong, and I'll take you to the doctor to find out why you've been nauseous for almost a month straight." Trina pinned her with a gaze that had potential defendants shaking and crying for mommy.

"Fine." Erin grabbed the box and headed for the private stall. Her hands shook so badly she was barely able to read, let alone follow the instructions, but a few minutes later, she and Trina were waiting in uncomfortable silence for the requisite pink or blue line.

As the second hand of her watch ticked slowly by, Erin thought about Cole. He'd deliberately steered clear of her in the time since their night together. When she'd see him at Cuppa Café, he'd nod his head and walk out the door.

The other day, while at Joe's on Ladies' Night, fighting against this ongoing nausea, a strange impulse had her approaching him. She'd attempted friendly conversation, ignoring the flutters in her stomach caused by being near him and his delicious masculine scent. With a long line of people waiting for drinks, he'd had no choice but to

20

indulge her.

She'd even made him laugh once or twice, giving rise to a stupid flurry of hope . . . that what? Erin refused to go there, which was smart, considering that as soon as his beer was served, he'd grabbed the bottle, treated her to that elusive nod, and disappeared. Cole made it clear that one night meant just that. They weren't even destined to be friends. Her stomach cramped at the reminder.

She couldn't pretend his indifference didn't hurt, and she wished he'd leave their small town so he wouldn't be a permanent reminder of her one step outside the lines. She *couldn't* be pregnant, and not with his baby. She couldn't think of a worse, more awkward scenario, and her stomach lurched at the possibility.

"Ding!" Trina's too-cheerful voice shook Erin out of her painful thoughts.

"You look." She wrapped both arms around herself, aware she was shaking.

Trina extended her hand, and Erin gratefully accepted her friend's support. She held her breath, her heart pounding so hard in her chest she could swear she heard the sound in her ears, while at this point she couldn't tell if the lump in her throat was from nausea or panic.

21

"Well?" Erin asked, unable to stand the silence or the suspense.

"It's positive," Trina whispered, no longer feigning upbeat excitement.

Erin let out a sound she didn't recognize and ran for the nearest stall, unable to contain the nausea she'd been holding at bay.

Two

Cole woke up to the sun shining through the window in his small apartment over Joe's Bar. As he did every morning since his return home from his last deep-undercover assignment, he catalogued his state of mind and concluded that today was no different than any other.

Yep, status quo in his world.

He took a hot shower, dressed, and headed downstairs to the coffee shop where every morning, Cole picked up his much-needed jolt of caffeine, ignoring the fact that most people in town gave him a wide berth. Most, not all — and *not all* included the owner of Cuppa Café, Trisha. Much like her bar-owning brother, Joe, Trisha could listen to anyone's tales of woe. Unlike Joe, she tried to use her charming personality to chitchat him into revealing something about where he'd been the last year and why he hadn't come around before now. When her well-meaning prying failed, she tried to get him to agree to let her set him up on a date with one of her friends. That wasn't happening either.

Cole was back in his hometown on standard R and R after a deep-undercover assignment. Usually he and one of his fellow agents did some traveling or he crashed at one of the guys' cabins in Montana, but Cole hadn't been back to Serendipity in a while. Much as it pained him to admit it, he'd missed the place where he'd grown up, if not all the people.

So here he was, back in good old Serendipity, where he had some family he liked, some he didn't, and a job to return to soon enough. At least he loved his job. Cole liked knowing he was taking down the scum of the earth, never mind that his father was convinced he was just like them. Jed Sanders hadn't approved of his son long before he'd gone into undercover work. He wasn't a replica of the old man and never would be. He was used to being a disappointment, but he couldn't deny the constant digs got to him, which was why he'd avoided coming home until now.

Cole figured the last job had gotten to him more than usual if he was back to thinking about Jed's opinion of him. He tried to avoid looking back on his childhood, taking stock, and learning that just maybe his father had a point.

His cell rang and he picked it up on the first ring. "Hey," he said to his cousin, Nick Mancini.

"Sorry to tell you, but we're not working today. Fire inspector's coming by, so everything's on hold."

Since his return, Cole had been working construction for Nick's company, and Cole appreciated knowing he'd always have a place with his cousin when he needed one. Working for Nick's dad had always been a way to stay out of the house and keep his father off his back. Too bad Cole hadn't been smart enough to work more and stay out of trouble, but he couldn't change the past. And since it had led his mother to take them both away from Jed and out of Serendipity, maybe his juvenile idiocy hadn't been such a bad thing. No matter what his father thought . . . or blamed him for.

"No problem," Cole said. "Any other sites you can use a hand on?"

Silence followed and Cole knew exactly what his cousin wasn't saying. Nick had already informed him that a couple of clients preferred that Cole wasn't on the crew who worked on their homes. As if he'd

25

steal from anyone, but old neighbors? Friends? Jeez. Much as he hated it, Cole had to admit they had good reason to be suspicious, and nothing he could do or say would dispel their mistrust. Undercover work meant he had to keep a low profile and live with the consequences.

"Don't worry about it. Call me when you need me again," Cole said, letting his cousin off the hook.

"My mother mentioned Uncle Jed needs some help around the house," Nick said. "I can handle it over the weekend if you want."

Nick's mother was Cole's mother's sister. Aunt Gloria had helped Cole's mom when she needed it most, giving her money to leave Jed, and Cole loved her for it. Nick was like his mom, giving and always there.

Much as he appreciated the offer, Cole didn't need Nick handling Jed's crap for him. "You spend the weekend with your pretty wife," he said of Kate Andrews, whom Nick had finally married a few months ago, a wedding Cole had missed because of work. It had been one of the few times he resented the job.

Because undercover defined him. It wasn't just what he did; it was who he was. He didn't have a real life: friends, habits, schedule, routine. He had his work, and his downtime before going back under.

"I don't mind. I'll get in and out with no shitstorm. You won't."

"Thanks, but as long as I'm in town, I'll pick up the slack," he told his cousin.

Nick's groan echoed through the phone. "No reason for you to deal with the old man."

"He's my father. I'm not going to let others do his shit for me, but thanks."

Nick cleared his throat. "Fine. Come hang out over the weekend?"

"We'll see." They both knew he wouldn't show. But Nick still asked, and Cole still gave him his standard answer.

He said good-bye, grabbed his coffee, and walked out of the shop. As much as Cole liked his cousin, family wasn't part of his makeup. He hadn't had a strong unit as a kid, at least until his mother married Brody Williams, but by then Cole had been almost seventeen, self-reliant, self-contained, and basically on his own. He'd taught himself not to want what he couldn't have. That mind-set served him well in his line of work, and he didn't see any reason to change now.

He stepped onto the curb as he caught sight of two women crossing Main Street. For a split second, he thought he saw Erin, then realized he was seeing what his subconscious wanted to see. The woman with reddish hair wasn't Erin, but the thought of her had been firmly implanted in his brain.

The first time he'd run into her after they'd slept together, he'd been abrupt. Curt. He'd wanted to make sure she knew he wasn't looking for her happy smile, flushed cheeks, or warm wave hello. Even if she had been the only good thing about his return home so far. That lack of interaction continued when they saw each other, and though he hated it, he understood keeping her at a distance was better than encouraging any thoughts she might have of a *them.* Because Erin was the kind of woman who would both want and deserve all the things small-town life entailed. Things Cole could never give her.

That changed a couple of days ago when, cheery smile on her face, Erin saw him at Joe's. She walked over and made polite small talk, which he managed to survive despite the scent of her perfume reminding him of their explosive night together in bed. It had taken fucking weeks for the arousing smell to dissipate enough to let him sleep in peace without those memories keeping him constantly hard and wanting her.

Since his beer hadn't been served, he'd had no choice but to wait. Talk. Let her put her soft hand on his arm, which brought back memories of those talented fingers cupping other places on his body.

As soon as Joe slid his drink across the bar, Cole had cut Erin off and bolted, getting as far away from her as he possibly could, heading upstairs immediately. She might think he was a bastard, and the hurt look on her face made him feel like one, but she didn't need the aggravation that came with being associated with Cole Sanders or the lifestyle he lived.

Even if she did tempt him with her good-girl persona, her creamy, soft skin, and the combustible chemistry that had taken him off guard. Not to mention the light laughter that warmed his chilled, dark soul.

"Enough," he muttered. Gritting his teeth, he headed to his old Mustang for the drive to his father's place.

Heaven help him.

He wondered what kind of mood he'd find his father in today.

After Cole and his mother left, his parents had divorced, just another one of the things for which Jed blamed his no-good son. Though his mother had remarried a good man, Jed remained alone and miserable. Cole normally stayed away, but his father was getting older, and as long as Cole was

29

in town, he'd do what he could to help, whether the other man wanted him there or not.

Cole pulled up in front of the house where he grew up, taking it in with a critical eye. Never mind the invisible loose floorboard over which Jed had tripped and broken his arm — the paint was peeling, the windows needed cleaning, and if they didn't get the roof fixed by next winter, his father would have his hands full with trouble.

For now, however, he'd focus on the smaller jobs, and if Jed was in a decent mood, Cole would try talking to him about moving into a condo that was smaller and easier to take care of, and where the maintenance was covered. His father had bitten his head off the first time he'd made the suggestion.

Cole walked up the driveway, surprised to see a sporty royal blue Jeep parked in front of the garage. He knew who owned that car and muttered a curse. For as much as he'd tried avoiding her in person and thoughts of her in his mind, it appeared luck wasn't on his side.

Erin put the two casseroles her mother had made for Jed into his freezer, and the other she placed on a shelf in his refrigerator.

Since Jed had been her father's right-hand man as long as Erin's dad had been police chief, her parents treated him like family. So before going on her monthlong Alaskan cruise vacation, Ella had cooked up meals to help him out while his arm was in a cast, and had asked Erin to take over her job of making sure Jed had a stocked freezer while they were away.

It was hard for men like Jed and Erin's father to accept illness or age gracefully. Erin's dad was in remission from lymphoma, hence her parents' decision to make the most of the years they had left. Jed's heart attack last year, his high blood pressure, and now his broken arm frustrated the hell out of him. He'd always been around when she was growing up, at both the house and of course the station, so helping him out wasn't a hardship.

Or it hadn't been when she'd agreed to do it. Now that she was pregnant with his son's child, she wasn't at all comfortable here.

She turned to Jed to go over the cooking instructions. "So all you need to do is heat the oven to 350 and put this in for about thirty minutes. Or you can cut pieces and microwave them individually. Got it?" Erin asked, turning as she closed the refrigerator door.

"You know I appreciate this, but I could have just ordered from The Family Restaurant." Jed sat at the kitchen table, drinking his morning coffee, a cast on one arm.

"And you know my mother wouldn't let anyone she cares about have to make do with takeout. Who would watch your salt intake?" she asked lightly.

"I'm taking those pills, which keep my blood pressure down, so I don't see why I can't eat whatever I want," he muttered with a frown, which did nothing to detract from his distinguished looks.

He had a full head of silver hair, his features masculine and well-defined. Cole definitely resembled his dad.

Erin shook her head, knowing better than to let her mind go there. "That's an argument for another day. I need to get to work."

"Is he giving you a hard time?" a familiar male voice asked.

Erin started at Cole's voice. "I didn't hear you come in," she said, her heart now racing at the sight of him.

"Came through the back door."

"Bastard still has a key," Jed muttered. "What the hell do you want?" he asked Cole.

Erin cringed, taken aback by the anger in Jed's tone and the way he treated his son. She hadn't been in the same room with them together since she was a child. All she remembered was Cole, the wild boy, drinking, getting suspended, and causing trouble, and her parents talking about Jed's threats to send Cole to military school. But surely all that was in the past? She narrowed her gaze.

"Morning to you too, Dad." Cole strode into the small kitchen, ignoring his father's words.

He leaned against the counter, dominating the room by sheer virtue of his presence. He was almost six feet tall, pure muscle and all male, and the small room shrank in comparison.

"So what are you doing here?" Cole asked her, those gorgeous ink-colored eyes penetrating her with his intent stare.

"My mom asked me to bring food over for Jed while she and my dad are out of town." And since she'd done just that, it was time to beat a hasty retreat. She grabbed her purse from the counter and her car keys, which she'd put alongside it. "I should be going."

"Don't rush off on his account," Jed said.

Erin tried not to wince.

Ignoring his father, Cole pinned her with his steady gaze, and she swallowed hard, resisting the urge to smooth her hair or look uncomfortable.

She didn't look her best. Morning sickness struck at odd times. She wasn't sleeping well and, of course, there was the anxiety over being pregnant eating at her. Carrying this burden alone wasn't smart, but she didn't know who she could turn to who wouldn't slip and inform her parents, her brothers, or worse, Cole himself. Erin wasn't in top form and she didn't want Cole looking at her too deeply and suspecting something was wrong. It was bad enough she'd have to deal with him eventually.

She clutched her car keys more tightly. "I've got to get to work."

"Driving off women now too, son?" Jed asked Cole, no hint of humor or joking in his tone.

Oh my God, enough already, Erin thought, dying to speak up but certain neither man would appreciate her interfering. Still, she couldn't help but glare at Jed, letting him know in no uncertain terms his comments were uncalled for. Whatever the difficulties between father and son, they deserved to remain private.

Erin didn't miss the deliberate way Cole

34

straightened his shoulders, as if he were bracing himself so the insults would bounce off him. But if the set of his jaw was any indication, his father's words clearly hit home. Worse, the ruddy flush in his cheeks told Erin it was as embarrassing for him as it was for her.

Which meant she'd make her escape before things became any more awkward between the Sanders men. She said another good-bye, and left the two wary men alone.

"Way to go," Jed said to Cole after Erin left the house. "You drove the lady off."

"You did that all by yourself, Dad." And though Cole was used to his father's attitude and was even proud of the way he'd ignored the obnoxious comments, it was clear he'd made Erin uncomfortable.

"You heard her. She wasn't itching to leave until you showed up."

Cole clenched his hands into fists. "Do we really need to do this? Do you have that list of things I can fix around here?"

"What? Did your cousin get smart and decide he didn't want to keep a no-good SOB like you around his respectable customers?"

Even with Erin gone, Cole didn't plan on engaging his father. Instead he pushed off the counter and headed for the front door. His tools were in the truck and at least he could get started on fixing the front step. Once outside, he realized Erin's car was still in the driveway.

Engine running, she sat in the driver's seat, arms on the steering wheel, head resting on her arms. Getting up close and personal with her was the last thing he wanted to do, but he couldn't leave her alone until he found out what was wrong.

He knocked on the window.

She jumped, startled, before lowering the window so he could lean closer.

"You okay?" he asked, though as he studied her, he realized she wasn't. Her skin was pale, and dark circles he hadn't noticed before shadowed her eyes.

"I just . . . got a little dizzy, but I'm fine now." She brushed her hair out of her eyes with shaking hands.

A flush of pink stained her cheeks and a hint of what looked like panic flared in her expression. Cole frowned.

"I'm going now." She started to buckle up.

"Uh-uh." Before she could put the car in gear, he opened the door.

"What are you doing?" she asked, her voice rising.

"When did you eat last?"

She shifted her gaze away from his.

"I'll rephrase. Did you have breakfast this morning?"

She might not want to look at him, but his body prevented her from closing the car door. If she wanted a battle of wills, he felt certain he'd win.

"No," she said at last.

"Mind if I ask why?"

"Mind if I ask why you care?" she shot back.

He couldn't help but grin. Even sick she had spunk. "Because I'm not about to let you drive off while you're feeling dizzy. Come back inside and I'll get you something to eat."

"That's nice of you, but no thanks. I have a breakfast bar in my bag." She riffled through her purse and held one up in triumph. "See?"

He nodded. "Good. Why didn't you eat it before you came over?"

"I wasn't feeling great when I woke up. Look, I'm going to be late for work. I have to go."

"Not until you eat and I know you won't pass out or swerve off the road."

She rolled her eyes, then peeled down the wrapper and took a bite. He watched her jaw work as she chewed, knowing he was making her uncomfortable and unable to stop staring anyway.

"You look tired. Are you sure you're getting enough sleep?"

She choked on a piece of her food. "What is with the third degree this morning?"

He didn't have a clue. He just knew something was off about her and he was concerned. Unlike him? Yeah. He didn't need another woman to worry about letting down, like he had Victoria, Vincent Maroni's wife.

Shaking his last case away, he focused on Erin as she finished the breakfast bar, then pulled out a bottle of water and drank a healthy amount. "There. I feel all better."

He didn't feel better, nor did he believe her, but whatever. "Good. Do you feel well enough to drive?"

She nodded. "Yes. Thank you," she said, eyeing him as if trying to see beneath his skin.

She wouldn't find much there; that he knew.

"Okay then. Take care." He patted the top of the car with his hand.

"You too." She paused. "Umm, Cole? Don't pay any attention to your father. He's just grumpy because of his arm."

"No he's not. He's Jed, expressing his low opinion of me, same as always." The minute the honest words escaped he could have bitten his tongue, mostly because he didn't want her pity.

But a glance at her narrowed eyes and tight expression showed anger, not sympathy. "He's wrong, then."

She wasn't defending Jed; she was sticking up for him. Warmth flooded his chest, but he ruthlessly squashed the good, clean feeling he wasn't used to experiencing. He didn't need her on his side any more than he wanted her to like him. He couldn't do anything but hurt her sweet-girl reputation. He couldn't do anything but hurt *her.*

"Go to work," he said gruffly, ignoring the flash of disappointment in her eyes at his response.

And though he wanted to keep her at arm's length, actually accomplishing his goal didn't make him feel like he'd done her the favor he'd intended.

After finishing up the porch and fixing a drawer in the kitchen he had noticed was falling off the hinge, Cole decided enough was enough. If he was going to live in this town, he needed more than his own company and the occasional conversation with someone on Nick's crew. Though he didn't know what kind of welcome he'd receive, Cole headed out to the police station for a visit with Mike Marsden.

He'd avoided this particular reunion because, like Jed, Mike, the current Serendipity chief of police, knew about Cole's past, old and more recent. And though Mike had done his share of undercover work, he hadn't ever been as deep as Cole. But he'd understand enough to empathize — and Cole hadn't wanted to discuss the last year in his life. But after his run-in with Jed, Cole needed a reality check and, if he was honest with himself, a friend. Even if that friend was Erin's brother.

Stupid. Stupid. Stupid. If Erin's head wasn't already pounding, she'd smack it against the car window for good measure.

Breathe, she ordered herself, trying to pretend the breakfast bar wasn't trying to force its way back up. What had she been thinking, sitting in Cole's dad's driveway, her head on the steering wheel, sick as a proverbial dog? Cole seemed to have bought the whole *I didn't eat* bit, so she exhaled hard. She needed to tell him and she didn't want to. Didn't know how.

With no meetings scheduled for this morning, instead of going to work, Erin decided to stop at The Family Restaurant to see her friend Macy Donovan. She decided it was time to confide in someone she'd known a long while and get advice on how to handle this from someone other than Trina, who Erin trusted, but who didn't go way back with her.

She pulled into the parking lot and paused, taking in the old building on the edge of town. Macy and her siblings had been trying to talk their father into remodeling and changing up the menu, but so far no luck. Still, the place was a town staple, and everybody seemed to show up here at one time or another, either for the food, the company, or a combination of both.

Today, Erin needed Macy's good old-fashioned common sense. She walked inside and settled at the counter, waving at her friend to let her know she was there. After seating an older couple, Macy made her way to the stool beside Erin and settled in.

"Hey, hon. Long time no see. How are you?" Macy asked, tapping her long hot pink nails against the counter.

"Truth?" Erin wasn't in the mood to segue into it or beat around the bush.

"Of course. What's wrong?" She narrowed her gaze. "I should have known when I didn't see or hear from you lately that something was up."

Erin nodded, leaning in close. The last thing she wanted was the Serendipity grapevine kicking in. "I need you to keep this quiet, okay?"

Eyes serious, Macy nodded. "Cross my heart," she said, doing as much with her fingers.

Erin swallowed hard. "I'm pregnant," she whispered, then immediately slapped her hand over Macy's mouth before her exuberant friend could scream her reaction.

Macy's eyes opened wide.

"Got a grip?" Erin asked her.

She nodded and Erin released her hand. "How the fuck did that happen?" Macy asked in her usual outspoken way. "I thought you said you used protection?"

"Shh!"

Macy nodded. "Okay, we need to talk," she said, this time in hushed tones.

"Nobody knows except Trina, who bought the test because I was too stupid to face reality, and Alexa. And now you."

"Oh, honey, what are you going to do?" Macy asked, her hand on Erin's arm.

"I'm having the baby, of course!"

Macy smiled. "I figured that. I just meant with the rest of it."

"I'm taking it one day at a time. I have to

tell him, but I thought maybe I'd wait until I'm past the first trimester." Which wasn't much longer. "You know, relatively safe and all that."

"You're young and healthy. I'd say you're going to be fine, and the longer you wait, the harder it will be. Yes?" Macy asked.

Erin nodded, tears forming. "Sorry. I'm just so damned emotional, on top of everything else."

"You know it takes two to make a baby, so don't be afraid to tell him. That man's bark is worse than his bite, and if you slept with him, I'm sure you'd agree."

"Yeah. Except we're not even friends. Ever since that night he's gone out of his way to avoid me." And Erin refused to admit out loud how much it hurt.

"He's got demons. He has to. Between how his father always treated him and the fact that nobody knows where he's been . . . You've seen the shadows in his eyes."

Except that night, Erin thought. All she'd seen in those dark orbs had been heat and passion. She shivered in her seat.

"Tell him," Macy said, patting Erin's hand.

Erin nodded. "I'll figure out when. And how."

She sat at the counter and drank a cup of

tea, which helped settle her stomach. Then she paid, hugged Macy, and headed for work.

The district attorney's office building was located adjacent to the police station and across the street from the courthouse. In the center sat a beautifully manicured lawn and gazebo, the pride and joy of downtown Serendipity. Though her office itself was small, Erin had always loved the view her window provided of her hometown. It made the hours she spent holed up in there easier.

Being late meant she had to park far from the entrance. Though it was August, today was an unseasonably cool day, and the breeze blew gently over her skin. She grabbed her briefcase in one hand and draped her suit jacket over her other arm, then shut the car door behind her. She was halfway to the office entrance when she heard a distinctive popping sound and whipped around to see what caused the noise. She didn't see anyone nearby. She took another two steps, then she felt a searing burning pain, unlike anything she'd experienced before, rip through her arm.

She glanced down to see that her silk blouse was now coated with blood. Her blood. Confused and suddenly dizzy, she stumbled.

Someone called her name and she saw the security guard from the front entrance running toward her. She opened her mouth to tell him she'd been shot, but the pain took over and she fell to the hard, asphalt-covered ground.

THREE

Cole walked into the Serendipity Police Station, ignoring the wary looks people threw his way. If they didn't know him from the past, they'd definitely heard of him by now. He squared his shoulders and continued through the precinct to the chief's office, raising his hand to knock, when he heard voices from inside.

A female laugh and a male chuckle.

Cole was backing away, not wanting to interrupt, when the door opened wide and Cara Marsden strode out. He had to hand it to her, she tried to pull off nonchalant, but her pulled-back hair was mussed from her husband's fingers, her lips were red from being kissed, and her cheeks were heavily flushed.

He shook his head, finding it hard to reconcile the serious Mike Marsden he knew with a man who'd fool around in his office. Cole tipped his head at the other

46

man's pretty wife, not saying a word as he nodded to her before knocking on his old friend's door.

"Come on in," Mike called.

Cole decided to take the offensive for this initial hello. "So you're married and settled in Serendipity. As chief," Cole said as he stepped into the room.

Mike had just finished straightening his tie.

"And apparently getting laid is a perk of the job. Good for you, man." Cole couldn't stifle a chuckle.

"That's my wife you're talking about," Mike said, coming around his desk.

He shoved his hand forward and Cole knew the other man wasn't angry, merely possessive. Go figure.

"Glad you could finally make time for an old friend." Mike shook with a firm grip.

"I had trial and prep in New York City, so I went back and forth for a while. Lately, I've been trying to decompress."

This, more than any job, had been particularly unpleasant. Maroni, the mob boss, had a clingy, needy wife who he ignored. In Cole's effort to protect her while taking down the drug-dealing, murdering bastard, he'd gotten close to Victoria. And she to him. Too close. And when her husband had

47

been arrested and Cole's role was revealed, she'd revealed her true feelings. Her neediness bordered on delusional, and she'd convinced herself that Cole had feelings for her that extended beyond the job.

Mike's penetrating gaze settled hard. "Take it from someone who's been there, and not as deep as you. It takes time to remember who you are."

Cole remembered. And when he didn't, Jed reminded him.

"How are you getting along with your father?" Mike asked, reading Cole's mind.

"Same. The man blames me for mom leaving him. He can't see past the punk I once was." And maybe the old man was right, Cole thought.

The truth hurt, but Cole didn't like the kid he'd been. The man he'd become after his mother remarried and Brody welcomed Cole in? That was a Cole he was coming to understand and maybe even respect. But even more than a decade later, it was hard to wipe away the vestiges of his father's negative influence.

"Hell, he blames me for breathing," Cole muttered.

"Jed always was a hard-ass. It's what let him do his job for so long," Mike said. "But that doesn't make him right."

Cole waved him away. "Forget it." Because if Mike ever found out about the one-night stand Cole had had with his sister, he'd be lining up against him with Jed.

Just because Mike knew what Cole's real job had been didn't mean he'd think Cole was good enough for his sister. There was the danger, a reality that Mike knew only too well.

Then there was Cole himself. Erin deserved a man who'd commit to being around. She'd grown up surrounded by love and with parents who cared, and no doubt she wanted the same. Cole's job meant he was gone for extended periods of time. This last job had taken a year of his life, excluding the trial that came after. He'd never had much in the way of family or friends outside of work and wouldn't know how to live that way, let alone blend the two.

Nor did he want to. Jesus, what was with him, constantly rehashing this shit in his head, over a woman he knew was all wrong for him and vice versa.

Before Mike could reply, a loud commotion sounded from the squad room. "Excuse me," Mike said, heading for the door. "What's going on out there?" he yelled out.

"There was a shooting in the parking lot," Cara said as she ran up to him and grabbed

49

his hand. "You need to get out there *now.*"

Apparently things weren't as quiet in his small town as Cole remembered. He followed the direction of the chaos and stepped outside in time to see cops swarming the scene and an ambulance pulling up to the middle of the lot, and for Mike's bellow to reverberate in Cole's head.

"What the hell do you mean, my sister was shot?"

Adrenaline spiked in Cole's veins and he started forward, but an armed cop restrained him. "No spectators, buddy. Clear the scene so everyone can do their jobs."

"But I'm —" He was what to Erin? Cole couldn't say family. And he wasn't a cop with permission to get past the barrier they were erecting.

Shit.

Waiting around helplessly wasn't his style, but bursting in and getting himself arrested wouldn't help matters. Neither would having to explain his actions to Mike. He forced himself to think clearly. Erin had been shot, which meant she'd be taken to the hospital, so that's where Cole headed, hoping for information from the family once they arrived.

University Hospital was a hustle of busy people running in all directions, even more so when the ambulance carrying Erin arrived. Cole stood back as they rushed the stretcher inside, but was relieved to see her eyes open. Being conscious was a damned good thing. He absently rubbed the left side of his abdomen, where he'd been shot in the final stage of his last undercover op. He wouldn't wish that pain on anyone, let alone someone as innocent as Erin.

Mike, who'd accompanied his sister in the ambulance, followed close behind the paramedics through the swinging doors. He didn't glance around, and Cole was grateful Mike hadn't noticed him. The other man would have questions Cole wasn't sure he could answer. Questions Cole had been asking himself since finding out the identity of the gunshot victim. Why was he so affected by the fact that it was Erin being wheeled in here? He had no concrete answers. He only knew that his gut was churning, and it wouldn't settle down until he knew she was okay.

He didn't know how much time had passed before he finally saw Mike come back out of the double doors. This time, the other man was more alert, and his gaze settled on Cole immediately.

"Hey, man. What are you doing here?"

Cole swallowed hard. "I was with you

when you got the news. I couldn't very well go home without knowing if you needed anything." The truth, as far as it went.

"I appreciate it." Mike ran his hand through his already screwed-up hair.

"How is she?" Cole asked, attempting not to show the craziness he was beginning to feel from wondering what was happening with Erin.

"They're assessing her now." Mike checked his cell, then met Cole's gaze. "You know, there is something you can do for me. I need to track down Sam," he said, referring to his brother. "Cara is out handling a domestic violence call so she can't do it for me. Since you're here, can you wait outside Erin's cubicle and get me as soon as there's news?"

"Sure." Cole hoped he didn't look as pleased as he felt, being given the opportunity to see Erin firsthand.

"Great. Come on. I'll walk you back." Mike led Cole back into the treatment area. "She's in cubicle three," he said. "I just want to go outside and try to call Sam again. I want him to hear this from me, and the cell service in this area sucks." Both of the Marsden brothers were protective of their sister.

"Just wait outside. When the doctor's

finished, you can go in. I'm sure she'll be glad to see a familiar face and not be alone."

Cole wasn't as certain, but he merely nodded. "I'll call you if I hear something before you get back inside."

Mike nodded. "I owe you one."

Cole didn't see it that way, so he didn't reply.

With Mike gone, Cole placed himself directly outside Erin's small cubicle, folded his arms across his chest, and waited. His pulse had sped up, and now his heart beat hard in his chest and he'd begun to sweat. He hoped like hell the bullet hadn't been lodged somewhere or she'd need surgery to have it removed.

Son of a bitch, who'd be firing a gun in the parking lot of the police station?

He stepped closer to the cubicle and the doctor's voice sounded through the curtain. ". . . bullet appears to have passed straight through, but we'll know more after some tests."

"Okay," Erin said softly, sounding weak, probably from loss of blood.

"Since you're pregnant, we're limited to what antibiotics and painkillers we can give you."

"What?!" At the doctor's words, the blood drained from Cole's head.

Before he could pull himself together, the curtain swung wide, and he came face-to-face with Erin's doctor.

Erin stared at him with a horrified expression on her pale face.

"Who are you?" the man in the white lab coat asked.

"It's okay." Erin spoke in a shaky voice. She glanced at the doctor, her hazel eyes dull with pain. "Can you give us a few minutes?"

"Of course." The physician stepped out.

And Cole forced himself to take the other man's place by Erin's bedside. He took in her ashen skin and the petrified look on her face and decided immediately the pregnancy discussion could wait.

"How are you feeling?" he asked.

"I'm okay."

"Liar." He chuckled even as he admired her strength. "Now, how are you really feeling?"

"It hurts like hell." She bit down on her lower lip and sucked in a shallow breath. Tears shimmered in her pretty eyes and he felt her pain deep in his gut.

"I know." He put a hand on her uninjured shoulder. To his relief, she didn't flinch or pull away.

"What are you doing here?" she asked.

54

"I was with your brother when he got word of shots in the parking lot. We ran outside, I heard it was you . . ." He shrugged. "And here I am."

He wondered exactly what he was confessing with the admission. His emotions were in turmoil and obviously they were about to be tossed around even more. "Erin —"

"Cole —" she said at the same time.

"Were you going to tell me?" Or was she too humiliated by the thought of being pregnant with *his* child?

He wouldn't blame her, but that didn't change the fact that the baby she was carrying was his responsibility.

Oh, man. Baby. Responsibility. Jesus.

"I was trying to find the right time. And the right words." Her cheeks turned pink. She still hadn't met his gaze, but now she looked him in the eye. "You don't question the fact that it's yours?"

He cocked an eyebrow, surprised. "I question a hell of a lot of things in life, but this? No."

Her lips turned down in a frown. "Because I'm such a good, sweet girl, huh?"

No, because he knew through the grapevine she hadn't been seeing anyone lately. He'd have expected her to be relieved he wasn't going to argue paternity. Instead she'd sounded more annoyed by her reputation.

He shook his head, telling himself this was no time to be amused or find her reactions cute. "If it helps, you weren't such a good girl that night," he said, memories and heat swamping him.

She managed a laugh, which had been his intent. Now for the harder stuff. "About the baby —"

"I'm keeping it." She attempted to fold her arms across her chest, but groaned in pain, tears finally leaking from the corners of her eyes.

His heart clenched in his chest. "Stay still, dammit." He curled his fingers into fists, feeling useless and unable to help her.

"Don't yell at me!"

"Then don't assume I'd ask you to get rid of my kid!" he barked right back.

They glared at each other and Cole realized they'd just had their first major disagreement . . . while still managing to come down on the same side.

"What the fuck did I just hear?" Mike asked, shoving through the closed curtain, his glare bouncing between Cole and Erin.

One look at her brother's horrified expression and Erin shrank lower in the bed. What a nightmare, and she wasn't talking about being shot. Shot! In her sleepy hometown, in the police station parking lot, of all places.

Although figuring out who fired at her and why should be her brother's biggest priority, Mike looked as if he were about to attack Cole, and Erin wouldn't allow that. "Mike?"

"What?" he asked, his voice gentling when he looked at her. "When did this bastard take advantage of you and why didn't you tell me?"

She pointed to his clenched fist with her good hand. "That's why. And he didn't take advantage of me. It was mutual."

"He should have damn well used protection!" Mike thundered, his voice raised.

Erin's embarrassment flew off the charts. "Shh!"

"Quit embarrassing your sister," Cole said in a more subdued voice. "Not that it's any of your business, but we did use protection."

Every time, Erin thought, but knew better than to say *that* out loud. "Accidents happen," she said instead.

"Well, I hope he intends to —"

"That's enough!" Erin used what strength she had left to yell at her brother before collapsing against the hard pillow behind her. "This is between Cole and me. I know you care, and I understand you're upset, but you need to stand down."

"Or take it out on me when we're alone. Back off your sister," Cole said, sounding more protective than she'd imagined him being.

Then again, she didn't know how he'd handle things. Considering the way he'd heard the news, so far so good.

"Sam's on his way, and so is Cara," Mike said, still obviously seething, but holding it in.

Erin sucked in a breath. "You can tell Cara when you're alone. I don't expect you to keep secrets from your wife, but I'd appreciate you letting me tell Sam myself. Same with Mom and Dad, and not until they come home." She pinned Mike with her most serious glare.

"Fine. How's your arm?" he asked, his voice softening.

"Hurts. I have to see what the doctors will let me take for pain since I'm pregnant." Before that could get him worked up again, Erin changed the subject. "Have your people found anything on the shooter?"

Mike shook his head. "They're working on it now, scouring the area. We're hoping to find the bullet so we can run ballistics. We're interviewing people who work in the area, and when you're up to it, I'll need to talk to you."

She nodded.

"Any cases you're working on that scream trouble to you?" Cole asked.

"I —" Erin began.

"Police business, Sanders," Mike interrupted before she could reply.

She rolled her eyes. "Cole knows what he's doing. Another set of eyes, ears, and experience might help."

"He knows what?" Mike asked Erin.

She opened her mouth and closed it again. Her brother was right. Just what kind of experience did she think Cole had, considering how little she knew about him?

"I don't know," she admitted. But she'd gone off and defended him like he'd been working for the Secret Service for the last few years.

Her brother and Cole eyed each other warily, as if in possession of some big secret. Erin had seen that look over the years between her two brothers when they wanted her left out of something — *for her own good.*

"What?!" she half yelled at them.

Cole inclined his head at Mike, obviously giving him permission to reveal *it.* Whatever it was.

"Your instincts are right," her brother said through gritted teeth. "Cole knows what he's doing. He's been doing undercover work for the NYPD."

Erin blinked in surprise. Not that her gut feelings about Cole had been on target, but because she hadn't any idea where he'd been, what he'd done . . . or seen. She still didn't have any inkling about the details, but with the darkness that surrounded him now being the beginnings of an explanation, she suppressed a shiver.

"When will you be released?" Mike asked, changing the subject from the shooter and from Cole.

"They aren't keeping me overnight, but the doctor still has to run some tests, clean the wound, and bandage it better."

Mike nodded. "Then Cara will take you back to our place."

"I've got her," Cole said, stepping close to the head of the bed, his voice firm.

"Whoa," Erin said. "I don't care who takes me home, but I'm going back to my place."

"Not alone," Cole said.

Erin scrunched her nose and looked up at him. "Why on earth not?"

The two men looked at each other, clearly coming to yet another silent understanding and agreement that didn't bode well for her. "Well?"

"You were shot and you were in pain, or has the burn suddenly worn off?" her brother asked.

"No."

"Then it's not safe for you to be alone," Mike said, sounding almost pleased.

Sadistic bastard, Erin thought, uncharitably.

"That's ridiculous. There's no way someone deliberately aimed at me. I'm sure I was at the wrong place, wrong time. I don't have any cases that would remotely lead to someone wanting to hurt me!"

"You think." Mike narrowed his gaze, his mulish expression one she'd seen many times before.

"You can't say for sure, so safety's an issue until we know it's not," Cole said, not only agreeing with her brother, but clearly taking charge. "You admitted to being in pain, which will get worse before it gets better, and if they let you take painkillers, you'll be fuzzy. Not to mention that you're immobile with the arm being bandaged and in a sling."

He leaned closer and met her brother's determined gaze. "I'll take her back to her place and stay. She'll be safe with me."

"The hell she will." Mike's expression morphed back to furious. "She's coming to my place until we can ascertain who shot her and why, and until *I* know she's safe." Mike straightened his shoulders, preparing for a fight.

Erin had had enough of their posturing. "*She* is right here. And she will decide what's best for herself."

Cole lifted her good hand, taking her by surprise with his gentleness. "While you're deciding, remember that's my baby you're carrying, which makes you my responsibility."

"I can take care of myself."

The two men did that silent communication thing again, but no way would they decide what was best for her. She'd choose for herself where she was going.

"I'm going home," she told them in the strongest voice she could manage.

Mike set his jaw. "Then Cole's going with you."

Erin whipped her head around and glared at her brother. "Weren't you the one who just questioned his ability to keep me safe?"

"I wanted you with me. I also know better than to think I'll win when you make up your mind. So if you insist on going home, you're not going alone. If you prefer, Sam can move in."

"No!" Erin and Cole spoke in unison.

Erin loved her brother, but if they were staying under one roof, she'd probably want to throttle him within an hour. "Mike, go do your job. Cole and I need to talk, okay?"

Her brother braced an arm behind her head. "Promise me you won't leave here by yourself?"

"I promise," she said before Cole could answer for her — because she just knew he would.

Mike leaned down and kissed Erin on the forehead. "I'll be by later." He spoke to her, but his intense stare was on Cole.

Then he took off, leaving Erin alone with the father of her baby. Who wanted to move in with her. Which made Erin wonder just when her life had gotten so complicated.

Just as Mike left, the doctor returned, which put off any conversation. Exhausted and in pain, Erin was relieved, but she knew the reprieve was temporary. She had a hunch she and Cole would have plenty to talk about once she was released.

FOUR

Seated in the waiting room, Cole watched
the clock while Erin was treated. Knowing
basic protocol, it would be a while before
they assessed the extent of the injury,
flushed and treated the wound properly, and
prepped her to go home.

He wasn't surprised when Mike returned,
cornering him in the hospital waiting room.

"We need to talk," the other man said.

Cole nodded. "I'm listening."

He owed Mike the respect due as Erin's
brother, but the decision had been made,
and he refused to budge. As for Mike's feelings on the pregnancy, well, Cole didn't
need to hear that either. Facts were facts,
just like done was done. He couldn't change
things now.

To Cole's surprise, Mike settled in beside
him in a chair, instead of remaining on his
feet to give himself the tactical advantage.

"You've been gone awhile so you missed

64

the drama with my old man," Mike said.

Cole hadn't expected this line of discussion. "Simon?"

"No. Rex Bransom."

Cole raised an eyebrow, then suddenly recalled old stories about how Simon Marsden had adopted Mike when he was a baby. Unsure where Mike was going, all Cole could do was listen. "Go on."

Mike groaned. "Rex got my mother pregnant when they were dating. He was always the bachelor, the charming guy, but not the one anyone could really count on for the long haul."

"Like me," Cole said, not missing the similarities — or the dig.

Mike eyed him intently. "I'm hoping the jury's out on that."

Cole appreciated even that much leeway.

Mike leaned back in his seat. "Look, I know what it's like to grow up feeling unwanted by my real father. It didn't matter that Simon did everything right; those scars remained. Do you understand what I'm saying?"

"I won't be abandoning my kid," Cole said emphatically. If he knew nothing else, he knew that.

He loved his job. It was dangerous and it took him away from any semblance of a real life, or even the chance of one. But it was all Cole knew. And it suited him. None of that meant he wouldn't provide for his kid.

Mike inclined his head. "That's a start. But it's not everything."

Cole swallowed hard. "Erin." He said her name before Mike could.

"This is my baby sister we're talking about. I know the hell my mother went through, loving Rex, or thinking she did."

"It's not like that between me and Erin."

Mike scowled. "Somehow I think getting pregnant from a one-night stand is worse."

Cole opened his mouth to speak, but Mike held up a hand. "Look, much as I love my sister, I respect that she's got to live her own life and make her own choices."

Cole narrowed his gaze. "But?" He heard the unspoken word.

"But she needs to have choices to make."

"That's between me and your sister," Cole bit out tightly. He wasn't about to be pushed into anything by her concerned brother.

Not only was it none of Mike's business, but the pregnancy had just been sprung on him. He wasn't denying responsibility, but whatever he and Erin decided, it wasn't Mike's call.

Mike rose to his feet. "She's got an entire

family willing to step up and help her. If you're going to break her heart, don't hang around."

The other man hovered over him, but Cole wasn't intimidated and refused to rise from his seat or take the bait. "Wasn't it you who just said bailing on a kid leaves lingering scars?"

Mike glared at him. "It sucked but I dealt with it. All it took was the love of a good woman. Take a hike if you can't handle it. Erin will find someone worthy of her to step up in your place."

Cole's stomach twisted, and he glared at the man he had thought was a friend. "And now we get to the real point. I'm not good enough for your sister."

"*You* said it, man."

Cole set his jaw, willing himself not to launch into anything physical. "I suggest you leave before we both say anything more we might regret. I'm that baby's father and I'll be around in whatever capacity Erin and I decide. Deal with it."

Cole chose this moment to rise to his feet.

"I'll be watching over my sister, Sanders. And over you." With that, Mike stormed off, leaving Cole alone to wait for Erin, his entire body tight and wired.

It didn't matter that half of what Mike

said echoed things Cole had thought himself. Hearing someone else say it only made it that much more real, and he was glad he had time to cool off before Erin was finally brought out in a wheelchair.

By then, Cole had calmed down, although her brother's words reverberated in his brain. Mike had said plenty, but the one thing that hit Cole hardest was the idea of Erin with another man. But with her in front of him, he had to focus on the present — taking a groggy, hurting Erin back to her place.

In the car, she remained silent, and when he glanced over at the passenger seat, he realized she'd fallen asleep.

Watching her, his lips curled into a grin. She was exactly the girl he remembered, innocent and sweet. That she'd been a wildcat in bed, a perfect match for him in every way, in no way detracted from the fact that she was still pure of heart. Her brother knew her well, whether Cole liked it or not. But she was in his life for good, that much he knew. So was his child. A lifelong commitment he hadn't planned — and the thought made him break into a sweat.

Pushing those thoughts aside, he gently woke Erin up and helped her out of the car and to her condo unit. Injured or not, he was way too aware of her as a sexy female. She wore a soft tank top under a cream silk blouse, which hung loosely off her slender frame. Thanks to the surprisingly cool August temperature, her nipples were puckered and visible through the sheer top, and he figured he was a pig for noticing when she was in such bad shape.

But he was a man, and she leaned against him as he walked her from the car to her house, upping his awareness of all things Erin. From the fragrant and still-familiar scent of her perfume to the way her hair fell loosely around her face, he was struck by her fragility and how much he wanted to take care of her.

The thought caused him to catch his breath and nearly trip. He ground to a halt, pausing for a minute.

"Bedroom's upstairs," Erin said, misreading his sudden halt.

He wasn't about to correct her assumption. "Thanks," he said, heading up the short flight of steps and into the master bedroom, where he helped settle Erin on the bed.

Around him, the room was a mixture of feminine touches, silk flowers, and small accessories, and sturdy light wood furniture.

"Cole?" She opened her hazel eyes and

focused on him.

"Yeah?"

"I just . . . Thank you," she said softly, and peered up at him with such trust that his entire body absorbed the warmth floating through him.

"You're welcome," he said. "Now rest."

She was out cold before he left the room.

Once downstairs, Cole ran a hand through his hair, feeling more like he was in the twilight zone with every passing minute. A pregnant woman. A stubborn pregnant woman. One he was more than attracted to, even in her disheveled, injured state. If anything, seeing her vulnerable and hurt triggered something in him he'd never felt before. Moving in with her was a mistake.

Unfortunately for him, he had no choice.

Erin woke, immediately aware of excruciating pain in her arm and the sound of male voices coming from downstairs. She dragged herself out of bed and stopped in the bathroom, groaning when she got a look at her face. One-handed, she washed off what was left of her makeup, brushed her teeth, and headed downstairs to deal with the men in her life.

She found Mike and Sam seated at her kitchen table, stacks of folders around them,

Cole hovering in the background. She recognized her work documents, many of them confidential, open in front of Mike.

Furious, she cleared her throat. "Just what do you think you're doing?"

Mike glanced up, his expression not the least bit remorseful. "I had your recent and open cases sent over. I want to figure out who'd have a stake in getting you out of the way or scaring you into backing off."

"And you couldn't wait until I woke up?" The pain in her arm became secondary to the blood boiling in her head at the sheer gall of her brother.

Sam jumped up from his seat and came up beside her. "You okay?" he asked, concern in his hazel eyes as they stared into hers.

He was her baby brother and he loved her, but like Mike, he took overprotective way too far. "I was fine until I found you two in my personal work files."

"Relax," Mike said, ignoring her concerns.

"You know we have a job to do —" Sam began.

"Then go do it!" She cut him off. "Don't you have a bullet to find? And if you want information on my cases, here's a novel idea . . . *ask me*!"

Ever the distanced observer, Cole watched

from across the room. His very presence in her small condo unnerved her, but she wasn't about to deal with him before she let her brothers know how unwelcome their meddling was.

The strain of yelling took a lot out of her, pulling at the muscles in her arms and the stitches, and she couldn't prevent the groan that escaped.

"That's it. You two heard her. You've done enough here, and Erin needs to rest." Cole stepped up, his tone brooking no argument as he faced down her siblings.

Most men in Erin's life lived in healthy respect and awe of her large, bossy cop brothers. Not Cole Sanders. When he faced them down, he dominated his space. Erin knew she'd be exchanging one set of over-protective males for another one, but at this point, she felt more comfortable handling Cole. He was right. She just wanted her brothers to give her some space for a while.

Mike rose to his full height, and Erin still felt Cole's presence loom larger.

"Look, just because you knocked up my sister doesn't give you the right to boss her — or us — around."

"What the hell?" Sam asked, obviously getting the memo about Erin's pregnancy for the first time.

"Thanks a lot," Erin muttered.

Cole clenched his jaw. "One, watch how you talk to or about your sister, got it? Two, I'm just backing her up since she told you to go away and you refuse to listen, and three, I'm here to protect her. If that means against you two, so be it." Cole folded his arms across his chest.

Silence echoed around the room in waves as Cole's words sank in. Erin knew her brothers, and if she didn't do something, she'd have a brawl in her kitchen. She exhaled hard. "Let's take a breather and talk again tonight or tomorrow, okay? I'll go through my cases myself, and you two go back to work."

"You're pregnant?" Sam asked, his mind still obviously reeling from the news. "By him?"

Erin nodded. "Yes. And that's a discussion for another time. I'll talk to you about everything. I promise. Just give me . . . us . . . some space now."

Sam straightened his shoulders, his body language obstinate. But when he turned to face her, he reached for her hand. "You'll always be the sister I protect, but I get it. I'll back off for now. But we will talk."

"Yes. And thank you." She kissed his cheek, then turned to her older brother.

"Mike?"

"Yeah," he muttered, clearly unhappy.

Erin would call Cara later and warn her she'd need to soothe her brother, the beast. "Thank you too," she said to Mike.

She finally got them out the door and turned to Cole. "Well, they're gone."

"Yep."

"So what happens next?" she asked, wondering just what he thought guarding her entailed.

"If you go out, I go with you."

She nodded. "And if I stay in and watch television?"

"I do that too."

Short and to the point, she thought. "Uhhuh. And . . . you leave at bedtime and return in the morning before I go to work?"

Cole narrowed his gaze. "I thought we went over this at the hospital. I'm staying here. With you."

"And I thought once I got settled you'd calm down and realize I can be alone. I'll respect the notion that when I'm out I need protection until we figure out who took the shot, but here?" She swept her free arm around the condo. "I'm perfectly safe."

"The alarm system looks pretty standard," he said with a scowl.

Erin shrugged. "It does its job. It'll dial

Central Station if someone breaks in. If the condo and its alarm was good enough for Cara when she lived here, it's good enough for me."

His frown deepened. "I'm staying."

From the determined set of his jaw, she decided not to argue. "Then let's see what I've got for lunch," she muttered, pulling open the refrigerator.

Cole came up behind her, his body heat warm, his masculine scent drifting toward her. She didn't know why he had such a potent effect on her, but just his nearness aroused her, despite the pain she was in. And arousal and desire for this man were what had gotten her pregnant to begin with. So why wasn't a complete one-eighty in her life enough to dampen her need?

He peered over her shoulder at the contents of the fridge. "That's it?" He sounded alarmed.

She took in the Greek yogurt, orange juice, eggs, skim milk, and fruit. Oh, and the multiple bags of Oreos she'd been craving when she wasn't nauseous. She preferred the cookies hard, cold, and crunchy. "What's wrong?"

"There's no substantial food in there, that's what. No wonder you were ready to pass out and starving," he muttered.

She blinked. "Uh, that was morning sickness," she informed him.

He cocked an eyebrow. "Maybe."

Stubborn man. "Fine. Go fill up a shopping cart to your heart's content."

"I plan to. And you're going with me when I do. I'm not leaving you alone, remember?"

She decided not to dignify that comment with an answer.

"We'll order in today so you can rest, and we'll go food shopping tomorrow. You're not working until next week. The doctor said you should take it easy."

Erin frowned. He might be right, but he was also bossy and controlling. "Any other orders for me?"

He lifted his head from the fridge and pinned her with his dark stare. "As I recall, you liked it when I gave orders."

Her heart skipped a beat. Yikes! The man went right for the jugular.

"It's rude to remind me of that," she muttered.

He chuckled and she turned to walk out of the room.

"Where are you going?"

"To take a painkiller and watch some TV."

"Not on an empty stomach," he said. "I'll make you some eggs."

She whipped her head around to face him.

"You cook?" Because she didn't.

"If I want to eat, I cook. Living over Joe's and the coffee shop, I haven't bothered much, but in this place? Yeah. I'll cook. How about you?" he asked.

Her mother always said she'd regret not spending any time in the kitchen with her, and Erin never thought she'd agree. "Umm . . ."

He raked his gaze over her. "Really? How the hell do you survive?"

"Takeout! Mom lives half a mile away. My best friend's family owns the diner in town. I'm hardly starving."

"You're skinny, though, and now you're eating for two." He opened and closed drawers until he found the skillet and other cooking utensils he was looking for. "Sit." He tapped the chair with a spatula.

She eased herself into the chair, unwilling to confess that her legs had been about to give out, the pain from her arm making her dizzy and weak.

"I hope you're always going to be this easy," he said, his pleased smile causing a distinct flip in her stomach.

"Don't count on it," she muttered.

"Considering you don't cook, your house is filled with all the right tools."

"What can I say? My mom still holds out

hope." Her mom. Whom Erin would soon have to tell she was pregnant.

Nausea that had nothing to do with hunger or morning sickness filled her at the realization, and she lay her head on the table to wait for her food.

Erin survived Cole's first night at her house by passing out and not waking up until late the next morning. Since she was in her bed with no recollection of how she got there, she realized she must have fallen asleep watching TV after dinner. Which meant Cole must have carried her to bed. *Quite the knight he's turning out to be,* she thought.

A dark knight who'd spent years undercover doing who knows what . . . or with whom. He obviously carried the emotional scars, and he'd been a brooding bad boy when she'd known him before. But now? She couldn't read his moods or feelings about their situation, but he was certainly stepping up and taking care of her.

For Erin, who'd never found a guy who treated her like she was precious or meant something to him, she found she appreciated being pampered when she wasn't feeling well. And that was the thought that had her ready to get up and back on her feet.

She couldn't get used to Cole taking care

of her. From here on out, she'd take care of herself and their child. He'd have a say in their baby's life, and she wasn't an idiot . . . she'd accept reasonable financial help. But for Erin, this pregnancy meant giving up the dream of having the love and marriage her parents shared. That her brother and Cara now had. That Alexa and Luke had. Finding a good man was hard enough. Finding one willing to take on another man's baby? Those were few and far between. But her reality didn't mean she could allow herself to mistake Cole's obligation to her baby as caring for her. He'd made himself clear each time she'd seen him post-one-night-stand.

The truth sent a knifelike pain to her heart, and as she climbed out of bed, the throbbing in her arm added to her torment. But she managed. Once again, she awkwardly used the bathroom and brushed her teeth with one hand, and she was starting for the kitchen when the doorbell rang.

Cole beat her to the front door. She heard him talking to someone outside, looking around before letting whoever it was inside.

Macy barreled past him, waiting until he shut the door and turned toward her before getting in his face. "What are you doing here, and where's Erin?" her friend demanded.

"I'm right here," Erin said from the top of the stairs.

Both Macy and Cole turned as Erin walked down the few steps to greet her friend. Macy's gaze ran over her, her wide-eyed panic subsiding when she saw for herself Erin was okay. "Oh, honey," she said, her gaze falling on the bandage and sling. "Come sit."

"I take it you heard what happened?" Erin asked.

"Good news travels fast," Macy said with sarcasm in her tone.

"I didn't know you were awake," Cole said. He hooked his thumbs in his jeans pockets and stared at her with that intense look that set her nerves on edge.

His black T-shirt showed off well-defined muscles. He hadn't shaved, and he was even more appealing scruffy than any man should be, while she looked like roadkill. She could only imagine the sight she presented, and she did her best not to wince.

"How's the pain?" he asked.

"Bad," she admitted.

His eyes darkened.

"Can you take anything given your condition?" Macy asked, startling Erin.

She'd forgotten she and Cole weren't

80

alone. Par for the course around this man, it seemed.

Suddenly Macy cleared her throat, her eyes widening in sheer panic. Erin managed not to laugh at her friend's distress. "He knows."

"Oh? Oh!" She whipped her head around to look at Cole, whose expression, true to form, was bland, giving nothing away. "So can you take anything?"

"Tylenol, definitely. And the doctor gave me a prescription for something stronger to take sporadically if I'm in agony but . . . I'm trying not to use it."

Macy squeezed her hand. "Well, I'm sure that makes rest all the more important then. You need to be still."

Cole nodded. "She's right. Sit. I'll go get you something for breakfast."

Macy narrowed her gaze, obviously not sure what to make of him yet. "I've got loads of food for you in my car. My mom sent me over with enough meals for you to heat up for a good couple of days."

Sonya Donovan, Macy's mother, was a sweet woman who treated her children's friends like they were her own. "Thank her for me."

"I will."

"Well, I've got eggs ready to cook, so you

can eat those this morning," Cole shifted his gaze to Macy. "Leave your car keys on the counter and I'll unload for you when I'm through." Without waiting for a reply, Cole turned and strode back into the kitchen.

"He always so chatty?" Macy asked, not bothering to hide the sarcasm in her tone.

"That was actually Cole at his most charming."

"So how'd it go when you told him?" Macy asked as she and Erin settled into club chairs in the den and Macy curled her legs beneath her and leaned forward in her seat.

Erin cringed at the memory. "He overheard the doctor say something about me being pregnant. He was shocked, obviously. But it's all taken a backseat to the shooting. We haven't really talked much about it yet." Erin bit her lower lip.

"Well, he's here and obviously taking care of you. So does that mean you two are . . . together?"

Erin shook her head. "Not even close. He's my bodyguard. He and Mike almost had a brawl over who would take me home and where I would stay. When I insisted on coming back here, Mike relented and let Cole play watchdog." And she hated being his responsibility just as much as she hated the idea that he was now saddled with her and a baby for the rest of his life.

When Erin envisioned her future, it was with a man she loved and who adored her in return. Maybe it was old-fashioned and silly, but she'd seen her parents together and watched her brother Mike fall hard for Cara, turning himself inside out to make her happy. She didn't want to settle for anything less. Like being a man's burden.

"What was that big sigh for?" Macy asked, too observant for Erin's liking.

"Nothing. No sigh. It's fine."

Macy's scowl let Erin know her friend didn't buy the lie. "For a man who's just your bodyguard, he's pretty concerned about you."

"Yeah, well, that's just a sense of obligation." She frowned. "As soon as I can get this sling off and move my arm a little, he won't need to hover."

"We'll see. Meanwhile, any word on the shooter? Word around town is that it was a stupid kid who shouldn't have been playing with guns."

Erin cocked an eyebrow. "Really? As far as I know, they have no idea, so until the police find something, the overprotective men in my life are calling the shots."

She laughed at her bad pun and Macy rolled her eyes. "He's unbelievably sexy. You know that, right?" Macy said of Cole, lowering her voice as she spoke.

"And brooding, and moody . . ." And occasionally charming and caring, but she wasn't giving Macy any ammunition. "And he's also a complete enigma who doesn't seem to want to let anybody in."

"Well, you're his baby mama. He's living here. If anyone can get through that gruff exterior, I'm sure it's my sweet, gentle, caring best friend." Macy waggled her eyebrows.

"You aren't warning me away?" Erin asked, surprised. She, too, kept her voice to a whisper. "Because my brothers are livid, my parents will freak, and nobody in town will socialize with him except his cousins."

"And you," Macy helpfully reminded her. "Besides, you weren't focused on that when you slept with him," she said with a grin. "I trust your judgment completely. I always have. So unless you've changed your mind about him —"

"No!" She wouldn't share with Macy what she'd learned about his past, but her friend was right. Erin had good instincts. She'd always thought Cole was a decent guy, and what she'd learned about him yesterday and his actions toward her proved it — no matter what he'd seen or done.

She drummed her fingertips on the chair. "Look, I know he'll be responsible for the baby, but I want more from life, from a relationship. You know that."

Macy nodded, her expression sober, as she met Erin's gaze. "Then I suggest you find a way to get it from the man who fathered your child."

Erin opened her mouth to reply, but Cole's voice calling from the kitchen stopped her. "Food's ready."

"He cooks," Macy said with an already devoted sigh. "He might just be a keeper."

Not wanting to argue with her friend, Erin pushed herself up from the chair with care. Cole Sanders wasn't a keeper. He wanted nothing to do with hearth, home, family, and most of all, love.

FIVE

Macy stayed with Erin through breakfast, then to help her shower without getting her bandage wet, as well as to wash and dry her hair.

Afterward, Erin collapsed onto her bed, exhausted. "Thank you so much. I don't know what I'd do without you."

Macy grinned. "My pleasure. Mr. Bodyguard might have his uses" — she wagged her eyebrows to emphasize the point — "but only a girlfriend can help with things like this. Unless . . . you wanted him to see you naked again?"

Erin peered up at her friend from her prone position. "Are you crazy? That's what got me pregnant," she muttered.

"Clearly his sperm is as potent as he is." Macy chuckled. "Need anything else before I go?"

"Between the food and the help, you've gone above and beyond." And Erin appreciated the bond between them more than she could express at the moment.

"Hey, I know you'd do the same for me. I'll check in on you later." Macy blew a kiss and started for the door, turning before she walked out. "If you're interested in more from Cole than him keeping you safe, you've got the man exactly where you want him. Do something about it," she said, then bounded out of the room before Erin could reply.

Not that Erin had a ready response anyway. She needed to think, not act spontaneously. Again. She placed her hand over her still-flat belly, unable to believe there was life growing inside her. Whatever happened between her and Cole, it wouldn't be because Erin pushed him beyond what he was capable of giving — or worse, more than what he wanted to give. No matter what Macy wanted to whip up in her fairy-tale-oriented brain.

As she thought about Macy, Erin bolted up in bed, groaning in pain as she did. "Shit!" She just realized Macy had gone downstairs alone, which meant she was free to corner and grill Cole.

Unwilling to let that happen, Erin rushed downstairs in time to hear her friend say, "Not that I'm one to meddle, but that's my best friend up there and if you hurt her, I'll come after you with a shotgun."

"Get in line behind her brothers," Cole said, arms folded across his chest, an amused half-grin on his sexy mouth.

Erin didn't know what he found funny, but *she* was plain embarrassed.

"This isn't high school revisited," Erin said to her best friend.

"What are you doing out of bed? You said you were exhausted." Macy shooed her away with the back of her hand.

Instead of taking the hint, Erin continued down the stairs. "I was trying to stop you from making an ass of yourself — and of me — but I see I was too late."

"Nothing wrong with someone having your back," Cole said to Erin, taking her by surprise.

"And I believe he's got yours." Macy nodded toward Cole.

"Message received," he assured her.

Erin rolled her eyes. "Go home, Macy."

Her friend blew a kiss. "Check in on you later!" With a wave, she let herself out the front door.

"You want to watch TV and rest?" Cole asked.

She nodded.

A few minutes later, they were in the family room, where they watched a half hour of television before her heavy eyelids drifted closed. Cole insisted she go back up to sleep, and instead of being annoyed by his bossy tone, she bolted to do his bidding, needing space from her ever-present awareness of him as a man. A sexy, potent, desirable man.

She was just about to head upstairs when her doorbell rang. Erin stood, but Cole held up a hand to stop her.

"I've got it. Stay here."

She scowled, but again let him take charge. Her arm throbbed and burned, she was exhausted, and appeasing him seemed easiest, at least for now.

Once at the door, Cole looked out the glass on the side and opened the door a crack, his hand on his holstered weapon.

Jeez, she thought. *Overkill much?*

He spoke to someone through the small crack in the door, then opened it wider and returned with a vase full of yellow roses. Her favorite.

"I wonder who they're from," she said, excitement in her voice, since what woman didn't like receiving roses?

Cole's expression darkened as he placed them on the table. She reached for the card, reading the short inscription:

Take care of yourself and don't rush back till you're up to it. Evan.

"Well?" Annoyance threaded through Cole's tone.

"No one important."

He reached out and snatched the card from her hand.

"Hey! That's private!"

"What if it's from the shooter?"

He read the words and his scowl deepened. "Who the hell is Evan?"

"Evan Carmichael. My boss."

Cole muttered something under his breath.

"What did you say?" she asked, attempting for civility. At this rate they were going to kill each other.

"Nothing." He sat back down in front of the television and didn't say another word.

Erin rolled her eyes. If she didn't know better she'd think he was jealous. But Cole's past actions taught her he wouldn't get jealous of anyone or anything in Erin's life. And he never would.

A couple of days into their new living arrangement, Erin's head cleared enough for her to remember she had someplace to be on Thursday night.

90

She knocked on the guest room door. "Come in."

She stepped inside to find him doing push-ups on the floor. He was wearing black gym shorts and no shirt, his muscles flexing and bulging with every move he made.

She swallowed hard. "I forgot, but I need to go out."

He easily maneuvered to his feet. "I see that." His gaze took in her jeans, black silk top, and ballet flats. "Where are we going?"

The *we* reverberated through her. "I meet clients on Thursday nights at an office downtown."

"You're not supposed to work for a week," he reminded her.

"It's just tonight, and I don't want to argue about it."

He raised an eyebrow and asked, "How far downtown?"

"All the way. Next door to Lynette's Diner."

He folded his arms across his chest. "Not a neighborhood I want you in at night."

"Too bad. I'm going. Which, as you so eloquently told me, means you're going. It's bad enough to bail on my day job, but these people count on me in a whole different way." Without explaining further, she started to leave, but turned back for a minute.

"Meet me downstairs when you're ready." She paused. "Please."

He hadn't expected to go out tonight, but one look at her determined expression and he decided not to fight this particular battle. A little while later, Cole parked Erin's jeep in a dimly lit parking spot and walked with her into a small office next door to Lynette's.

When he reached the entrance and looked up at the writing above the door, the name explained everything. "Pro bono, huh?"

Erin shot him a proud grin and grabbed the door handle before he could do it for her.

Inside, the waiting room was full of people, mostly women, many of whom had young children with them. Although some didn't look up when they walked in, and others glanced warily at Cole, the kids all perked up when they saw Erin.

"Erin!" A little girl with two missing front teeth ran up to her with a huge grin.

"Hi, Merry!" Erin knelt down so she was eye level with the child. "How are you?"

"Good. Mommy said if you can get money from my dad, then maybe we can leave the shelter soon and find a real 'partment of our own."

"I'll do my best," she promised the child.

Cole's heart clenched at the seriousness of the girl's words. Such huge hope and such a sad situation. Yet she looked up at Erin with such faith, even Cole wanted to believe she could perform miracles.

He accepted her request that he sit outside her door, client confidentiality being of paramount importance, especially to this kind of client. And he waited for the next four hours as she worked with as many people as walked through her office, never turning anyone away. Not even when her eyes were closing from exhaustion and he caught her mid-yawn when she walked her second-to-last client out.

He knew it was her second-to-last client, because he'd turned the lock on the front door. She was pregnant, had been shot, and needed rest. She'd have to forgive him, assuming she even realized. But thankfully she didn't.

"Arm hurt?" he asked, as he helped her get settled in the car after the final client of the night.

"Badly."

He managed not to growl at her for overdoing it, and climbed into the driver's seat and got them on the road. "Those women rely on you."

"They do." She leaned her head against

the window.

"Makes me wonder what my mom would have done if she'd had a place like this to come to," he said, staring into the dark night as he drove.

"What?" Erin lifted her head.

"Never mind." He didn't like to talk about those years.

She studied him through wise eyes. "The one thing I always knew was that I had it good growing up. And my mom? She had it good because Simon stepped up when Mike's real father wouldn't. But what would have happened to her if there had been no Simon? If she had been pregnant, alone, with nowhere to turn? I want to make sure these women know they have somewhere. Someone."

Oh, man, she was too good to be true. His mother would love her. "They're lucky to have you."

She shot him a grateful smile. "That's nice of you to say," she said through a yawn.

"I'm not nice."

She rolled her head to the side. "You have your moments," she countered.

Thankfully he pulled into the driveway of her condo before he had to reply.

Somehow Erin survived the first week of

living with Cole. They made little progress in any kind of breakthrough in their relationship, which made her uneasy, as she'd have a future of dealing with him. Neither of them discussed her pregnancy, though she sensed he was taking the time to process his new reality. And since she, too, had needed time after she'd found out, she couldn't deny him the same.

For now, Erin had enough to deal with, including the immobility of one arm and the pain from the bullet, which was getting slightly better day by day. For the baby's sake, she took as little medication as possible, which meant she hadn't slept much.

Still, she returned to work, grateful to be getting out of the house and even more grateful to be back in the office.

Trina greeted her with a welcome-back cake, which nearly brought Erin to tears. She blamed it on hormones. Her first two days back were harder than she'd anticipated. She tired easily, a combination of lingering pain and the drag on her body from the injury combined with the pregnancy.

Always observant, Evan noticed and stepped in, assuring her that he'd spread out her workload until she could handle everything again. She appreciated it and stopped insisting she could do more when she knew better. This unexpected pregnancy had certainly shown her limitations, and accepting them was better than thinking she was Superwoman.

Her biggest problem at the office was Cole. His hulking presence outside her door had everyone talking, providing an endless source of gossip and speculation among the women. Erin, who'd always been a private person, told them he was her bodyguard because of the shooting and he'd stay until they figured out who'd shot at her and why. She could only imagine how her colleagues would react when her stomach ballooned and the truth about her and Cole came out.

Especially Evan. He postured around Cole, and Cole returned the favor. And for what? Yes, Evan had asked her out in the past. Yes, they'd gone on one date when he moved back to town, before he'd been elected and become her boss. But no, she hadn't found the chemistry needed to go out with him again. Not that he didn't keep trying, but it had become a game between them. She was his challenge, and he enjoyed the chase. But Evan respected her legal abilities and she felt the same about his, and that was that. Harmless. Not that Cole understood.

Since the flowers had arrived, Cole acted like Evan was both the enemy and direct competition who needed to be chased off. Unfortunately, Evan treated Cole the same way. In reality, neither man had a claim on her, and the endless stress of the two men's reactions was slowly driving her insane.

As for her shooting, the bullet had been found lodged in a nearby car, as well as the shell casing, near the woods. Only an amateur would leave evidence behind, but at least they had something to work with. Mike sent the evidence to the state police crime lab, which was backed up with *more important cases,* and that news sent her brother over the edge. To calm him while waiting on ballistics, Erin had given in and gone over her cases with her brothers, even though she believed the possibility was ridiculous. Still, the Serendipity police were questioning people she was prosecuting — and, as Erin had predicted — with no results.

With Cole around, a reminder of his presence in Erin's future, her brothers were in constant bad moods just as she was in a constant state of awareness. How could she not be? A sleepy, just-awake Cole was as sexy as a ready-for-bed, sleepy-eyed man. Knowing he was just a room away added to her tossing and turning.

At least she was now allowed to remove the sling and use her arm as far as was comfortable, which helped her feel better and improved her mood.

She glanced at her watch, noting it was time to leave for her three P.M. appointment. She walked out of her office and nudged her bodyguard. "Time to go."

"Where are we off to?" he asked.

"It's a long story," she said as they made their way out of the office and to the elevator.

"I'm not going anywhere," he reminded her.

She sighed. "I'm doing a favor for Macy's aunt Lulu. You see, she had an argument with her sister, Macy's grandmother, over the pies at the restaurant. So Aunt Lulu applied for a job at the new supermarket that just opened in town."

She glanced at Cole to see if he was really listening and was surprised to see his eyes on her, rapt and attentive. With a shrug, she followed him onto the elevator. Cole hit the ground-floor button, and while they took the short ride down, she continued her story.

"So while Aunt Lulu was setting up the cake displays at the supermarket, a portion of the roof collapsed and she ended up with a concussion and some bruising. She sued, of course, and it should have been settled quickly, but instead the parent company sent in a high-powered law firm, who immediately slammed Lulu's attorneys with paperwork and discovery documents in an effort to get her to drop the suit." Erin frowned, hating how the older woman was being railroaded by a big corporation.

"You're a criminal prosecutor. What does this have to do with you?" Cole asked, pausing by the security desk in the lobby.

Erin shrugged. "I promised her I'd look into why a small workers' comp case has turned into some legal nightmare. Maybe throw my weight around and pull some strings. It makes no sense to hound an older woman." Erin had already made some phone calls prior to being shot, but nobody at the supermarket's main office had returned them.

Cole nodded and turned to Edgar, the afternoon security guard stationed in the lobby. "Has it been quiet?"

"Very few folks in and even fewer out," Edgar said, patting the log-in book in front of him. "How are you feeling, Miss Erin?"

She grinned. An older, grandfatherly type, Edgar had been at his post longer than Erin had been of legal age. "No worries. I'm better every day," she assured him.

Edgar hadn't been on duty when she was shot, but he'd been as distraught as Murray, the morning guard. She tried not to think about that day, but as she waved goodbye to Edgar, she paused by the front doors. Those were bulletproof, but Erin had been outside when she'd been shot.

Shaking off the thought before she stepped outdoors, she gripped the handle — and froze, suddenly unable to push open the door, let alone walk through it. Though she'd promised herself not to give in to fear, ever since the shooting, a simple walk through the parking lot was more traumatic than she'd like to admit.

"Erin?"

From a distance, she heard Cole's deep voice calling her name, but all she could hear was the chirping of birds that fateful morning and the popping sound of the rifle.

Dizziness assaulted her and dark spots danced before her eyes. Mentally, she was back in the moment, and not even the knowledge that it wasn't happening now helped her move. Without warning, her knees buckled beneath her.

Strong arms lifted her, and when she finally focused, she was wrapped in warmth, protected by a hard male body and enveloped in a purely masculine scent that triggered memories of a night she couldn't forget.

"Cole?" She blinked up at him, surprised to find his face so close, his lips near hers. Concern and worry marred his handsome face.

"You okay?" he asked.

He'd obviously caught her before she passed out and had taken her to a private corner of the lobby. "I am now." She fought off the embarrassment of nearly having fainted, instead appreciating the safety she felt in his arms.

"Panic attack, huh?" His serious gaze never left hers.

She shrugged. "I guess."

"I know."

The certainty in his tone intrigued her. How was he so sure this wasn't pregnancy- or nausea-related?

"Miss Erin?" Edgar's voice sounded from above her, interrupting before she could ask Cole that question. "Are you okay?" the elderly man asked.

"She's fine," Cole said gruffly.

"Can I get you something?" Edgar asked.

Erin nodded. "Water would be great. Thank you."

"Be right back."

Cole refocused on her. "Dizziness better?" he asked.

"Yes." She ran her tongue over her dry lips, noting he hadn't made a move to shift her out of his lap. And given that once she moved, she'd lose his warmth and security, she wasn't in any rush.

"The open parking lot scares me," she said softly.

"Jesus," Cole muttered at the admission, his arms tightening around her. He'd taken one look at her pale face, recognized the signs of panic, and grabbed her before her knees buckled. "Nobody's going to hurt you again." They'd have to go through him first.

The trust in her eyes humbled him, and he hoped he could live up to it. The same thing working in his favor also weighed against him. Cole was protecting a woman in whom he had an emotional investment — a definite problem. But instead of making him weak, he swore to himself his emotions would make him stronger, more vigilant and aware, instead of less.

Knowing she needed him, whether she wanted to or not, gave him a type of fortitude he hadn't known was in his genetic makeup. *She's mine,* he thought, tightening his arms around her. *Mine* to protect, he amended, knowing the distinction was of the utmost importance in both keeping her safe and giving him the distance he needed to do his job and not hurt her when he left on his next case.

"I know my fear isn't rational; it's psychological." She glanced down, her long eyelashes dark against her pale skin.

"It's like PTSD," he explained, attempting to keep a detachment from the subject he didn't feel. He'd gone through a rough case of post-traumatic stress disorder after his first undercover op ended. And though his superiors and the department shrink had assured him that most felt it at one time or another, Cole had fought like hell to overcome the debilitating reaction.

"What do you mean?" Erin asked.

"Rationally you know everything is okay, but your mind takes you back in time and you have no control over your body or its reactions." Just the explanation had him gritting his teeth, knowing how close to the surface his own memories actually were. His fingers curled into tight fists, until Erin's soft groan of pain alerted him to the fact that he was pinching the skin beneath her blouse.

He ran his thumbs over her arm by way of apology.

"How do you know so much about it?"

she asked.

"Water, just like you wanted," Edgar said, shoving a bottle at her.

"Thanks," she said.

Cole opened the bottle and she drank, leaving him well aware that he'd been granted a reprieve from her question. Much of his work was confidential; more of it was shit he didn't like or need to talk about. He had the required shrink sessions for that and he'd learned to put it behind him when he walked away. But Erin was persistent, and he wondered how long it would be before she pushed him for answers he wasn't ready to give, or how long he could hold out against the pull she had over him.

She wasn't deliberately tempting him, that much he knew. If anything, she was keeping her distance, or had been until he drew her into his lap, wrapped her in his arms, and shielded her from her own fears. It was part of her appeal, the way she held on to her dignity and pride. But living with her, taking care of her — hell, just being around her twenty-four seven — Erin was becoming harder and harder to resist.

Six

The rest of the week passed with no repeat of Erin's panic attack, though she couldn't stop thinking about that out-of-control feeling — and the sense she had that Cole knew more about what she'd experienced than he'd let on. She'd asked, he hadn't offered up information, and she'd let it go. Just as she'd let it go when he'd wondered aloud what his mother would have done had there been a pro bono clinic back when she'd left his father.

She still hoped for answers one day, but he was so self-contained, she doubted they'd be forthcoming.

Neither Cole nor her brothers wanted her out in public, in places like Joe's Bar, where she was an easy target, and Erin wasn't used to being confined. Having Cole for company definitely helped her when she was feeling cooped up or antsy.

As she readied for bed, washing up, brushing her teeth, and moisturizing well, she glanced in the mirror at her bare stomach. Not quite flat anymore, there was a slight roundness now that clothes still hid, and her breasts were more sensitive and slightly fuller. She swallowed hard, knowing no matter how not-ready she felt, she'd better get there and fast. Her parents were coming home Wednesday, and she'd have to tell them about her pregnancy, the shooting, and her new roommate-slash-bodyguard.

She climbed into bed and listened to the sounds of Cole in the next room. Familiar noises she was more than growing used to hearing. The creak of the floor as he walked, the sound of him opening, then closing, the bathroom door in the hall. If he worked out, doing sit-ups, push-ups, and chin-ups from a bar he hung in the bedroom doorway, he'd shower before bed.

Erin didn't know what was harder for her, knowing he was a few feet away, naked in her shower, or catching a glimpse of his bare chest and flexing muscles as he pulled himself up and lowered himself down from the bar, working out the definition she'd once felt beneath her hands. Hot skin she'd once run her lips over, then followed with her tongue.

Yes, bad-girl Erin was latent and begging

to come out, especially now that the morning sickness had begun to subside, just as the doctor promised, around fourteen weeks into her pregnancy. To make matters worse, her sexual desire returned full force, although she could also attribute that to Cole's invasion into her life. At first, she'd been in too much pain from being shot to think much about sex. Then she'd been too shaken up to focus on anything beyond one day at a time. But slowly, life had returned to normal . . . except for Cole living in her home.

And her mind consistently rewound to the day she'd panicked at work — and his immediate reaction. Not only had he been aware of her emotions but his reaction had gone over and above what a bodyguard would — or should — do. There were other ways he could have taken care of her dizziness and panic, starting with sitting her on a chair and placing her head between her knees. Instead he'd pulled her onto his lap, cradling her in his warm body and protecting her with every breath he took.

His gentleness did more to affect her than his potent arousal, and she'd felt the swell of his erection pressing against her core. Nothing had been the same for her since, not with her hormones so crazy, her emotions all over the place, and desire raging like a furnace inside her. So it was no surprise that she tossed and turned in her bed, unable to fall asleep — and when she did, panicked dreams took hold.

She went to the mall, where someone was stalking her, so she ran to her car and nearly missed being shot at again. She drove to the police station, but even there, someone was firing a gun at her in the parking lot. She woke up with a scream, bolting upright in bed, her heart pounding as she looked around the darkened room.

Without warning, the lights switched on and Cole burst in, gun drawn, which only caused her to choke out another shriek.

He lowered the weapon immediately. "Easy," he said, placing the gun on the dresser across from her.

She managed a nod.

"You okay?" he asked, coming up to the side of the bed.

"Yeah," she whispered, once again feeling ridiculous for overreacting. "I had a nightmare." Goose bumps raised on her arms as she trembled with the aftereffects of the dream.

He sat on the edge of the bed, and Erin suddenly realized he wore a pair of tight boxer briefs . . . and nothing more. It took everything she had to keep her gaze above his waist, where the dark strip of hair trailed below the waistband. She flicked her stare to his chest, but his bulk and muscles didn't help either, so she looked at his face. Concern etched his handsome features.

"Want to talk about it?" he asked.

She managed a nod. "Everywhere I went, someone was after me. I couldn't escape the gunshots or this stalker. I know it wasn't real, but I felt like I was being hunted," she said, mortified when a tear fell.

He leaned in and brushed at the moisture with his thumb. "Maybe you should talk to a professional," he suggested.

She shook her head. "No. It's stupid and it'll go away. Nobody's after me anyway. I still think the shooting was random, but until the police call it closed and you don't need to guard me anymore, I'll continue feeling on edge." But believing she hadn't been targeted and feeling safe warred in her mind, still heavy with the remnants of the dream.

She shivered and curled deeper under the comforter, not wanting to be by herself again, not knowing how to ask him to stay. She was feeling too vulnerable, and if he said no, she might embarrass herself and burst into tears.

She took in a deep breath, letting it out with a small shudder. He placed a hand on her shoulder and she felt that strong touch deep inside her.

She turned and looked up at him, drawing on courage she didn't realize she had. "Please stay."

He sucked in a surprise breath. Erin held hers but she refused to take the words back. From the moment she found out she was pregnant, she'd been alone — with the shock, with the morning sickness, and on her own again when she'd been shot. She was only so strong, and that strength had fled with the nightmare. She needed comfort and she wanted it from Cole.

Even if it was just for one night — and Lord knew they were experts at that.

She held her breath as he pulled down the covers and climbed in behind her, too far away for her even to feel his body heat. That wasn't going to work for her. She cleared her throat and rolled onto her other side, facing him.

"I can't sleep. Tell me a story," she said, getting a chuckle from him.

She liked his laugh, more because he didn't do it often and she had to work for the ones he gave her.

"What do you want to hear?" He propped

himself up on his side.

"How about what you've been up to the last few years?" she suggested, knowing he wouldn't like the subject. "In general, if you can't discuss specifics."

His frown told her she was right. "I don't like to talk about it."

"Since you're my baby's father, I want to know more about you, and I don't think asking about your past is unreasonable. You said you were undercover, so it must be serious."

"It is, when I'm living it. When a case is finished, it's over."

She held his gaze, looking into his handsome face and refusing to let him off the hook. "I don't think it is. At least not for you."

He cocked an eyebrow. "Aren't you the one who had the bad dream? So shouldn't we be talking about who or what could possibly be upsetting you?"

Erin bit the inside of her cheek. "Good try. But I asked about you. How do you know so much about anxiety attacks and PTSD?"

"I just suggested it as a possibility," he muttered.

"When most people would have attributed it to pregnancy. Come on, Cole. I'm not stupid. I see that something haunts you."

He shook his head and groaned. "You're so damned stubborn," he muttered.

"It's part of my job to push — but I really want to know you," she said.

"Then you must be damned good at it," he said, and she knew he was close to cracking.

"I am. Now talk."

"There's not much to tell. It sure as hell isn't glamorous. It's dangerous, spending great lengths of time pretending to be someone else, living a fake life. It can blur the line between who you're pretending to be and who you really are. Sometimes we have to do . . . things that are legally and morally wrong to ensure the greater good. As a result, stress reactions are normal."

Erin knew he was giving her a clinical reaction and description of his work, not the emotionally true one, but she'd take what she could get. "Go on," she said softly, not wanting to break whatever spell had him revealing things to her.

He stared at the ceiling and continued. "We're trained to go in, to deal; and when we get out, we're debriefed and shrinked until they believe we're stable and can go back under. That's how I know what you were feeling, and that's why I suggested help."

She swallowed hard. "I'm getting help."

He raised an eyebrow.

"I am! From you." She answered his unspoken question. "You're here for me. You diagnosed me," she said with a grin. "That explanation helped me understand. And I haven't had a panic attack since you held me in your arms afterward." She stared into the face she trusted and released a contented sigh. "See? Feeling better already."

He narrowed his gaze, clearly uncertain if she was feeding him a line. She wasn't. Not by a long shot. Everything about this man soothed her in ways she didn't understand. Not when those very things screamed danger, both to her life and to her heart.

"Anything else I can do to help?" he asked.

Erin's mind had already moved on from her nightmare to her greatest desire. He'd opened up to her and she felt closer to him emotionally, but it wasn't enough. They'd been living together, tiptoeing around the past, the sexual tension, the yearning she could no longer deny.

She was independent and would remain so during Cole's stay as well as after his departure, but right now, she was female and she had needs only he could fill.

He was here and he was offering to help . . . not that he knew what was on her mind. She wanted him — and she had every intention of getting what she needed.

Wide green eyes with flecks of gold stared at Cole as he waited for her to tell him what he could do to help calm her.

"You can hold me," she said, her boldness shocking him.

When he hesitated, she grinned. "Okay, that's too much for you too?"

"Wiseass," he muttered, stalling for time. Everything about her drew him in — her strength and beauty, her independent spirit and sense of self-worth.

She was single, pregnant, and not complaining. Standing up to her bossy brothers, not to mention going toe-to-toe with him. Only when her subconscious took over did she allow normal human frailty to show.

And man, did Cole get that. So how could he deny her this moment of peace?

Especially when he wanted it too.

"Turn around," he said, sensing he was approaching a threshold he really shouldn't cross, especially with her wearing a short camisole nightie with lace, all her satiny soft skin showing through.

Her eyelids fluttered, and she flipped over,

immediately scooting backward until she pressed against his chest and her ass snuggled into his crotch. His cock, which he'd managed to maintain some control over in her presence, reacted immediately, and now he was hard as nails.

With a sigh, she relaxed into him, while he was now totally tense as well as erect.

"I haven't been sleeping," she said quietly.

His arms tightened around her. "Probably because you haven't felt safe."

"I feel safe with you." She snuggled closer against him.

Her words made him uneasy. She had too much faith in him that went beyond basic protection. If she trusted him, she was doomed to disappointment. But he couldn't push her away. Instead, his hand settled on her stomach.

He couldn't get over the fact that his baby was in there, and at the thought, something warm and unfamiliar settled inside him. Made him wonder what kind of parent he'd be. He didn't have the best example of what to do. More like what not to do. He figured that was a start.

"How are you feeling?" he asked her.

"The nausea's almost completely gone. I'm just really tired." As if on cue, she yawned, and he forced himself to try to relax.

He listened to the sound of her breathing even out, and soon she'd fallen asleep. It took Cole another hour before his heart rate evened out and he chilled out enough to get drowsy with her in his arms, and at least another thirty minutes before he finally drifted off.

Erin awoke, her body plastered against a hard male one. She knew at once where she was, who she was with. She shifted and registered the fact that her silky boxers had ridden up her leg and she was brazenly rubbing against Cole's hard, muscular thigh. Mini explosions ignited inside her as she climbed a steady peak that felt so good. Mortified, she immediately stopped wriggling, and the delicious sensations pouring through her body receded.

She wanted to weep at the loss.

They were generating so much heat. The kind that was impossible to resist. And they were living together. More important, and as she'd pointed out to him, she felt safe here in his arms. She didn't care if it was temporary; she wanted him and she knew he still wanted her. Even the good girl inside her accepted that something had to give between them sooner or later.

Why not sooner?

Her overly hormonal body craved not just sex, but sex with *this man,* and she no longer wanted to deny herself. Drawing a deep breath, she ran her hands over his bare chest, following the same path with her lips, hoping he'd wake up and accept what she was freely offering.

She inhaled, breathing in the musky scent of his skin, and memories of another night assailed her, memories of him taking her hard and fast. That night he'd been in control.

This moment was all on her. She slid her fingers beneath the elastic of his briefs and wrapped her hand around his rigid shaft. Steel covered in silk, she thought, marveling at the magnificent feel of him. This was exactly what she wanted. What she needed.

She slid her thumb over the head and moisture slickened her finger. He jerked in her grasp and her hips writhed in response.

"What the hell?" He bolted upright in bed and caught her gaze. "Erin." His tone held a serious warning.

"Mmm?" She pulled down the comforter with her free hand, then pushed at his briefs, wanting them gone.

"We shouldn't do this again," he said, his

voice thick with arousal.

She paused and looked up, knowing from his gruff tone he was fighting with himself and his desire. "Why not? It's not like you can get me pregnant."

His eyes darkened. "You're going to be the death of me," he muttered.

"But what a death it'll be," she teased, tugging on his briefs once more, urging more action and less speech.

He held his body stiff, drawing her attention. "As long as you understand that I'm here for you and the baby, but as far as the future I don't . . . I mean, I can't give you —"

"Happily ever after," she said before he could put his own spin on things.

"Exactly." He breathed out, sounding relieved, and shifting his gaze away from hers. "I have a job that takes me away for long stretches of time. It's dangerous and I just don't —"

Erin didn't need to hear any more about why he couldn't provide her with the family she craved. Instead she pulled her pride around her like armor. "What makes you think I'd want that kind of future from you anyway?" she asked, deliberately nonchalant.

Which was true, for right now. Combustible chemistry and joint parenthood weren't enough to base a lifetime commitment on.

But the fact that he already knew he wouldn't want her *that way* hurt.

More than it should. So she pushed the thought out of her mind and focused on the present and on him.

"Lift your hips," she said, and was shocked when he complied.

She drew his briefs down his muscular legs and tossed them aside. When she came up next to him once more, she found him propped on his elbows, waiting. For her.

Completely nude, his erection now freed, he was hard and big and all hers.

"Be careful what you wish for," he said, studying her until her face flushed with heat.

He thought she was uncomfortable? That she'd change her mind? Then he probably forgot the woman she'd become that night. Emboldened by her memories, she ran her finger down his long, hot length until he shuddered.

She grinned and lowered her head until her hair brushed his thighs and her breath heated his skin. His groan told her she was getting to him — and she hadn't really touched him yet. Not the way she wanted to. Closing her eyes, she licked him once, twice, and then finally slid her tongue down the same path her finger had taken. His hips bucked upward and she let out a pleased sigh. Finally, she grasped him with one hand and slid her mouth over his waiting erection, enclosing him completely.

With his acquiescence, she gave herself permission to do the same, to lose herself in his taste, his scent . . .

In him.

One lick and Cole's entire body lit up. And when she pulled him into her warm, wet mouth, he thought he had died and gone to heaven. His arm gave out and he fell back against the mattress. Apparently the surprising seductress took that as a *go* because she started to work his cock in the most perfect combination possible.

Her hand cupped his length, twisting up and down while her mouth, that unbelievable mouth, took him deeper than he thought she could handle until he almost swore he touched the back of her throat. Then she eased off, her delicate tongue circling the head with an occasional hum that vibrated along his shaft. Up and down with her hand, accepting every thrust of his hips that pushed him deeper into her waiting mouth. Faster than he thought possible, his climax drew closer, his cock grew harder. His balls drew up tighter. He saw stars behind his eyes.

Reaching down, he tugged at her hair, letting her know he was ready, but instead of backing off, she kept at it, maintaining that delicious suction. And when she grazed her teeth along his shaft, he was done for. His hips jerked up and he came, his entire being thrown into the strongest, hardest climax of. His. Life. Erin accepted everything he gave, slowing her movements but not stopping until she'd wrung every last shudder from his body and every drop of moisture from him.

Cole lost all sense of time and place. When he came back to himself, she was staring at him with glassy eyes and a pleased smile on her swollen lips.

Hell. Why did they have to be so damned good together in bed? He could have kept his distance if they didn't go and do . . . *this.* But they had.

And they weren't finished. Not by a long shot. The hell of it was, Cole didn't want to be done. What man could turn down a sexual dynamo like Erin?

He crooked a finger her way. "Your turn."

"I don't think you're quite ready," she said, her cheeks pink with embarrassment.

Cole closed his eyes and groaned. That cute little blush encapsulated why Erin

Marsden was everything Cole should stay away from. Beneath the woman who'd given him the best blow job he ever had was a sweet girl who could still be embarrassed by what she'd done. Cole was dark where Erin was light, his past ugly where everything about her was beauty and grace. She'd remain that way long after he went under again . . . as long as he didn't destroy her first.

Still, he'd gotten them into this position, and he didn't just mean in bed. They were connected by more than just sex. But as long as she knew not to build white picket fences around him, they'd be just fine. They'd already had that conversation, he reminded himself. So he could feel free to just enjoy *now*.

"I said, come here," he told her.

Her eyes glazed a bit more at his command and she shifted until she was beside him once again. He pushed her tangled hair off her face. Without makeup, she was even more innocent-looking, more sweet.

He'd tasted that sweetness before and he intended to do it again now. "Lay back."

She raised her eyebrows and complied without question. He grasped one of her legs and pulled it open, then the other, until she was spread wide for him. With shaking hands and little finesse, he yanked her silk shorts down, shocked to realize she wasn't wearing underwear beneath.

"You're just trying to torture me," he muttered.

"Not really. I sleep like this every night," she informed him.

"Of course you do." He'd already decided to torment her the same way she'd done him and lowered his head, allowing only his hot breath to touch her bare mound.

He took in her feminine scent and his entire body stiffened in response. In record time, he was ready to go again. But he wasn't giving her that treat too quickly. If he was going to allow himself this, knowing that whatever he and Erin shared in bed had to be temporary, he wanted memories to keep with him in the future.

So when they played nice for the sake of their kid, when she finally looked at him and saw the real Cole Sanders, the one his father raised, Cole would have them to hold on to.

Right now, he wanted her begging him to take her.

Her legs were trembling and he braced a hand on either thigh before dipping his head for the long-awaited treat, and sweet heaven, she tasted good. He slid his tongue between her wet folds, lapping at her over and over, savoring the unique flavor that was Erin. He remembered exactly what made her moan, made her writhe in need, buck her hips and call out his name. He knew where to lick, where to suckle and when to ease off with teasing flicks of his tongue.

Only when she was shaking, straining against his mouth for release, did he give her what she wanted, thrusting one finger into her moist heat and nipping the tight bud with his teeth. Erin's body went from trembling to stiff as she came, crying out his name long and hard. He suckled her clit through her entire orgasm, waiting for the tremors to subside before easing off her and giving her a minute to return to reality.

"Cole," she said in a husky voice.

"Yeah, honey?" he asked, sliding back up on the bed.

"As awesome as that was? It wasn't enough. I need you inside me."

Oh, hell, this woman was practically made for him. She wasn't begging, but it was damn close enough. His body was near to bursting.

"I can do that." He lifted himself over her and paused, calculating how fast he could get to the bathroom and back.

"You don't need protection," she said

softly, surprising him. "I mean, not just because I can't get pregnant, but . . . I'm . . . you know." That blush covered her cheeks again.

Yeah, he knew. She was clean. In so many more ways than him. "I am too. I had a complete physical when I came out from undercover."

"Okay then." She nodded, her expression dazed but certain.

"Okay," he said, and looked into her eyes for the first time.

As soon as he met that wide-eyed gaze, the emotion he'd been holding at bay slammed into him hard. Yeah he'd been with her before, but this time was different, and not just because he didn't have to wear a condom. She was carrying his baby.

Jesus.

He glanced at her pale stomach, mostly flat, but there was a slight bump he hadn't noticed before. He jerked his head up and she laughed.

"You won't hurt me — or the baby."

She'd read his mind. He knew that, but for some reason it helped to hear her say it.

"Do you not want to do this?" Her voice dipped low. Her lashes fluttered down and she looked everywhere but at him.

He'd never been with a pregnant woman,

but he'd had buddies whose wives had been pregnant, and he knew all about raging hormones, feminine insecurities over getting bigger. Cole had never enjoyed those beer-induced conversations, but he was glad for them now.

"Honey, you are so damned beautiful. Of course I want you." His gaze traveled from her stomach, to the breasts he intended to explore later, then to her mouth.

Which he realized he hadn't yet kissed. Maybe that connection would reassure her that no matter what he couldn't give her in the future, right now, there was nothing he wanted more than to get inside her body.

He leaned down and trapped her mouth with his, and what he'd intended to be a soft seduction flared into a raging inferno. He devoured her, knowing he was not only giving her a taste of him, but showing her what she tasted like on his tongue. She groaned beneath him and threaded her fingers through his hair, pulling at the same time she kissed him back, matching him in both desire and need.

Unable to stop himself, he rocked his hips against hers, letting his erection swell and thicken against her soft folds, arousing her with a slow, stroking glide.

"Mmm," she sighed into his mouth, and

arched her back up for better friction.

He shifted his hips from side to side, giving her some of what she needed, but not everything. Not yet. Even if he was killing himself, he thought, there was more he wanted from her first.

He trailed his lips from her mouth, down the side of her cheek, neck, throat, pausing to dampen a patch of skin that begged for a taste.

She tugged at his hair. "Inside me. Now."

"Greedy," he said, chuckling. "Not yet."

He slid lower until he reached her breast, licking around her soft flesh, noting she was bigger than he remembered. Not much, but enough for him to notice. He plumped one full mound in his hand, before pulling one tight nipple into his mouth.

She whimpered. Obviously she was more sensitive too, but since she wasn't complaining, he took advantage, flicking his tongue back and forth over her nipples.

"Please, please," she said, bending her knees to entice him.

Her hips gyrated beneath him and he loved the way she cradled him in her thighs and her slick moisture dampened his cock. He grinned and moved to her other breast, giving it the same treatment, prolonging her sweet agony, only this time he used his teeth, grazing her sensitive nipples.

She nearly bucked him off her as she writhed and cried out. "I need you inside me," she said, her voice almost breaking with the depth of her need. "Now, Cole. Please, I need you now."

"That's what I wanted to hear." He braced his arms on either side of her, readying himself.

Her eyes were bright, her face glistening, desire making her even more beautiful. Fuck.

He poised at her entrance, unable to tear his gaze from her face as he entered her, even as he knew he shouldn't look. That watching her eyes soften as he pressed inside, felt her heat and warmth cushion him, would only make complicate things. *As if they aren't complicated enough,* Cole thought, and thrust into her completely.

"Oh my God," she said, her body clamping tight around him.

He knew exactly what she meant. It was just them. Skin to skin, no barrier. He'd never felt anything like it before. Never not used a condom. With this woman, he never planned to use one again.

Unable to remain still, he slid out and back in and suddenly he wasn't thinking; he was feeling. An avalanche of sensation hit him from all sides, taking him higher, faster than ever before. She met his thrusts, her moans and sighs telling him she was right there with him. No way would he come without her, but he didn't have to worry. As quickly as his climax approached, hers did as well, her body slamming upward with each thrust he made inside. She came beneath him, her nails digging into his back, and when he heard his name on her lips, he followed her right over the cliff.

SEVEN

Erin woke up wrapped in heat, her body totally sore in the best possible way. She enjoyed every aching muscle, especially when she recalled the reasons behind each one. A glance at the clock told her it was almost time to get up for work, but she had a few minutes before her alarm went off.

Time enough to think about last night. A night she wouldn't trade for the world. Right now Cole slept beside her, having pulled her into his arms in his sleep, but she had no doubt he'd wake up, remember . . . and withdraw. She swallowed hard, deciding her best defense was to expect the behavior and act like she just didn't care. If she was going to play in his league, she'd have to accept his rules.

Even if she was developing feelings for the self-contained man who held her close in sleep and pushed her away during daylight hours. She already knew she was one of

130

those girls for whom sex wasn't just sex. She couldn't help it. She'd been raised to take it seriously, and when she did sleep with a guy, it was because she was ready to deepen the relationship.

Cole was the one man for whom she'd broken her rule, but that had been the first time they slept together. This time she'd had time to think. And this time she knew him better. If not details about his past, she understood more about the kind of man he'd become and she'd discovered her instincts about him were correct. He had a protective streak, he knew how to take care of her, he did it without complaint, and he anticipated her needs.

How could she not have begun to appreciate his finer qualities? But she'd agreed that this was about sex, not commitment. Their future held child custody agreements, joint parenting — when he was in town — and other things she hadn't begun to contemplate.

All she needed to do was act cool and remind herself his caring was about his protective streak and not anything he felt for her beyond a sense of duty. Yeah, that hurt. But it was the truth and she'd do well to remember it.

On that thought, she lifted the covers and

rolled away from Cole in an attempt to get out of bed before he woke. Unfortunately her alarm went off before she made her escape.

"Running again?" he asked in a sleep-roughened voice.

She shut the alarm on her cell phone. "Nope. Just getting up for the day. It's not like I can disappear on you this time."

"Are you okay?" he asked, surprising her.

"I'm fine. Why?"

"You haven't looked at me, for one thing."

Forcing herself to turn over, she met his gaze. And wished she hadn't. First thing in the morning, Cole Sanders was even more sexy than ever. His hair was mussed and stood at odd angles, razor stubble darkened his jaw, his brooding eyes assessed her through heavy lids, and all she could think about was climbing on top of his broad chest and kissing him senseless.

"Pregnancy hormones," she muttered.

"What?"

"Nothing. I'm hungry. I need to shower and get something to eat before work."

"Okay, well, I'll jump in the shower real quick and make us something while you get ready." Throwing the comforter off, he rose, perfect in his nudity.

From his muscled arms and defined abs

to the tattoos on his biceps and upper back, he was simply amazing. If she allowed her gaze to travel lower, there were even more things she could ogle, but she refrained. Because she, on the other hand, had pulled the blanket back over her and now held on for dear life.

She wasn't one to flaunt her body on a good day. At four months pregnant, she wasn't feeling particularly comfortable with herself, the curves she was developing, or the lack of a waist that had suddenly occurred. Last night she'd been too caught up in the moment to be shy, but that wasn't the case this morning.

"Go ahead." She waved him away, indicating he should use the shower first. And quickly.

His gaze dropped to her fingers, clutching at the blanket. "Erin?"

"Hmm?" she asked too brightly.

"You're gorgeous, and if you didn't need to get to work, I'd strip that cover off you and pick up where we left off last night."

A small moan escaped her lips, but he was gone without indicating he'd heard. A few minutes later, she heard the creaking of pipes and the sound of water running in the shower. She was dying to join him.

With a groan, she snuggled deeper into

the blanket. How she was going to keep her distance was beyond her, but she had no choice if she wanted to survive their enforced closeness with her emotions intact.

Cole was making breakfast in the kitchen. He removed the bread from the fridge and was opening the bag when Erin's scream from the other room startled him.

He dropped the bread and bolted for the front door. "What happened?"

"I went to get the newspaper from the porch. I opened the door and . . . look!" She pointed beyond the entry, her hand shaking, her face pale.

He shifted her behind him and pulled his gun from his back holster before cautiously checking outside. A dead animal that looked more like roadkill than a pet lay on her porch in an open shoe box.

A gagging noise sounded behind him. He turned to see Erin run for the bathroom in the hall.

"Shit," he muttered. Not wanting to taint evidence, he left the box outside and headed to help her first.

He stood in the doorway of the half-bath downstairs while she dry-heaved into the toilet. He cringed, something too near the region of his heart twisting at her pain and discomfort.

Without asking, he stepped inside and wet a damp towel, then knelt beside her.

"Go away," she moaned into the toilet.

Cole ignored her, merely lifting her hair so he could lay the cold towel over the back of her neck.

"Feels good," she said begrudgingly. He understood she was more embarrassed than angry at him for not giving her privacy.

"If you're okay, I need to call your brother and get someone over here to process the . . . evidence." Since her retching had stopped, he didn't mention the dead animal specifically.

"Go." She waved a hand and this time he listened.

A few minutes later, both Mike and Sam arrived in separate cars, Mike in an SUV, Sam in his patrol car. Erin was in the kitchen sipping ginger ale, and Cole met the men at the door.

Sam, in uniform, knelt in front of the box and frowned. "Jesus," he muttered. "What kind of sicko would scoop an already dead animal off the road?"

"One who doesn't want to do the dirty work herself to make her point," Cole said.

"Her?" Erin came up behind him.

He glanced over, noting she was still pale.

Unable to help himself, he wrapped a steadying arm around her shoulders. "Let's sit down inside so we can talk this through," Cole suggested.

"One of our forensics people will be here to process things any minute," Sam said.

They all headed for the family room, where Erin curled on the couch. Her eyes were cloudy and shadowed, a far cry from the sexy, teasing minx from last night, and he realized how badly he wanted that Erin back, not this worried, fearful one.

"I suppose I should be grateful they didn't throw it through the window I just had replaced," she said.

All three men's heads came up at that. "What window?" Cole asked.

"A baseball destroyed my front window a few months ago. I had to replace the broken glass."

"Any reason you didn't mention it?" Sam asked.

Mike cocked an eyebrow, pinning his sister with an annoyed glance.

"Get that look off your faces. It was a baseball! I'm sure some neighbor kid had an accident and was too scared to admit it. It happened way before the shooting and I forgot all about it until now."

Cole frowned, not happy about any of

this. Something niggled at the back of his mind, something that made him uneasy, but he couldn't pinpoint what. Or why.

"Let's get back to this morning's . . . gift," Mike said.

The doorbell rang, interrupting them. "That'll be forensics." Sam rose to answer.

Erin, Mike, and Cole sat in silence, waiting for details, while Sam observed the evidence collection outside.

Sensing Erin's stress, Cole placed a hand on her stocking-covered ankle. She'd been dressed for work when she came downstairs and opened the door.

Mike's gaze immediately shot to the intimate contact and he scowled.

Cole ignored him. Mike's sister needed comfort, and Cole was the closest one who could give it to her. He didn't give a damn if Mike liked it or not.

"Erin, did you call in sick to work?" he asked her.

"Oh God. I can't afford to miss more time."

"More?" Cole turned to face her.

"She had morning sickness but thought it was a stomach bug. But it figures you wouldn't know anything about that, considering you were nowhere to be found." Mike eyed him with a healthy amount of disgust.

"Can you just lay off?" Erin said to her brother. "I can't deal with this right now. Give me a phone. By the time we're finished here, I won't have time to go in to work before my appointment."

"What appointment?" Cole asked. They hadn't yet discussed her schedule for the day.

"I have a doctor's appointment at noon."

"Is something wrong?" he asked, concerned.

She shook her head. "Regular monthly appointment. Every pregnant woman has them."

He nodded. They could discuss this further later. He handed her the portable receiver lying on the table.

While she dialed and called in sick, Mike's furious gaze didn't leave Cole's. Ah, well. He knew better than to think the Marsden brothers would give him any kind of pass on the situation with Erin. He didn't have a sister, but he imagined he'd react the same way, so he let it go.

He wasn't too thrilled with himself at the moment. He hadn't known Erin missed any work because of the pregnancy, hadn't thought about what she'd gone through the first three months alone. He closed his eyes and fought for calm.

138

"Let's discuss what we know," Mike said, drawing his attention back to what was important. "First a shooting, then a warning."

"That's de-escalation," Cole said. "Normally the warning would come first."

Mike nodded. "Unless . . . maybe the softball through the window was a warning."

"Possibly, but that doesn't explain going from shooting to another warning."

Erin's gaze traveled between them. She was listening. Processing but not participating — and that concerned Cole. In the short time he'd known her, he wasn't used to her being a bystander in her own life.

"Shell casings left at the site, leaving roadkill in a condo neighborhood. Both of these things seem like they were done by amateurs," Mike continued.

"Cole, you referred to the person who left the — present — as female before. Why?" Erin asked.

And there she was, Cole thought with relief. Erin was speaking up, which meant she was okay.

"Because a man would have no compunction killing a cat or a dog to make his point. A female would have more trouble with it. A woman is more likely to use an already dead animal. It's easier to justify to themselves."

Erin pulled in a deep breath. "But what woman would scoop up roadkill herself?"

Cole could tell she was trying to control her breathing and gag reflex response to the dead animal she'd seen.

"She probably has an accomplice," Mike said. "A male who would do that kind of dirty work."

Erin nodded. "That makes sense, but who? Who would shoot me? Who would target me like this?" she asked, her voice rising.

Cole squeezed her ankle in reassurance that he was there. Not going anywhere while she was in any danger.

"Hey, you might want to see this," Sam said, returning with a sealed plastic bag, a note inside.

Erin scrambled to a sitting position. "What is it?"

"A note. Handwritten."

"What's it say?" Mike asked.

" 'Leave him alone,' " Sam said.

Erin wrinkled her nose. "Him who?"

"That's the thousand-dollar question." Sam sounded as frustrated as the rest of them.

"Someone's telling me to leave *him* alone.

140

That's further confirmation we're dealing with a woman, right?" Erin glanced at Cole, her confusion clear in her tight expression and troubled eyes.

He nodded. "On the roadkill, yes. On the shooting? I'm not so sure." Something felt so off about this whole thing. It could be because the person was unstable —

"Are you suggesting it's two people after me?" Erin asked, sounding more panicked by the second.

Cole kept a firm hand on her leg. "It's possible, that's all. Mike?" He looked to her brother for confirmation. They'd gone through similar training and they'd both been undercover. Both been given the same behavioral courses.

"Rifle shooting doesn't sound like a woman," Mike agreed. "This does. But like I said, could just be an accomplice or someone doing something on their own, not listening to the woman."

"My head hurts," Erin muttered.

"Look, let's get this processed, see if we can pull any prints. You two didn't touch anything?" Sam asked.

Cole shook his head.

"Are you insane?" Erin asked, obviously doing her best not to gag again. "I want answers," she said. "I hope the lab can work faster than they've been doing on the gun."

"They will." Cole agreed and he'd already taken steps to ensure it. "I have a call in to my people along with a promise to get things moving. We should know something soon." He'd given everyone involved time to work without stepping on toes, but he'd gotten tired of waiting and he was finished tiptoeing around her brothers' egos. While Mike had contacts high up in Manhattan, Cole had people who owed him more recent favors, both federal and state. Erin was worth pulling them in for.

Mike looked ready to argue but obviously thought better. "Thank you," he said begrudgingly.

"No problem."

Mike rose from his seat and walked over to Erin. "You okay, sis?"

She nodded. "I thought morning sickness was over, but that just . . ." She closed her eyes against the memory.

"Yeah. But I didn't mean just that."

"He meant with me being here," Cole clarified for her.

Erin let out a long sigh. "I'm fine. If I wasn't, Cole wouldn't be here. End of discussion." She folded her arms across her chest, a sign she was digging in her heels.

Cole had come to know that about her at least.

"Fine." Mike raised both hands in a gesture of defeat. "Just know —"

"You're here for me. I know. And I love you for it." Her voice softened. "But if you want me calm through this, I suggest you accept that Cole's part of my life — my baby's life now. Whatever we work out between us will have to be okay with you too."

Mike inclined his head, then leaned over and kissed Erin's cheek. "I'll call you as soon as I know something."

She nodded.

"You." Mike stood and Cole did as well. "Don't let her out of your sight."

"They'll have to go through me to get to her," Cole told the other man. They might not agree on everything, but when it came to Erin's safety, they were one hundred percent in accord.

Mike inclined his head, obviously satisfied.

Once he left, Cole turned to Erin. "Let's get you reshowered and changed. You'll feel better, and then maybe you'll want to eat."

Erin rose. Her color looked better, a touch of pink in her cheeks. "I can handle myself. I'll meet you back in the kitchen in a few minutes."

He backed off, recognizing that despite everything, she was still in withdrawal mode. He'd noticed it this morning but let it go without a fuss. Although he preferred her soft and giving, he understood self-protection only too well.

Besides, he didn't want Erin getting attached to him, and her accepting how things needed to be was a good thing. He'd laid out the rules — no commitment, just sex — and today she was giving him the space that defined those boundaries. Part of him approved because it was safer that way, for both of them. But damned if her turning away from him hurt more than it should.

And it grated that she'd pulled into herself, since she so obviously needed someone to lean on. Another thing he liked about Erin: She might need him, but she wouldn't let herself depend on him in that needy way some women did. His thoughts immediately traveled to Victoria Maroni and her begging him not to leave or to take her with him. It'd been a goddamned case, and she had made it sound like he was bailing on an actual relationship. He hadn't slept with the woman or sent her mixed signals, that he knew for sure.

He refocused on Erin, guilt riding him

that she'd been alone through three months of misery, when he was equally responsible for causing her pregnancy. Now she'd mentioned a doctor's appointment he'd known nothing about. He was shocked by how possessive he felt about her in such a short time, warning signals going off in his brain. She didn't want him hovering, but suddenly he needed to be there for her, to take care of her, to show her she wasn't alone.

Which went against every instinct he had that told him to encourage her to preserve her independence because she'd need it when he was gone. But he couldn't let her go through this alone when he was here, now. Especially because once he was gone, she'd be needing that independent streak of hers once more.

Already exhausted before her day had even begun, Erin made her way back downstairs, her nerves shot from this morning. What kind of sicko would leave a dead animal outside her door and not get specific about what they wanted from her? Leave *who* alone? Which case? Why?

Her stomach grumbled and she realized she was so hungry she could barely think. Well, at least the nausea had passed.

She found Cole in the kitchen with a delicious-looking breakfast of French toast and orange juice waiting for her at the table. "You really missed your calling," she said with a grin.

He'd shocked her with his culinary skills, and she suddenly had an urge to learn how to feed herself this well. Not to mention her child.

"Not really. I just like to eat," he said with an endearing grin.

"Would you teach me?" she asked. "You know, so I can give little him or her the kind of Sunday meals my mom gave us?"

Cole's eyes warmed as she spoke. "Yeah, I can do that."

She reached for the maple syrup and smothered her French toast. "I remember how my dad would go get the papers, and when he came home, mom would have the most amazing pancakes waiting for when he came back and we all woke up." Erin would love to have that in her future.

Of course Cole wouldn't be part of that scenario, and she quickly glanced down at her plate, not wanting him to see the disappointment in her eyes.

Instead she cut herself a piece and tasted. "Oh my God, you are a magician."

He laughed and began eating his own

food. "So tell me more about this doctor's appointment you have today."

She shrugged. "Nothing much to tell. Just a normal monthly appointment. You can just drop me off at the hospital. My doctor sees me there, and I'll call you when it's time to pick me up."

"Erin," he said, a distinct edge to his voice. "Just because you were alone before doesn't mean you are now."

She glanced up, noticed the tight set to his jaw, and realized he was worried about her safety. "You can sit in the waiting room if it makes you feel better, but nobody's going to hurt me in a hospital." She drank a long sip of orange juice and her body thanked her by perking up a bit more.

"Try again, sweetheart."

She narrowed her gaze. "Surely you don't want to sit in the same room while the doctor examines me!"

His grip tightened around his fork. "That's exactly what I want."

"But it's just me and my doctor! Nobody can get near me!" Not even her brothers would make such a ridiculous demand, and they were as overprotective as they came.

"This has nothing to do with someone being after you."

She placed her glass back on the table.

"Then what? I don't get it, and you're going to have to lay it out for me."

"Did it occur to you that I might *want* to be there for you? For our baby's doctor appointment?"

No, she thought. It hadn't occurred to her. She'd gone into this thinking she was alone. Even after he'd said he'd be there for her and the baby, she thought he'd meant just financially.

He was only living here now because she might be in danger, not because he wanted to be with Erin. He'd made that clear last night. Given a choice, he'd be in his room over Joe's, ignoring her when they saw each other in town. Sex was a perk, nothing more. Even as obvious hurt and frustration flashed in his expression, she couldn't understand it.

"You don't have to go through this by yourself. I'll be with you today, and I want a list of future appointments. I'll be going with you from now on."

"Umm, okay." Maybe?

She wasn't sure how she felt about his proclamation. She doubted he knew either, considering the conflicting messages he was sending her.

No future. You aren't alone. Two very different concepts, and her head was spinning, but one thing stood out. She'd hurt his feelings by not including him, but she'd never have thought Cole would be interested in the little things her doctor discussed with her about the baby.

She thought he'd . . . what? Hand her child support and walk away? Was that the kind of man she believed him to be? And if that was the conclusion he'd drawn, no wonder he was insulted by her assumption.

They finished eating and cleaned up in silence, Cole dealing with a mix of warring feelings. His emotional reaction to her doctor's appointment caught him off guard. Way off guard. Since when did he want to be involved in things like doctor's appointments? Where did these protective instincts for Erin even come from?

Yeah, he was the baby's father, and he'd planned to do right by her and the kid, but even he hadn't considered what that entailed. Maybe she hadn't either, which meant he'd overreacted. But when her brother slammed him with what she'd gone through alone, something inside him had shifted, leaving him confused.

His head pounded and he decided he needed to talk to someone who could give him clarity, but who could he turn to? Not her brother, Mike. The man would likely throttle him. There was his stepfather, but he wasn't ready to have that conversation with him just yet. Or with his mother either. And he sure as hell wouldn't turn to his father. Cole let out a low laugh, knowing that the shit would hit the fan when his old man found out Erin was pregnant and Cole was responsible. He'd like to put that conversation off as long as possible.

Maybe his cousin Nick. The man was recently married, so he might have more of a handle on something like this than Cole did. He'd get in touch with his cousin soon. Because what Cole was feeling and what he was capable of giving were two different things. So was what Erin deserved. They might be completely compatible people on paper, and when they were together they were explosive, but Cole didn't know how to live the family life Erin obviously craved. The one she'd grown up experiencing. The one she clearly desired — and he wanted her to have.

EIGHT

Dr. Reed squirted warm gel on Erin's skin, then placed the ultrasound wand on her stomach. By now, the procedure was a familiar one, as he searched for the baby's heartbeat. In a few seconds, the reassuring *whoosh*ing sound echoed throughout the room and Erin let herself relax. From the moment the doctor was able to let her hear the heartbeat, she held her breath each time the man did his scan.

"And that is your baby's heartbeat, Mr. Sanders," Dr. Reed said to Cole.

He sucked in a sharp, surprised breath and reached for Erin's hand, squeezing it tight. His excitement was palpable, and she understood the feeling all too well. Unfortunately there were other emotions rushing through her too. Ones that made her feel fragile, raw, and vulnerable. With Cole beside her, Erin felt as exposed as her bare belly, his presence making her wish for things he'd flat-out told her she would never have.

At least, not with him.

Of all the reasons she hadn't let herself think about including him in her doctor's appointments, this overwhelming emotional pit in her stomach was the main one. Erin had dreamed of a family in her future, and one night had suddenly changed and complicated everything. She swallowed over the lump in her throat, determined to get through this with her dignity intact, and that meant no crying.

"Erin? Did you hear me?" the middle-aged OB-GYN asked.

Erin smiled at the man. He'd come highly recommended by her regular doctor, and so far Erin was pleased with his practice, his partners, and her choice.

"I'm sorry. Can you say that again?"

He smiled back indulgently. "You're somewhere else today. I asked if you two would like to know the sex of the baby. You're at the right time and my view is pretty good, so I'd say I can give you a pretty accurate answer. It's up to you."

Erin's heart skipped a beat. In her excitement, she was about to answer when Cole's voice stopped her.

"Can we have time to talk?" he asked the

doctor, taking her by surprise.

"Of course. I'll be back in a few minutes." He placed the wand in a holder and draped a paper sheet over Erin's stomach before leaving them alone.

"This is overwhelming," he said, taking her by surprise.

And, of course, with his admission, her heart melted. How could she keep him at a distance when they were sharing something so fundamentally important and deep?

"That's how I felt the first time I heard the heartbeat and saw the baby on the screen." She met his gaze, startled to find softness where there never had been any before.

"Makes me want to take a second look at myself. And a third and a fourth."

The surprises kept coming. "Why?" she asked him. "I like what I see. We wouldn't be in this situation if I didn't."

His lips turned down. "Then you see something my old man doesn't and your brothers sure as hell don't."

Anger at Jed surged through her. She definitely wouldn't be bringing him any more of her mother's casseroles. As for her brothers, they would come around once they got over the shock of her pregnancy.

"Your father's a harsh, unforgiving man

who obviously wanted a clone of himself. Nothing less would make him happy. That's not who you are. Your mom wouldn't have left town with you if she didn't want better for you both." He still held her hand and she squeezed tighter.

"My mom's great," he agreed.

"And she took you away from Jed, right?" She held her breath, hoping he'd tell her more. That the intimacy of her lying here on an exam table, of seeing the black-and-white sonogram of their baby, would help him want to confide in her.

"I was a handful, make no mistake. The harder Jed pushed at me, the more I rebelled. So when he threatened to send me to military school, going so far as to make the calls and hang the brochures on the refrigerator, I knew something had to give."

"What happened?"

"Got myself arrested. It was stupid. I was drunk. Me and another guy graffitied a wall downtown." Cole grinned sheepishly, as if the memory had the power to embarrass him.

Despite the seriousness of the subject, Erin laughed. "What happened?"

"I wasn't calling my dad." He let out a harsh laugh. "I called Mom. She came and talked to me through the jail cell bars. She

154

said she'd take me away from here and we'd make a life somewhere else, but only if I swore getting away from Jed would turn me around."

"Wow."

He nodded, his expression pensive and pained. "I promised. Hell, I wanted nothing more than to get away from the old man. Imagine my shock when I found out she felt the same. Her sister, my cousin Nick's mother, gave her start-up money and the name of a friend in New York who'd promised to rent her an apartment. She took a secretarial job at a local PD and met Brody. He's my stepdad."

Erin fell a little in love with his mother at that moment, even if she barely remembered her. "Cole?"

"Hmm?"

She knew she was treading in dangerous territory, but the doctor hadn't returned and she wanted so badly to get inside his head and understand him better. "If your mom was so good to you, why doesn't her belief in you overshadow your father's lack of it?"

Cole ran his free hand through his hair and groaned. "There's only so many times you can hear negative shit before you start believing it yourself. By the time we got out,

I'd had sixteen years of disappointing Jed under my belt."

His words seared through her and she decided to change the subject to a more pleasant one. "Tell me about your stepdad."

"That's easy. Brody Williams is a good man. He fell hard for my mother, and she must've been miserable long before she left Jed because she was open to a new relationship pretty fast."

"Was he a good stepfather?" she asked, hoping Cole had had a positive male role model in his life at some point in time.

He nodded, his facial muscles relaxing with the new topic. "The best. He did everything he could to turn my head around. He got my arrest expunged from my record. If not for him, I wouldn't have gone to the police academy, that's for damn sure. I didn't want anything to do with a legacy that was my father's."

"What made you change your mind?"

"I wanted Brody to be proud of me." Cole shrugged his shoulders, indicating it was that simple.

Maybe it was. Erin had certainly always strived to please her parents, though they hadn't pressured her into her good-girl mode. For her it came naturally.

"Then you need to focus on the things

Brody said to and about you, not the things Jed said."

Cole treated her to a rare smile, and her stomach flipped at the sight.

"You can be damned sure *he'll* be my role model for how to be a good parent," he said, and Erin nodded in understanding.

She hurt for the childhood he'd had and the way his father emotionally abused him. Cole had so many more scars and dark places than Erin had realized, and it made her mad. Unlike Cole, she'd been blessed with a loving family. Sure, they had their share of dysfunction — her mom had been pregnant with Mike, another man's child, when she'd married Simon Marsden. And just last year, Mike's real father, Rex Bransom, had surfaced, bringing painful secrets with him. But her family had pulled together and survived because of the love they shared and the solid background her mother, Ella, and her dad, Simon, had given their children.

Erin wanted that same sense of security for her baby, and she just knew Cole felt the same way. He didn't believe they could provide that environment together because he'd return to undercover work, but so what? Did that mean he couldn't come back to her when he was finished? If that's what they both desired? They wouldn't know unless they tried to make things work between them before the baby was born.

She was scared, she admitted to herself, and suddenly she was ready for her parents to come home so she could confide in her mother. Ella had been through something similar . . . Why hadn't Erin realized it before now?

The recognition made her smile.

"What are you grinning at?" Cole asked.

"I just realized some things." Things that helped her look at her situation differently, just as Cole needed to do the same. "Don't let Jed's feelings define you as a man or as a parent, Cole. Just be yourself. Our son or daughter will be lucky to have you." She tightened her hand around his.

His dark eyes heated, and corresponding warmth settled in her chest.

"Speaking of the kid, do we want to know the sex?" he asked her, breaking the silent but charged moment.

"I thought I did, but now . . . I think I'd like to be surprised. You?"

"Whatever you want works fine for me."

Erin nodded, wishing the rest of her life with him could be as easily decided.

Cole sensed Erin's unease when she arrived

at work on Monday. Cole didn't blame her. After all her arguing about the shooting being a fluke, she'd finally been forced to accept that for some unknown reason, a crazy person was after her. Maybe two crazies. Cole hadn't wrapped his mind around which.

Ballistics should come in today, giving them answers, or at least a lead. In the meantime, he settled into his chair outside her office door, satisfied with knowing he had a firsthand view of whoever went in to see her. Especially when that smarmy boss of hers arrived not too long after she did this morning.

Dressed in a suit and tie, his brown hair expensively cut, the man looked like he'd stepped out of a magazine ad. He was too slick, and Cole had disliked him on sight. Carmichael walked past him without a word, which just made Cole want to give him a hard time — because he could.

Rising, Cole placed his arm across the doorway and cleared his throat.

Carmichael turned. "What's wrong, Sanders? Need to pat me down before I'm allowed entry?"

"Evan, come on in," Erin called, interrupting.

Probably on purpose. Cole lifted his arm

and Carmichael shot Cole a smug look before stepping inside.

"What can I do for you?" Erin asked, sounding pleased to see him.

Cole insisted she keep her door open, enabling him to hear whatever went on when her boss commanded an audience. In Cole's opinion, based on Carmichael's fake charm and the way he constantly self-promoted, the man was the consummate politician, a man wrapped up in appearances only.

"I just wanted to remind you about our date Saturday night."

Cole stiffened — despite the fact that he had no claim on Erin and made no bones about his lack of intentions regarding marriage and the happily ever after he knew she wanted. And regardless of the fact that his own choices might push Erin into the arms of another man.

One day.

In the very distant future, if ever.

But not this bastard. And not while Erin was sleeping with Cole.

"Oh no," Erin said, sounding truly upset. A riffling of papers followed. "I completely forgot. And it wasn't a *date* date, it was me accompanying you to the annual Bar Association dinner."

"Call it what you want, I've been looking forward to it. And you know it's important that we're seen at this, what with me planning to run for state attorney general and you the logical successor to my office."

"Evan, I never said —"

"Hush," he said in an affectionate tone that made Cole's skin crawl.

He itched to storm in there, but knew there was only one way *that* would end — badly. So he held his anger and frustration in check, bit his tongue, and waited.

"We both know you're the perfect choice to take my place. Together we're a power couple in this town, or we could be."

Damn the man. He obviously viewed Erin and her family connections in this town as the perfect way to take his next career step. They'd be a power couple over Cole's dead body. She was pregnant with *his* baby, and he wondered how Mr. Family Values would take that bit of news.

Tell him, Cole thought, with uncharacteristic possessiveness and need.

Erin whispered something Cole couldn't hear.

"Just think about it. In the meantime, I'll pick you up around seven. I want to get there in time for cocktails and schmoozing."

"Umm —"

Cole had had enough. He rose and stood in the doorway, glaring at the other man. "Just how did you factor her bodyguard in to this occasion?"

Evan turned to face Cole. "Frankly, I didn't. She'll be perfectly safe with me for the evening."

Cole raised an eyebrow. "Because you're trained to protect her?" He folded his arms across his chest.

"Cut it out," Erin muttered.

"Well?" Cole pushed, determined to verbally shove the other man out the door. "If someone shoots again are you willing to throw yourself in front of a bullet to protect her?"

Evan paled.

"Because I can assure you, I am. Trained, capable, and willing."

Evan assessed Cole with a different look on his face now. "I still think you belong at this event, Erin. But maybe your . . . bodyguard is right. You need protection I can't provide."

And Cole could see what it cost him to admit it. For the first time, he dredged up a modicum of respect for the man.

"Your safety is of paramount importance, but so is your career. Having nothing to do

162

with me, you need to be there this week-end."

Erin rose to her feet. "I don't even know if I want your job."

"Doesn't matter." Evan stepped to the desk, ignoring Cole and meeting her gaze. "I don't know what's going on between you two, but remember something for me?"

She glanced up at him, her hazel eyes soft as if she sensed he had something important to say. Vulnerable, Erin was even more beautiful.

"What is it?" she asked.

"I don't know what kind of game he's playing, but trust me, he's playing one. He's been gone from here for how many years? And now he's back, acting possessive and staking a claim, but he'll be gone again soon. Everyone knows it, including your brothers."

Erin straightened her shoulders. "Evan, you're overstepping —"

"Maybe, but I'm not finished. He will leave, or at the very least, leave you."

Cole had enough. "Do not presume to speak for me," he said, holding on to his anger for Erin's sake. If it were up to him he'd take the arrogant SOB down a peg, but she didn't need added stress.

Evan didn't react to Cole. "Mark my

words, when he's gone, you're going to want your career to fall back on. Not to mention your friends, and no matter how I come off, I am that."

Erin's eyes glistened and Cole realized the bastard had hit a nerve.

"You're finished, Carmichael." Cole started for the man but Evan held up his hands.

"Take it easy. I'm going. And if you really cared about what was best for Erin? You'd do the same thing." Carmichael stormed out of the room, his shoulder deliberately bumping Cole's on the way out.

By the time lunch hour rolled around, Erin still hadn't processed the scene in her office, and wasn't sure she wanted to. Both men infuriated her. Good thing she already had lunch plans with Macy, the one person she could really talk to. And since she'd already given Cole her schedule when she came in this morning, there was no reason to speak to him now.

She strode out of her office. "I'm going to lunch," she told him, and kept on walking.

He rose to his feet and kept pace with her as she made her way to the parking lot. The one good thing about her fit of pique was that she didn't stop to worry about being scared, just pushed the thought out of her head and headed for the car.

"Are we going to talk?" he asked her.

"I have nothing to say." She still couldn't believe he'd gotten in the middle of a work discussion with her boss, any more than she could believe the personal comments Evan had thrown at her about Cole.

Knowing it was an exercise in futility, Erin had long since stopped arguing with Cole over letting her drive.

He settled in the driver's seat of her Jeep. But instead of starting up the engine, he turned to face her. "You're mad."

"You think?" she asked, voice rising. "Where did you get off answering Evan for me? We were discussing plans we'd made, plans that had nothing to do with you."

She stared at her clenched hands, willing herself not to get into anything personal with him. He merely needed to respect her boundaries, and he'd crossed over them today.

"What did I tell you when I moved in with you?" He didn't wait for her reply. "Where you go, I go. I was just making that clear to *Mr. I Want to Be One Half of a Power Couple in This Town.*"

She swung around to face him, all her earlier resolve to remain calm flying south in the face of his words. "Careful, Cole. You almost sound jealous, and we both know that's not the kind of relationship you want, because you can't promise me any kind of happily ever after. No commitment."

He sucked in a sharp breath at her sudden fury. Well, let him get used to it, because she had more to say. "Well, guess what? Evan or some other man can give me what I want," she said, on a roll and unable to stop the flow of words spouting from her mouth. "Just because we're going to be raising a child together doesn't give you the right to dictate whether I can see other men!"

His eyes narrowed to mere slits, the navy irises turning nearly black as a low growl emanated from his chest. "Let's get something straight, okay? As long as you're in danger, I damn well can and will dictate who you see. And if you're sleeping in my bed, you sure as hell won't be going on a *date,* business or otherwise, with some other man." A muscle ticked in his jaw, his anger a match for hers.

But his possessive tone startled her, and he wasn't finished. Before she could blink, he'd wrapped his hand around the back of her neck and pulled her across the center console, sealing his lips over hers.

Erin lifted her hands to his chest, to push the arrogant man away, even as a part of her was unreasonably affected by his jealous display. His mouth made it perfectly clear this was about more than mere obligation, that he was more affected by her than he'd let on. While she'd been fighting to keep her feelings out of the equation, just maybe he'd been doing the same thing.

She didn't shove him away, but she didn't welcome him either.

Until he licked his tongue over her lips and whispered, "Open for me, honey."

Accepting that in this, they were equally affected, she did as he seductively asked, letting him inside. His kiss was as possessive as his words and she melted into him, allowing him to overwhelm her common sense with sweeps of his tongue and nibbles on her lips. She lost herself in his delicious scent, the amazing way he kissed, as if she were the only thing that mattered.

He finally lifted his head and looked into her eyes. "Are we clear?"

"Arrogant son of a bitch," she muttered, finding it hard to believe she could be falling for this man. Finding it impossible not to.

He looked after her, protected her, cooked her meals, and kissed like a dream — but he also came with a boatload of issues and warnings.

Did she dare give in to this thing between them on the mere whisper of hope that he could get beyond his past and let her in? When she had no doubt that taking that risk would leave her heart shredded if — and when — his own words came true?

"Erin? I said, are we clear?" He still held the back of her head in his strong hand.

As long as he touched her, she couldn't focus. She desperately needed to think.

"We're clear," she said, buying herself time to decide what her next step ought to be.

They walked into The Family Restaurant and Erin immediately headed for Macy, leaving Cole alone. Good thing for him that when he'd seen Erin's full schedule, he'd asked Nick to meet him for lunch. He settled into a seat with a decent view of both the front door and Erin's table, his head swimming from how badly he'd fucked up this morning with Erin and her boss. Then continued to screw up worse in the car ride over here.

What the hell had he been thinking, staking any kind of claim? He hadn't been using the right head, that was for certain. Cole needed a strong drink to get his thoughts

168

straight, but since that wouldn't be happening, he'd settle for a swift kick in the ass. He hoped he could count on his cousin to give it to him and remind him why he needed to keep his distance from Erin.

A glance at Erin told him she and Macy sat with heads bent together, and though Erin hadn't looked at him since they walked in, Macy did. She glanced up at him and waved. Her grin had a calculating look that had the hair on the back of his neck standing on end.

"Hey," Nick said, drawing Cole out of his brooding thoughts.

"Thanks for coming."

Nick settled into the chair across from him. "Well, you look like hell." Nick gestured to the waitress, a young woman neither of them knew.

She walked over and smiled. "What can I get you?"

"I'll take a Coke and the meat loaf special," Nick said without looking at the menu.

"You?" She turned to Cole.

"Same."

The redhead scribbled their orders and walked away.

"So what's got you in knots?" Nick leaned back in his seat, looking more relaxed than Cole had ever seen him, and considering

Nick's easygoing personality, that was saying something.

Cole didn't pretend not to know what his cousin was talking about. "I am so screwed," he said out loud.

Nick barked out a laugh. "That's got to refer to a woman, and since the whole town knows you're watching out for Erin Marsden, I'm guessing she's the one."

Only the waitress's return with their sodas prevented Cole from answering.

When she walked away, Cole tipped his head toward the women's table. "Those two? I think they're plotting something."

Nick turned Erin and Macy's way and burst out laughing. Again. "I can see why you'd think that, but seriously, what gives?"

Cole debated how much to tell Nick, then decided that since Erin had already confided in her best friend and her brothers wanted his head, Cole might as well have someone in his corner.

He leaned closer to his cousin. "Erin's pregnant."

Nick choked on his drink. "No way. This is Erin we're talking about. The chief's daughter. The same girl who never stepped out of the lines a day in her life."

"Doesn't make her a nun," Cole said, sounding defensive even to his own ears.

"Point taken." Nick paused, probably to digest the information. "Man, I don't envy the father. Her brothers are going to string him up by the . . ."

"Balls," Cole finished for him. "Yeah, they probably would if they didn't need me to watch out for her twenty-four seven."

Nick's eyes opened wide. "Oh, shit," he muttered, the revelation sinking in. "What are you going to do?"

"Support her and the baby. What else?" At least he had a healthy savings account, courtesy of living undercover and not spending what he earned.

"Oh, I don't know." Nick raised an eyebrow, looking at Cole like he was an utter moron. "You knocked up about the sweetest girl in town. Did you even consider mar—"

"Do not say that word." Cole's mouth grew dry at the mere thought of tying Erin to him in any legal way. She deserved so much better, so much more than he could ever hope to give her.

Nick scowled. "Come on, man. You need to at least consider it."

Cole shook his head. "Think about what you just said. She's sweet and good. Then you've got me. The bane of my father's existence, coming out of a world that's dark and ugly, with plans to head back under. What part of me and my life is good for her?" he asked, laying the truth out for his cousin and for himself.

Because sometimes Erin got to him so badly even he needed a reminder.

"Are you seriously going back under?" Nick asked. "I was hoping you'd give it up and try living a normal life."

Cole let out a harsh laugh. "What the hell do I know about normal? Did my father come home to family dinners with my mom like June and Ward Cleaver? Or did he come in slamming doors, grumbling about her crappy cooking and whatever shit he could throw at me? I don't have real friends other than you, because I'm not in one place, living my own life, long enough to make any. Is that the kind of life you think she wants?" he asked, his tone harsh but his voice low.

"I think that's up to her to decide."

Cole set his jaw. "She deserves better."

"Sounds like bullshit excuses to me."

"Shut up. I know what I'm talking about. Even her brothers agree."

Nick assessed him with a knowing stare. "Again, it only matters what you want and what Erin agrees to accept for herself."

Cole didn't reply. Circular arguments weren't his thing.

But Nick being Nick, he wouldn't give up — which served him well, since that's how he had finally convinced Kate he meant it when he said he wanted her. And only her. Cole still liked to give him shit about setting Kate up to spend time alone with him. He had to give his cousin credit for ingenuity.

"Unless it really is just sex for you, in which case, let her go. Give her up, see your kid on occasion, when Erin and whichever schmuck she marries give you time."

Yeah, like Cole thought, Nick didn't give up. "Leave it alone," he told the other man.

Nick braced his arms on the table and leaned in close. "Somebody has to spell things out for you, because you're too stubborn to see things clearly. In that way, sorry to tell you, you're just like your old man."

Cole's hands clenched into fists.

"Chill out. Just giving you something to think about. So I suggest you take the next however many months until she's due to sort through your issues. A kid's not something to take lightly," Nick said, as serious as Cole had ever seen him.

"I'm not taking anything about this lightly."

Nick shook his head and let out a groan. "You'd better not be. Take it from someone

173

who had to fight for the woman he wanted. It's worth it. And so is she." He tipped his head toward Erin.

She was worth it, Cole thought. And that was the exact reason he was sticking to his plan. But for now? While he was here, living in her house, protecting her, taking care of her?

She was his — until he had no choice but to let her go.

NINE

Because Erin was starving, Macy, being a good pal whose family owned The Family Restaurant, went into the kitchen and returned with a big hunk of chocolate seven-layer cake that had Erin's name written all over it.

Erin eyed the dessert and sighed with pleasure. "I have so earned that baby." She picked up her fork, ready to dig in. "Come to mama," she said, and whisked the plate from Macy's grasp.

"Okay, if you need chocolate, you must not be getting sex."

Erin paused, her fork halfway to her lips. "I'm getting. Sort of," she said, shoving the fork in, hoping Macy would change the subject.

Macy snatched the plate away. "Spill."

Erin scowled at her friend, but knew she wouldn't get her cake back until she explained. "Fine. We slept together again, but before we did, he made it perfectly clear it didn't change the future. And I agreed."

Macy shook her head sadly. "And here I thought the man had potential."

"Not finished," Erin said, eyeing the cake longingly. It was her dessert. "I backed off the next day. There's no way I'm going to let myself get emotionally involved when I know the outcome ahead of time. But then he'll say and do things that lead me to believe he feels more than he's admitting to me or to himself."

"Such as?"

Erin shrugged. "Acting all possessive. I mean, get this: He *forbade* me to go to the Bar Association event with Evan. He said, and I quote, 'If you're sleeping in my bed, you sure as hell won't be going on a *date,* business or otherwise, with some other man,' " she said in a baritone imitation of Cole's voice.

Macy chuckled but her eyes opened wide. "Did you kick him in the nuts for ordering you around?"

"He was driving. Can I have my cake back now?"

"I'll rephrase. Did you want to kick him in the nuts for ordering you around?"

No. No, I did not, Erin thought, knowing her reaction had been a shock to herself at

176

the time.

"You're blushing!" Macy squealed.

"Shh!"

"So . . . you liked his command."

Erin resigned herself to the inevitable mortification. "It turned me on," she whispered. "Now give me my cake!" Her voice rose in direct relation to her frustration.

Macy grinned and returned the plate.

Erin dug in. "Thank God, Aunt Lulu is back with you. This cake is something else."

"Aunt Lulu is still hoping for a settlement from the grocery store. What do you think her chances are?"

"Good, actually. Turns out there's a family feud going on over who should be able to run the business. The high-powered legal team was one brother's way of trying to manipulate the other brother into caving. Long story. Anyway, when I found out what was going on, I called the father who'd left his two moron sons fighting over the running of his business while he retired in Florida."

"Family-run businesses can get hairy." Macy shuddered, knowing that truth from experience.

Erin nodded. "I told the father that if he didn't come home and choose, his sons would bankrupt the business in no time."

She grinned. "I'm betting Aunt Lulu gets a nice settlement and the whole thing goes away."

Macy's smile grew wider. "Thank you. She'll be thrilled!"

"You're welcome." Erin licked the back of the fork and placed the utensil on the plate, finally full.

"Now that you're sated . . . so to speak . . . let's talk about what you're going to do to get the big lug to see if you two can make a go of any sort of relationship." Macy waggled her eyebrows.

"Not happening. He made that clear."

"But his actions are saying something else, yes?"

Erin shrugged. "Doesn't matter. He's stubborn."

"So, my friend, are you. The way I see it, you can go all in, sleep with him as long as he's staying with you and seems interested, go through the baby thing together and hope that he sees what an amazing woman you are and what a great life he could have. Then if he doesn't come around, you can kick him in the nuts." Macy grinned. "Or you can give up now without ever really trying."

Erin wasn't a quitter. She didn't give up when things got tough or she wouldn't have survived law school or the bar exam. She understood she'd had it easier than many of her friends, no major drama in her life. *Until now, that is,* she thought, glancing down at her stomach.

"So which will it be?" Macy asked. "And decide quick, because he's on his way over here. You in or out?"

Erin straightened her shoulders and set her jaw. "In." She was in.

"Hello, ladies," Nick Mancini greeted them before Cole said a word.

"Hi, Nick. How's the wife?" Macy asked.

"Pretty damned good." And from his wide grin, Erin figured he more than meant it.

"Which reminds me, Kate and I are having a small get-together on Sunday for family and friends. We'd love it if you two came."

"You are?" Cole asked. "You didn't say a word to me."

"Because you always turn me down. But if this lovely lady says yes, you'll have no choice, because you're her shadow these days." Nick laughed, obviously pleased with his way of thinking.

Cole's low growl of annoyance didn't surprise Erin, and she swallowed a chuckle. Obviously Nick knew his cousin well.

"So can I let Kate know you'll both be

there?" Nick asked.

Erin glanced at Macy. It had been so long since she'd been out with friends, just having a good time.

Her friend inclined her head and nodded. "I'd love to come."

"Same!" Erin said excitedly, but without meeting Cole's gaze.

"I'll call Kate and see what she needs in the way of food," Macy told Nick.

"And I'll bring one of Aunt Lulu's cakes," Erin said before Macy could take over that idea.

"Because we all know you can't cook." Macy snickered.

Erin shook her head. "I'll have you know that Cole promised to teach me," Erin said, knowing that in that instant, she'd mentally and verbally committed to her course of action. She'd drop her guard and let him in, hoping he'd do the same.

And if things fell apart? Well, like Macy said, at least she'd know she'd given it her best effort. Then when he left, she'd have a baby to raise and a job to keep her so busy she wouldn't have time to miss him when he was gone.

It was a nice lie she told herself, anyway. The distinct ringing of a cell phone broke into Erin's thoughts.

She looked to where the sound came from as Cole pulled his phone from his pocket. "Sanders," he said. "What do you have for me?"

He listened, his steady gaze never leaving Erin. It had to be answers on the ballistics from her shooting. Her stomach in knots, she leaned forward, waiting for him to finish the call.

"Yeah, I got it. I'll pass it on to someone who can run down the lead. Expect a call from a Mike Marsden. Thanks. I owe you one." He ended the call and looked at Erin. "They traced the bullet to a gun used in a shooting last year. With a little luck, the guy who owns it is someone for hire or he can tell us where he unloaded the gun or who has it now. It's a long shot, but it's all we've got."

Erin drank a long sip of water to ease the dryness in her mouth. "At least it's something."

"I'm going to step outside and call Mike. Let him get the information and start to run down the lead. I'll be right back. Don't move," he ordered Erin.

Since she was suddenly dizzy and shaken, she wasn't about to argue with the command.

■ ■ ■ ■

Although Erin had decided to go all in with Cole, after his possessive show about sleeping with her and her not seeing other men, she'd also expected him to act first. But in the last forty-eight hours, he'd been on his best behavior, leaving Erin with the decision about how to start showing him the kind of future he could have with her. It wasn't all about sex; that much she understood.

A life with her included friends, family, dinners out, and work functions. She had the latter coming up Saturday night and she'd already informed Cole he'd need a suit and tie, which had necessitated a mall trip after work the other day. They had Nick's party on Sunday, which was another place she could out them in public by being affectionate in front of others, *if* that was her intention. But she couldn't do any of those things if she and Cole didn't establish a change in their relationship here. At home.

It would have to be tonight, then, Erin decided, nerves making her stomach dance and flutter. But first she had to deal with welcoming her parents home, and of course telling them her news. From the shooting to her pregnancy, they were completely in the dark.

She had no desire to have such a personal conversation in front of her brothers, who were already biased against Cole. In fact, she decided she'd have to talk to her mom alone, and discuss how to break the truth to her father. She didn't think her brothers would have the nerve to be the ones to tell Simon that news.

Erin changed from her work clothes, choosing a sexier panty and bra set than normal because she planned to end up in Cole's bed. But when she attempted to button her jeans, she had no luck closing them. Overnight they had stopped fitting. She stripped them off, walked to her closet, and began a systematic trying-on of her casual clothes, only to have the same result.

Frustrated, she tossed item by item onto the bed.

"Erin, almost time to go," Cole called from the hallway, knocking on her door.

"I'm not going anywhere," she yelled back, eyeing the pile in disbelief.

He entered without knocking.

She didn't bother to cover up. First, he'd seen it all before. Second, she was too upset with herself for not thinking ahead about buying maternity clothes. And third, she had a plan, and belly or not, she might as well see if he responded.

He did. One look and his eyes glazed with desire, and relief flowed through her. She did everything she could not to squeeze her legs together in an effort to alleviate the sudden ache in her core.

"What's going on?" he asked, his voice gruff, the raspy sound setting her nerve endings aflame.

"Umm, I'm having a . . . malfunction."

He cocked his head to one side, his gaze never leaving her exposed body. "Explain."

She gestured to the bed. His gaze followed the direction of her hand and blinked in shock. "Whoa. Your closet explode?"

"Along with my middle," she muttered. "Nothing fits."

He was gentleman enough not to comment. "Why not wear what you had on for work?" he asked, rather diplomatically, she thought.

"That was tight too." She felt her cheeks heat. "I had to unbutton the skirt and then untuck my shirt so the blouse covered the waist. The skirt kept falling down and it wasn't comfortable." She knew she sounded like a grumbling, whiny pain in the ass.

She didn't care.

Cole chuckled, annoying her further.

"What's so funny?" she snapped.

"Nothing." He held up both hands, the nervous expression of a man dealing with a hormonal female on his face. "Look, I don't think your parents would appreciate it if you showed up in my sweatpants. Don't you have something you can put on until we can get you shopping?"

"We?" Though she ought to be used to him grouping them as a couple whenever she needed to go somewhere or do something, he always caught her off guard.

Or maybe it was the lurch in her chest when he used the term *we,* causing hope to settle in her heart, that upset her so much.

She folded her arms across her chest while he attempted not to look down at her bare legs and the slight swell of her stomach that peeked beneath her silk camisole.

"If you need to go shopping, I'm going to have to drive you, so yes. We. Now, are you going to get dressed for your parents, or is show-and-tell the way you want to break the news?" Cole studied her patiently.

Contrarily, she threw up her hands in frustration. "Fine. These seemed the loosest." She grabbed a pair of black pants from the pile. "I'll just leave them unbuttoned and hope nobody notices."

She waited, but he didn't leave so she

could dress, so she started pulling on her pants anyway.

"Erin?"

"Hmm?"

"I meant it earlier when I offered to go with you to talk to your parents." He'd offered on the drive home from work and she'd put him off, needing time to think. "I know you don't need my protection while you're there with your brothers and father, but you don't have to face your parents alone."

His words disarmed her irrational — and yes, hormonal — anger over her lack of wardrobe. As usual when dealing with Cole, her emotions ran the gamut from being frustrated to being thrown completely by his kindness and concern.

"Talk about facing a dad with a shotgun." She couldn't help but tease him.

He grimaced and she got serious. "I appreciate you being willing to step up," she said softly, admiring his courage in his willingness to face her father, the police chief. She drew a deep breath before explaining her decision to go alone. "I just think since we're not a couple, this is something I need to do on my own."

Erin might want them to be one, she might be planning to use everything in her

186

arsenal to get him to come around and see things her way, but she wouldn't set her parents up for disappointment by showing up with Cole to announce her pregnancy. Not when the reality was that she'd be mostly doing this alone.

"Fine," he bit out, obviously hurt by her answer.

Erin understood, but she hadn't made her choice lightly. In fact, she'd talked it over with Sam, who so far had been the more rational brother to deal with, and he'd agreed.

Cole stalked to the door and turned, bracing a hand on the frame. "Just come on down when you're ready. I'll drop you at your folks' before I head over to Joe's. You can ring me when you're done and I'll get you on the way home."

Erin bit down on her lower lip, knowing she was about to dig the knife in deeper. "Umm, my brother called a little while ago. He offered to pick me up and bring me home. I figured I'd give you a break from babysitting me and said yes."

Cole's hand tightened on the doorframe. "Fucking Mike."

Erin winced. "Actually, it was Sam." She just hadn't had a chance to tell Cole he was off duty before her clothing dilemma sidetracked her.

He shrugged as if he didn't care, but she knew the damage was done.

"I'll be at Joe's, enjoying my break. Make sure you call or text when you're on your way back and I'll meet you here." He walked out, his footsteps ringing as he hit the hall, leaving Erin with a stomachache and a tiny hole in her heart.

It was so good to have her parents back and the whole family in one place. Sam, Mike and Cara, and Erin were all at the house. Erin didn't realize how much she'd missed her folks until she found herself wrapped in their welcoming embrace. Suddenly the stress of her life caved in on her and she burst into tears.

Ella Marsden stepped back and braced her hand on Erin's shoulders. "I'm here now." She looked over Erin's shoulder to Simon, Mike, and Sam. "We'll be back. You all catch up without us." Then, taking Erin's hand, Ella led her to the kitchen, her mother's domain and sanctuary.

"You know what that's about?" Erin heard her father ask her brothers.

She cringed, not knowing what they'd reveal, but after her emotional outburst, she figured *everything* was a fair guess.

"What's going on?" her mother asked.

Erin looked at her mom, who appeared healthy and happy. The wavy auburn hair she'd shared with Erin framed her face. If possible, the stress of Simon's cancer last year had dissipated, thanks to their overdue vacation, and Erin was pleased.

"I guess you wouldn't rather tell me about your trip?" she asked, hoping to stall the inevitable.

Her mother shot her a look that, when Erin and her brothers were kids, had meant *Talk now, or else.*

"Okay." Erin glanced down at her hands, which she'd begun twisting together. "The night of Mike's wedding, I was feeling . . . out of sorts."

"Lonely," Ella said softly.

Eyes filling again, Erin nodded. "It seemed like everyone around me was finding that special someone. I guess I was feeling sorry for myself, so I stopped at Joe's on the way home and . . . Cole Sanders was there."

Ella's face remained understanding just as she kept silent, letting Erin tell the story at her own speed.

"We danced. One thing led to another and . . . we had a one-night stand." Erin didn't meet Ella's gaze. Discussing sex with her mother wasn't exactly comfortable.

"And it was just that one night." No need to mention how many times that evening, Erin thought. "He barely spoke to me in the days afterward."

"And that hurt your feelings," Ella said with a woman's wisdom and a parent's understanding.

Erin nodded. "A lot. But I understood. He'd just come back to town and he obviously had been through something bad before coming home." She drew a deep breath. "About a month later, I started getting nauseous."

"Oh my God." Ella clasped Erin's clenched hands. Obviously there was no need to go on. Her mother got the point loud and clear.

"I guess I didn't want to face it, because I didn't let myself make the connection, and as a result I didn't take a test for a while. Anyway, I couldn't bring myself to tell anyone, because I needed to process it myself."

"Does Cole know?"

Erin exhaled a long breath. "He does now, but he didn't then." She lifted her head, met her mom's gaze. "There's more."

"I'm listening." To her mother's credit, she held on to Erin's hand and didn't say a word, not judging or asking questions.

"The day after you left, I was on my way to work when I was shot in the parking lot."

"What!" Ella's face leached color.

"I'm fine, Mom. I promise. The bullet passed through my arm. No permanent harm done. And I'll explain everything I know about the shooting, which isn't much, in a few minutes. Anyway, I was taken to the hospital, and when Mike went to find Sam, he had Cole wait outside the cubicle where they were treating me. Cole heard the doctor mention I was pregnant. That's how he found out."

"Good Lord, I don't know what to react to first."

Erin winced. "How about you let me finish."

Her mother's eyes opened wide. "There's more?"

"Not too much. Cole and Mike argued over who would take me from the hospital. I insisted that I was going home. Cole said he was going with me. Mike wanted me to have round-the-clock protection and finally agreed to Cole staying with me, which I thought was ridiculous, since I figured it was a random shooting."

"It wasn't?" Her mother's voice took on a harsh, yet worried, tone.

Erin shrugged. "It doesn't look like it."

She told her mother about the roadkill delivery to her front door. "In the meantime, Cole told me that Mike and Sam have a lead, thanks to the ballistics on the gun. But now they're not sure the two things are related, because a shooting is major and roadkill is a de-escalation. It doesn't make sense. Plus the note with the animal said, 'Leave him alone,' and that's just odd."

Ella stood and began pacing the kitchen. "First, you should have called me."

Erin exhaled long and hard, having expected this. "You were on a cruise. You'd just gone through a hellish year and you deserved the time away with Dad. Besides, you're here now."

"And not a minute too soon. You need your mother." Ella held out her arms and Erin gratefully went back into her mom's embrace. Her familiar scent eased the anxiety Erin had been living with for so long.

"Now, tell me what's going on with you and Cole Sanders."

Erin's face heated at the mention of Cole's name, while her body still reacted to the mere thought of him.

"I see," Ella said thoughtfully.

Knowing her mother, she probably did. "He said he can't make promises for the future beyond him taking care of both me and the baby. We haven't defined anything, but I'm guessing that's financial. And he'll want to see his child when he's home between jobs." Erin crossed her arms in a comforting self-supplied hug.

Ella made a humming sound while she pursed her lips in thought. "It's more than Rex gave me," Ella said, speaking of Mike's biological father.

Erin swallowed hard. "The thing is, his actions are so opposite from his words. He's decided he's in charge of everything, beyond the bodyguard thing. He cooks meals. He makes sure the fridge is stocked and that I eat well. He was insulted I didn't ask him to come to my monthly doctor's appointment and insisted he'd be there for the rest of them. And he had a jealous fit when Evan Carmichael reminded me about the event that we're supposed to attend together on Saturday night."

Her mother's eyes opened wide. "Not the actions of a disinterested man."

Erin shook her head. "He holds himself back from me emotionally. And he's definitely scarred by how Jed treated him growing up. How he still treats him. My God, Mom, it was awful." And she was pretty sure Cole hadn't been in touch with Jed since he'd moved in with her.

With a sigh, her mother lowered herself back into her seat. "Jed's a hard man. Very set in his beliefs and in his ways." She shook her head. "He had little patience for a child, let alone an independent one with a mind of his own like Cole was. They butted heads so often I wasn't surprised Cole went out looking for trouble when he was younger."

"That's so sad." She couldn't imagine growing up without a loving father. "I guess I was too young to realize how bad things were."

"As deputy police chief, Jed was loyal and good to your father, and our friendship stemmed from there. We tried to tell him the damage he was doing in his private life, but he didn't listen. To be honest, I was glad when Olivia took Cole and left Serendipity. But I didn't realize how much he'd already hurt Cole by then." Ella paused. "Does Jed know about the baby?"

Erin shook her head. "I'm sure Cole's avoiding that conversation until the last possible moment. He doesn't need to hear what a crappy father he'll make from the man who still makes digs every chance he gets."

Her mother's face showed her disappointment. "I'll have your father talk to him."

"No. We should all mind our own business and let Cole deal with Jed. Speaking of fathers, I think Mike and Sam might be telling Dad everything." Erin placed her hand over her belly.

"We're not going to judge you, honey. Especially not me. That would be like the pot calling the kettle black. I just want to know if you're happy."

Erin looked into her mother's wise eyes. "I was shocked. Now I'm scared. I'm excited too." She drew a deep breath. "I'm on my way to being happy, but . . ."

"What is it?" her mother asked.

"Cole. I want to try and see if anything that's between us can be real. So far it's just pieces of a relationship that he's unwilling to string together into something that makes sense. It's like, I can feel how right we could be, and then *bam*, it's gone." Erin's chest squeezed tight.

"I'm sure he's scared, just like you are."

"I know. But it's more than that. He's alluded to the fact that someone like me deserves better. More than he can give. But nobody could treat me better than he does, and that's without emotional commitment or involvement."

"Oh, honey, you're in love with him?" Ella asked.

Erin sniffed, her throat full. "I can't know

195

that yet, but I think I could be." If he opened himself more. If he could accept that he was meant to share in life, not just live undercover. "But I'm afraid he'll never give us a chance."

"Honey . . ."

Before Ella could finish, Mike strode into the room. "Sorry. I couldn't help overhearing. I came to see if you were ready to join us yet."

Erin shook her head, annoyed by the interruption. "In a few minutes."

"Can I say something before I go?" Mike asked.

"Can I stop you?"

He settled into a chair next to her. "Umm . . . I might have overstepped and hurt the situation between you and Cole."

Erin narrowed her gaze. "What did you do?"

"Michael?" Ella asked, her voice low.

"Back when you were shot? I confronted him at the hospital. I said a few things and he took them to mean I thought he wasn't good enough for you."

"And you didn't correct him?" Erin asked, her voice rising.

Mike shook his head. "I agreed with him" — he held up his hands — "but you have to understand I'd just found out you were pregnant. And you'd just been shot." To his credit, her brother appeared embarrassed, but he sure hadn't bothered to fix things either.

"It's not like you've done anything to make him feel better about things since, so cut it with the puppy dog eyes. I'm not buying the whole contrite act."

"Erin, Michael, stop. What's done is done. But Michael, you of all people know what it's like to doubt yourself. What were you thinking, talking to Cole that way?" Ella asked, sounding disappointed in her son.

"I've been worrying about Erin."

Erin rose to her feet. "Well, if you care that much, you should have been listening to me the last few weeks when I asked you to ease up on Cole. This is my life, and whatever happens, it's up to me."

He exhaled hard. "I know. Cara said the same thing on the way over here."

Erin knew how fragile Cole's psyche was in general, thanks to Jed. Undercover work suited him, yes, but it also let him avoid reality and people who could love and care about him.

Erin had decided to make her move with Cole tonight, back home. After hearing what Mike had done, she decided any move she made had to be now.

197

And it had to be public. "Take me to Joe's," she said to Mike.

He raised an eyebrow. "We all just got here."

Erin glanced at her mother, who waved her away with a smile on her face. "Go do what you have to do. I'll talk to you tomorrow."

"Don't you want to talk to Dad before you go?" Mike asked Erin. "He's barely got the gist of what's going on with you."

"I'll handle Simon," Ella said. "Michael, take your sister and stay out of the way," she said in the authoritative voice she'd used on them as children.

Despite how upset she was, Erin couldn't help but laugh.

"And keep my baby safe," Ella said sternly.

"Yes, Mom." Mike kissed Ella's cheek.

Of course, it took longer than Erin would have liked to get out of her parents' house. Simon insisted on talking to her about stalker safety and assuring her he would be there for her and the baby, no judgment. The same way he'd been there for Ella when she'd been pregnant so many years ago. Simon was a good and decent man, and Erin was lucky to have him as her father. She just wished Cole had been as fortunate.

Finally, Sam stayed behind with their

parents, while Mike, Cara, and Erin headed for Mike's truck for the short ride to town. As they pulled up to Joe's, Mike turned to Erin in the backseat.

"You do realize Cole's got more issues than just the things I said to him, right?" he asked.

"Erin's a grown woman," Cara reminded Mike. "Give her the time and space to handle things without always having to stick your nose into her life."

Erin bit the inside of her cheek. She loved how Cara took her husband in hand.

"Thank you," she said to her sister-in-law. "Mike, yes, I know. And I believe I can handle everything about Cole." She just needed to make sure he wanted to be handled.

Because if she went all out only to discover Cole really didn't desire anything to do with settling in Serendipity, with her — in whatever capacity they worked out between them — Erin couldn't change his mind.

Still, she wouldn't know unless she tried. Tonight, she decided, it was time to do just that.

TEN

Cole had forgotten Wednesday night was Ladies' Night, which meant it wasn't a quiet evening at Joe's. Instead, Cole took in the various groups of people, some of whom he remembered well, some he merely recognized, and others too young for him to know at all.

He spent some time shooting the shit with Joe. The other man's wife, Annie, friendly since Cole had moved in, tried chatting, and though Cole gave it his best shot, he wasn't in the mood for small talk that inevitably led to the subject of Erin's shooting and Cole playing bodyguard. Annie seemed perceptive and backed off, which left Cole as he usually was. Alone.

He nursed a beer for most of the night, trying unsuccessfully not to brood over things he couldn't change. He didn't blame Erin for not wanting him with her when she told her parents — and did he really want to put himself through that kind of torture? Still, sooner or later he'd have to face Simon, a man Cole had always respected, who'd now look at him with disgust and disappointment. He was used to it from his own father and from ignorant people who didn't know him at all, but it would bother Cole coming from Erin's father.

And he couldn't forget the look on her face when she'd given him her reason for going alone. *Since we're not a couple, this is something I need to do on my own.*

So hurt. And so very brave, pretending everything in her world was okay. He ran a hand over his burning eyes and glanced around the crowded bar, watching people dance to music from an old-fashioned jukebox.

Time crept by slowly.

A glance at his watch told him he still had a good stretch before he expected Erin to call to meet her back at the house, so he was surprised when he heard her voice. Sure he was imagining things, he turned to see Erin walk up to him, her eyes blazing with determination — over what, he hadn't a clue. She was followed closely by Mike and Cara.

Mike stepped around his sister. "Got a minute?" He spoke before she could.

Erin narrowed her gaze. "You were just my ride. I don't need you opening your big mouth any further."

Uh-oh. Looks like brother and sister had had an argument.

"Mike, let's go dance." Cara tugged at her husband's arm.

"In a second." Mike turned to Cole. "Look, what I said at the hospital after Erin was shot? And the way I've acted since? I was out of line. Everything going on is between you two. Whatever happens, I won't get in the way."

Cole narrowed his gaze, wondering what brought on the apology, other than maybe Erin's wrath over her brother's feelings about him. "I don't blame you for looking out for her."

"We were friends a long time ago. Maybe when things settle, we could . . . I don't know. Have drinks?"

Cole wasn't one to hold a grudge. Especially when the other man had a right to his feelings. "Sure." He held out his hand and Mike shook it.

"One more thing before I go. We ran down the trail on the gun that was used in the shooting."

"Yeah?" Cole sat up straighter in his seat. "What'd you find out?"

"The weapon was stolen from the legal owner and used in a robbery last year. Guy's out on parole. Says he sold the gun to a guy named John Brass, a drug addict who'd do anything to get cash for a fix."

"Did they find him?"

Mike nodded. "So high it didn't take long for him to confess to the shooting. Says a brunette hired him. She didn't say why and he didn't ask. Idiot didn't get a name, either. She just showed him a picture of Erin and told him where to find her."

Erin's eyes opened wide.

Sensing her distress, Cole acted without thinking. He snagged her hand and pulled her close. "Did your people get a look at the photograph?"

"Didn't have it anymore."

"Shit. Where's this Brass guy now?" Cole asked.

"Detoxing in a Bronx jail cell. They'll take another crack at him in a few days, but I have a feeling we got all we could from him." Mike scowled, his frustration evident.

"So whoever this woman is, she's still out there." Erin shivered.

Cole slid his hand up her shirt, along the soft skin of her back. From where she stood, with her back to her brother, nobody could see the private touch, which eased her trembling and pleased him. When she didn't pull away, he was even more thrilled.

"We'll get her. I promise you that," Mike swore to his sister.

Erin nodded. "I believe you."

Whatever problems the siblings had been having, it was obvious Erin trusted her brother. A part of him wished for that same faith, even as he knew he'd never deserve it.

"You okay for me to go?" Mike asked.

"I'm with Cole. I'll be fine." She glanced back at him, her eyes startling in their certainty.

Mike hesitated, as if he wanted to add something, when Cara stepped in. "I'm stealing my husband now." She grabbed Mike's hand and led him to the dance floor.

Erin waited a beat before turning to face Cole.

"So what brings you here? I thought you were having dinner with your family."

When she'd bolted out of her parents' house, she hadn't had a plan. She only knew she needed to see him. Now she was here — and she still didn't have one, so she fell back on her old standby.

Honesty. "I didn't like how we left things earlier and I wanted to see you."

He raised an eyebrow. "You broke up a family gathering for me?"

A hint of . . . vulnerability mixed with pleasure flashed across his handsome face.

No more dancing around the issue. Erin drew a deep breath and nodded. "I did."

He beckoned with a crook of his finger. "Come here."

She stepped into the V of his legs, and without caring who was looking, she looped her arms around his neck.

His eyes opened wide. "What are you —"

"Shut up," Erin said, and she leaned in close and kissed him full on the lips.

He stiffened at first, not, she knew, from lack of desire, but from shock that they were in a public place. *Well, tough luck,* she thought, beginning phase one of her suddenly formed plan: getting Cole Sanders used to being a part of her life.

Determined, she ran her tongue over the seam of his lips. With a groan, his hands gripped her waist and he kissed her back with a passion that matched her own.

When they parted, Erin felt pleased with herself . . . until she looked into his wary eyes. "What's going on?"

"I just don't see a reason to hide what's happening between us. I mean, it'll be obvious soon enough." She patted her stomach.

"We agreed —"

"About the future, yes, I know. But wasn't

it you who said if I was in your bed, I wouldn't be dating anyone else?" She fluttered her eyelashes in a not-so-innocent gesture.

A muscle ticked in his jaw. "You haven't been in my bed the last few nights."

"But I plan to be from now on."

His eyes darkened, desire blazing in the inky depths. "You want people to know about us."

"Yep. Whatever it is, for as long as it lasts —" She wouldn't tell him what she really hoped for. That would send him running. But to acclimate him to her Serendipity life, she needed him on board. "Yes. I want to be able to go out. To act on impulse. And when it's over, we'll figure out our parenting plan and go from there. Are you okay with that?" she asked, her tone deliberately challenging.

He shook his head and her stomach flipped over, disappointment filling her. She hadn't expected him to turn her down, not when everyone would know he was her baby's father eventually anyway.

"Fine. Forget it." She whipped around before he could catch a glimpse of her tear-filled eyes.

He grabbed her wrist. "Whoa. You didn't let me finish."

She hesitated before turning back.

"I shook my head because you never cease to surprise me, challenge me, and take me off guard."

She swallowed hard. "Is that a good thing?"

An unexpected grin curved his lips. "I'm still working that out. But as to your question? I may live to regret this, but yeah. I'm in."

Her eyes opened wide. "You are? Why?"

He let out a laugh that had people around them staring. "Because only an idiot would turn down what you're offering."

"Yeah?" she asked with what she figured had to be a goofy smile on her face.

"Yeah." He brushed her hair off her cheek in a tender gesture that had her eyes burning all over again.

"Want to dance?" she asked.

He nodded.

A few minutes later, he'd settled up with Joe, and Erin found herself on the dance floor, surrounded by a crush of people, Cole's hard body pressed deliciously against hers while a slow, old Air Supply song crooned from the jukebox. Cole held her tight, her curves molded against his harder muscular form. She lay her head on his shoulder and let herself pretend, just for a moment, that everything she was feeling was real.

Permanent.

That this tough man with his protective alpha ways could actually come to care for her just as she was beginning to care for him. And maybe he could, but she understood on a pragmatic level that caring didn't mean he'd trust her to accept or live his kind of life — because he'd been ingrained with the belief that he wasn't worth it.

The next hour passed in a blur of stares and cautious conversation from friends and acquaintances of Erin's who were obviously surprised by the public display of affection between her and Cole. Erin played it cool — and real — introducing Cole with an easy, "You remember Cole Sanders, don't you?" and letting them draw their own conclusions about them together based on the way they danced and the way she stayed by his side. She hoped to acclimate the people of Serendipity to Cole and vice versa. Everyone seemed polite, even with Cole acting as wary as she would have expected, leaving Erin satisfied with her night's work.

"Okay, we played things your way. Now it's my turn." Cole's low growl reverberated throughout her body, already primed from dancing so close to him. "Let's go home."

Cole was a man of few words to begin with, so when Erin walked into Joe's, swung her arm around his neck and kissed him senseless, in front of Joe and all of Serendipity, she stunned him into silence.

And then she seduced him with her mouth and her words. She wanted to be in his bed? He had no problem taking her there. Not long after leaving Joe's, they were back at Erin's. He did a quick perimeter check and a sweep of the house before opening her car door, scooping her into his arms, and carrying her through the house and upstairs to her bedroom.

Cole lowered her to the bed. He stripped off his clothes until he was completely nude. It was easy enough to rid her of a skirt that was partially open anyway, before removing the rest of her outfit. Soon, he had her where he wanted her, in nothing but a flimsy pair of panties and a sexy bra with her lush cleavage spilling over the lace cups, staring up at him with pure desire in her hazel-green eyes.

As hard as it was to accept what the idea of the pregnancy meant, the future it tied him to whether he'd planned it or not, the changes in her body cemented him in reality. Right now, when he looked down at her, he didn't feel panic but rather tenderness. He wasn't experiencing dread but rather a pure bolt of desire.

He bent to ease one bra strap off her shoulder, but instead of reaching for the flimsy material, he found his hand covering her stomach, gently caressing the slight swell there now. Eyes wide, Erin watched him, wonder and awe in her gaze. He knew the feeling — was experiencing it himself — of knowing it was *his* baby inside her. And it made him want her even more.

He planned to go slow, to taste every last inch of her exposed skin, until she was a writhing mass of need.

"How much longer are you going to make me wait?" she asked in a husky voice. "I mean, I was happy to let you do your control thing, but if you're not going to move, I suppose I should take over." A wicked gleam lit her gaze and suddenly he wanted nothing more than to change places.

He flipped over and braced his hands behind his head. "Go for it."

Erin grinned. She looked her fill of his gorgeous body, his olive skin appearing tan, a dark sprinkling of hair on his chest running down his abdomen to the thatch of hair between his thighs. His thick, pulsing erection called to her, and she couldn't wait to touch.

So she did, wrapping her hand around his straining shaft and pumping her hand up and down until a drop of moisture pooled at the head. She licked her lips and moaned.

"Like what you see?" he asked in a hoarse voice.

"I most certainly do." She continued to slide her hand back and forth, as she lowered her mouth and took him inside, tasting his unique flavor — salt and musk, his erection so hot and smooth as it passed her lips and glided through her mouth.

She'd loved doing this to him before, had reveled in the power she possessed to bring this big, strong man to a mind-blowing orgasm. Her, Erin Marsden, the good girl. The one who never before loved sex the way she did with him. More important, she'd never enjoyed giving to a man the way she did with him, like his gratification meant as much if not more than her own. Because giving him pleasure did the same for her.

She swirled her tongue over the sensitive head, down his shaft, then back up again. He thrust his hips, and she accepted all of him, would give whatever he needed or even demanded.

She was shocked when he reached down

and lifted her off him, pulling her up his prone body.

"Hey! I was busy," she said, teasing him.

He kissed her damp lips. "I am not coming unless I'm inside you."

"You would have been." She chuckled, a sound he cut off by sealing his lips over hers.

He kissed her long and hard, telling her with his mouth and his roaming hands how much he wanted her. Erin didn't need the words, she just needed him. Even on top, she handed back the reins, taking direction as he pushed at her hips until she was poised over his waiting erection.

She aligned their bodies and started a slow downward glide. At the same time, he cupped her breasts in his hands and fondled her nipples, toying with them together. Every pinch and pull went straight to her core, and she thrust downward, engulfing him completely.

"Oh God, you feel good." Erin couldn't hold back the words; the feelings swamping her were too strong, too incredible.

"So do you." He jerked upward and groaned. "So hot and tight."

His words inflamed her and she began to rock against him, taking her pleasure, and from the tightness in his cheekbones and the rough sounds coming from deep inside him, giving to him as well.

Suddenly he managed to flip them, Erin flat on her back, Cole above her, a predatory gleam in his eyes. As he slid out, then into her once more, Erin felt him everywhere, in a deeper way than ever before. She tried to close off her mind to the emotions building and open her senses instead but it wasn't easy, and it wasn't working.

He grasped her hands over her head and pumped into her hard. "Feel good?" he asked, picking up the pace, thrusting faster.

She moaned in reply, and Cole did the one thing guaranteed to shake her to the core. His gaze met hers and held on as he continued to make love to her — and though she'd never say the words, never admit aloud to feeling them, he loved her with his body.

More than sex, more than primal lust and thrusting, she felt the way he took his time, never breaking eye contact, making sure the ripples inside her body were real before letting go and taking his own pleasure. And his orgasm, when it came, caught up with hers, matching the intensity and the sheer explosive pleasure shredding her to pieces before she slowly came back together in his arms.

Long after her breathing evened out and

Cole fell asleep, Erin lay awake, accepting some hard truths. What happened in that bed meant more to her than it had to him.

But she also sensed they were bound together in a stronger way than they'd been before, giving her something to build on. She knew it. Even if he didn't.

Saturday arrived before Erin was ready. The Bar Association dinner dance was at the Pierpont Hotel, thirty minutes from Serendipity. This yearly event was important to her, though not for the reasons Evan had said. She enjoyed her job and even if she didn't plan to take over Evan's position or run for political office, she had a reputation to maintain. And she would need her career after the baby was born.

She didn't kid herself that tonight would be easy, not with Evan determined to make a statement and Cole equally insistent on keeping her away from her boss. Still, Erin had a statement of her own to make. She'd begun on Wednesday night at Joe's, and she'd continued at work, no longer treating Cole like the man who guarded her but like one she cared about. Had a relationship with.

At first he'd seemed uncomfortable with her public touches and endearments — as if he'd never had a girlfriend before, one where they were committed and outright affectionate, but he'd slowly warmed to the idea.

In the meantime, she'd gone maternity shopping with her mother on Friday's lunch hour, Cole hovering in the background as her bodyguard. Thanks to the salesgirl's expertise, Erin now had stylish clothing to go forward with this pregnancy, and she felt better about herself when she walked out of the house than she had before. She was still able to disguise her slightly swelling stomach with flowing tops, but she knew soon enough that wouldn't work. For now, she had time.

Early Saturday evening, she showered and dressed for the event, taking special care with her hair and makeup, wanting to make an impression on the man in the other room. She'd chosen a formfitting lapis-colored dress, held up with a gorgeous crystal brooch on one shoulder, draped in the right places to accent her breasts and not her stomach, and which hit above the knee. Sparkly silver shoes picked up the glitter on the brooch. Appropriate for a work event, yet a touch sexy enough to appeal to the man who was now officially sharing her bed.

■ ■ ■ ■

Cole waited for Erin in her family room. He paced, acknowledging to himself how uncomfortable he was with the idea of going out in public as her date. This wasn't a part of his normal life. Hell, he didn't have a normal life outside of undercover work. But if he was going to have a kid, he supposed he should get used to various conventional situations and events. Dating Erin — well, it wasn't something that would continue once the baby was born. They'd agreed on that.

The sound of a door opening drew his attention and he turned to the stairs. Erin stood at the top, glowing from head to toe, in a gorgeous blue dress that showed off her long legs, set off by high heels. Her face was made up in a way he'd never seen before, and though her fresh-faced look appealed to him on a gut level, this Erin took his breath away.

He walked to the bottom of the stairs, held out his hand and grasped it when she met him at the bottom.

"You look spectacular."

Her beaming smile was the only thanks he needed.

216

"You look pretty hot yourself, Mr. Sanders. Ready to deal with a room full of stuffy lawyers?"

He let out a laugh. "I don't think I'll ever be ready for that." But for her he was making an exception. Not just as her watchdog, but as her date.

He refused to delve too deeply into that.

On the drive over, Erin surprised him by bringing up the stalking. "The longer we go between incidents, the more worked up I get." She placed a hand over her stomach.

He reached over and grabbed her, lacing her fingers through his. "Don't think about it. Stress isn't good for you, and as long as I'm around, all he or she can do is try to scare you. Nobody will get near you, remember?" He squeezed her trembling hand.

"Thank you," she said in that husky voice he liked so much. "And tonight? Whatever Evan pulls, ignore him, okay?"

Cole remained silent, unsure he could make that promise.

"Cole? He's all bluster. A true politician."

"Who wants you."

"I'm not so sure about that." Erin laughed. "He's only stepped up his rhetoric about us as a power couple now that you're around. I think he likes getting to you because he knows you're a worthy opponent. Don't give

217

him the satisfaction."

Cole let out a rumbling growl.

"I'll take that as an okay."

"For you? I'll do my best." He slid his hand to the exposed skin on her thigh and ran his thumb back and forth over the silky flesh.

"Thanks." The sound came out reed-thin.

He grinned and kept his eyes on the road. He was adept enough without looking. "So tell me what to expect this evening." He inched his hand higher, until the pad of his fingers hit the elastic on her panties.

She squeaked. "Cole!"

"Yes?"

Before she could tell him to stop, he brushed his thumb over the front of the silken material, pressing downward on her sensitive nub. She stiffened, sighed, and gave in, spreading her thighs as far as the tight dress would allow. Beneath his touch, she was warm, damp, and aroused.

A glance told him she'd leaned her head back against the seat, eyes closed, lost in sensation. He maintained a consistent pressure until the hotel came into view.

He withdrew his hand and cleared his throat. "We're here," he said, his voice none too steady.

"Noo—"

"Look at it this way. You have something to look forward to during the boring speeches and Carmichael's posturing."

She shifted, straightening her dress. She opened the visor and checked her makeup and hair in the mirror, all without saying a word.

Though he had a hunch he'd pay for his sensual torture later, for now, she was hot, bothered, and thinking only about him. Just the way he wanted her for the rest of the night.

Erin had been to events like this before, but never with her entire body quivering with need and arousal. She stepped from the car on wobbly feet. Handed her coat in with shaking hands. Took Cole's elbow to join him as they walked into the cocktail area, wondering how she'd survive the night. Beside her, Cole, in a navy blue suit with a dark red tie, looked scrumptious and good enough to devour whole, something she intended to do when they got home. First she had to maneuver among her colleagues.

They walked the room, Erin greeting her coworkers from Serendipity and others she knew from various conferences in other jurisdictions. She introduced Cole and accepted the surprised looks from the locals who knew him and figured out from Erin's body language that he was more than just her bodyguard.

Instead of letting him drift behind her, she included him in conversation, and soon, her friends and colleagues did the same, and it wasn't too long before he was involved in a baseball conversation with a group of men. Even as he spoke, Cole kept a possessive hand on her back.

Erin had just finished talking to one of the judges when Trina arrived. She greeted Erin with a huge grin, her eyes focused on where Cole's hand remained possessively on her back. His touch burned through the dress.

As if aware Erin's focus had changed, Cole excused himself from the men and turned to Trina, remaining beside Erin the entire time.

"Well, well, well, look at you two." She leaned in to hug Erin and whispered in her ear. "Doesn't look like it's for show to me."

Erin pinched her friend in response.

"Ouch!" Trina squealed and stepped back, scowling at Erin.

Erin merely grinned in reply, knowing they'd talk about this another time.

"How are you, handsome?" Trina asked Cole.

Erin rolled her eyes. "Trina's quite the flirt, if you didn't already realize it in the office," Erin told him. But a non-threatening flirt. Her occasional outrageous behavior fit her personality.

Cole merely grinned. "I'm fine. You?"

"Oh, you know. Surviving this yearly event." She grabbed a champagne glass from a passing server's tray. "I know you can't have one," she said to Erin. "But how about you?"

Cole shook his head. "On duty."

"How are things on that front?" Trina asked, sobering.

"Quiet in a way that scares me," Erin said, repeating what she'd told Cole on the way over.

He pulled her closer, the move not getting lost on Trina, whose eyes lit in approval.

"Well, on to schmooze," she said. "Catch up with you later. We're all sitting together since the D.A.'s office took one table."

"Now *that* you neglected to mention," Cole growled.

Erin laughed. "I figured the less you knew, the better."

"I can handle sitting at Carmichael's table. Because I'll be sitting next to you." His eyes darkened, bringing her back to that moment in the car, when he'd had his hands beneath her skirt and she'd been so close to coming . . .

She shook her head, focusing on his words and not the sizzle behind his eyes. And it was his comment that had her beaming. She knew it and didn't try to hide how much his words pleased her.

She leaned over and kissed him on the cheek. Guessing her intent, he turned his head and her lips met his. It was a brief kiss, but one that was public and filled her with absolute contentment.

"So that's how it is," a familiar voice said.

Cole placed his hand on her hip and lifted his head. "Carmichael."

"Sanders." He slid his gaze to Erin. "You look beautiful. In fact, you're glowing."

Cole's grip tightened.

"Thank you, Evan." Before she could continue any conversation, the lights above them flickered.

He glanced up. "I guess that's our cue to move on to the next part of the evening."

Erin nodded. "See you at the table?"

Her boss met and held her gaze. "I wouldn't miss it for the world."

"What was that all about?" Cole asked when Evan walked away.

Erin shrugged. "Beats me. The man's always got some agenda."

Cole's gaze followed the path Evan had taken to the main ballroom. "Then I guess it's time to see what he's got planned now."

ELEVEN

As always during these sorts of dinners, which Cole had been to in many guises and disguises over the years, the speeches and awards portion of the evening came first. It tended to be a dry, boring, yawn-inducing event no matter which association hosted the festivities. Erin's Bar Association dinner, which encompassed quite a few New York counties and jurisdictions, was no different.

More than once, Cole was tempted to reach beneath the table and pick up where he'd left off with Erin in the car. Only respect for her prevented him from acting on his dirty inclination, but that didn't stop him from creating his own fantasies about the idea. Sliding his hand into her warm, wet heat, toying with her while the speeches droned on . . .

"You might want to pay attention now." Carmichael leaned over and spoke to Cole, snapping him back into the present.

"And now we get to the last award of the evening," the speaker on the podium said.

Cole didn't know why this should matter to him but he refocused his attention.

"The recipient of this year's Rising Star Award, given by the Young Lawyers' Section of the Bar, is a woman with remarkable legal skills who shows exceptional promise for a bright future in our profession. A graduate of New York University School of Law, our honoree went on to work as an assistant district attorney in the town of Serendipity, Putnam County, where she has worked for the last five years."

Evan Carmichael spoke once more. "She's special. Don't hurt her."

Before Cole could tell the man to mind his own business, Erin's name was announced as the recipient of the Rising Star award.

From the way she sucked in a startled breath beside him, she was floored by the news.

"Congratulations," Cole whispered as she turned to him, her eyes wide.

"I had no idea!" She glanced over his shoulder. "Evan?"

"You earned it," he assured her.

From the podium, the speaker continued

to list her credits and accolades. She sat on a number of young lawyer committees for the state bar association and she had a record number of prosecutorial wins to her credit. But what seemed to sway the votes in her favor was the establishment of a pro bono office in downtown Serendipity, where, among other things, poor and often abused women obtained divorce settlements and property owners caught in the recent recession found legal help in an attempt to retain their homes. And to staff said office, she'd recruited attorneys from all facets of the law and coaxed them to donate their hours. For free.

No wonder she'd insisted she not miss her weekly night there. She wasn't just a volunteer; she'd founded the thing. It was her baby. Another reason Carmichael saw her as a political asset. Family connections aside, Erin Marsden was indeed special. Cole had merely sensed it in her giving nature. Tonight had shown him concrete proof.

A few minutes later, they called her to the podium; a round of applause followed, and Erin stepped up to thank the audience and accept her award. As she spoke, a lump formed in Cole's throat. And stayed there.

He hadn't planned on having children,

but he was, and he couldn't ask for a better mother to his son or daughter, a better role model, or a finer woman than this one. He wasn't sure what to do with the feelings rolling through him and was grateful when she stepped down from the podium, rejoining him at the table.

He reached over and squeezed her hand. "I'm really proud of you."

Her eyes sparkled with pleasure. "I don't know what to say. There are so many worthy candidates. I didn't even think —"

"Don't. Just enjoy." Before he could say anything more, the speech portion of the evening drew to a close, and Erin was surrounded by colleagues who came to the table to issue their congratulations.

He let her have her moment in the spotlight, in awe of the easy way she had with people, the genuine pleasure she took in helping others, and just everything about her.

By the time they pulled back up to her condo, Erin was still floating. The award was such a proud moment for her, a validation of all the hard work she'd put into her career over the last five years. To have Cole by her side was icing on a very special cake, and she looked forward to continuing the celebration in private.

Once they were back upstairs in her room, Cole picked her up and laid her down on the bed. "Do you have any idea how proud I was to be the one by your side tonight?"

"No, why don't you tell me?"

"Beyond." He kissed her hard on the lips. "Zipper?" he asked.

"Right side."

His fingers went unerringly to the fastening and he unzipped, then peeled her out of the dress, his gaze never leaving hers. Bra came next. A flick of his fingers undid the front clasp, sliding the cups open and the straps down her arms. She was more than eager to maneuver herself to make his life easy, and soon she lay before him in nothing but her strappy high-heeled sandals.

He bent his head and pulled one of her sensitive nipples into his mouth, taking his time to pleasure her with his tongue. With every long lick, she moaned. With each tiny nibble she arched her back, pushing her breast farther into his eager mouth, wanting more of the fiery darts of pleasure shooting through her body and centering at her very core.

Without releasing her breast, he used his hands to cup and mold its twin, rolling the peak between his thumb and forefinger, until she cried out, unable to stand the dual sensations on both breasts.

"Shh. I've got you," he promised. But instead of release, he merely switched sides, tugging her other nipple with his teeth, while working her damp other breast with his large hands.

She writhed beneath him, lifting her hips, silently begging him to touch her where she needed relief the most. Without her having to ask, he slid his hand down her belly, taking deliberate care to lay his hand over the swell where her child lay, a move that never failed to touch her deeply.

He lifted his head and she stared into his handsome face, knowing full well she was dangerously close to losing her heart to this man, if she hadn't already. And there was nothing she could do about it except pray with everything she had that he'd be there to catch her when she fell.

He finally cupped her mound in his large hand, applying pressure with his palm and delicious friction with his finger, spreading her moisture over and around her sensitive flesh.

"You are always so wet for me," he said, his voice laced with approval.

His husky tone and the obvious satisfaction he took from her body had her wanting him even more. She bent her knees and whimpered out loud. "What are you waiting for?"

He spread her legs and eased himself between them. "I'm drawing out your pleasure. And mine," he said, dipping his head for a too-leisurely taste before settling in to bring her to heights she'd only imagined. While he worked her clit with his mouth, licking the hardened bud with the tip, he slid one long finger inside her.

"Cole." She moaned and tried to pull him in farther, clenching her walls around him, needing him harder and deeper.

"Need more?" He added a second finger and nipped at her harder, causing the first wave of sensation to hit. He was so in tune to her body, he knew the instant the first tremor began and flattened his tongue against her clit, pumping his fingers in and out while she came hard around him, against him, and for him.

Erin didn't know how long she rocked against his mouth and hand, only that he drew out her orgasm as long as possible.

"You're incredible," he murmured, sliding away from her only long enough to undress.

She bent, intending to unhook her shoes, but he stilled her with a strong hand on her leg.

"Leave them on. With those heels, you're

a goddamned fantasy come to life."

As if to prove his point, he stood before her, completely naked, his erection rock hard, protruding from his gorgeous body. While raking his hot gaze over her body, he wrapped his hand around his cock, pumping once, then twice, before joining her.

He bracketed her, one knee on either side of her, as he poised his erection at her damp, pulsing entrance.

Erin looked up at him, afraid everything she felt for him showed in her eyes. Not wanting to lose him because she was becoming emotionally invested when that wasn't what he wanted, she drew on bad-girl Erin as she met his gaze. "Fuck me, Cole."

His eyes darkened to a stormy black and with a strangled groan, he plunged hard and deep. Erin cried out, taking all of him, feeling all of him as he laid claim to her with a punishing rhythm that somehow felt so very right. Her body, which had been sated seconds before, came alive once more, taking a fast climb to an inevitable end that arrived in an explosion that encompassed everything that was Erin. She held nothing back — couldn't — as he demanded and took all of her with him when he came.

Cole stood in Erin's kitchen cooking breakfast. A mundane task he'd begun to enjoy because she appreciated and liked his food so damn much. Another thing he wasn't used to. Doing things for someone else on a daily basis. Giving and receiving approval for little things. Someone else coming to expect things from him.

And him learning to rely on things from another human being. Erin had begun to do his laundry, something he'd tried unsuccessfully to prevent. She was doing hers anyway, and since she came home from work and had a routine she followed, he'd started to let her scoop up his towels and things along with her own. She left him the newspaper to read because she only scanned the comics and "Dear Abby," a weird choice for such a bright woman, but it amused him to watch her small smiles as she read while she devoured his food.

Little things that he'd miss when he was gone. None of which meant he wanted this psycho to continue to toy with her life. The very thought made his blood boil. Nobody wanted to catch this bastard more than he did, but her brothers were at a standstill.

To top things off, he'd gotten a couple voice mail messages from his boss, asking when he'd be ready to go back under. Normally the answer was yesterday, but no way would he leave Erin alone when she was being stalked. And with the baby on the way, he admitted to needing time to get his head on straight. Not that he'd tell his superiors any such thing. He wanted space, and after the years he'd put in, he was entitled.

He'd just served them both and was about to call Erin when the doorbell rang. Knowing she'd learned not to answer, he felt for his weapon and headed to see who was there at ten o'clock on a Sunday morning.

A look outside and he froze.

"Who is it?" Erin asked from the top of the stairs.

"Jed." Cole didn't turn around.

"Oh. Umm, I'll let you handle it," she said, and he sensed rather than saw her head back to her room. He appreciated the privacy, since nothing about this visit could possibly be good.

Cole opened the door and faced his old man.

"You took your sweet time letting me in."

"Good morning to you too. What brings you by? Want to see Erin?" he asked, on the slight chance he could avoid the inevitable confrontation.

He shook his head. "I had breakfast with Ella and Simon. 'Course I knew you were

233

here playing bodyguard. Despite it all, I figured you'd take decent care of Erin, but damn it all, couldn't you keep it in your pants?"

Cole grabbed his father by his good arm and pulled him inside. In a public condo unit, he didn't need Erin's older neighbor coming outside and getting an earful.

"None of this is any of your business," he said, shutting the door behind Jed.

His father ran his good hand through his hair. The cast had been removed on his other arm, leaving him with just a sling. "You feeling okay?" Cole asked him.

"What do you mean, it's none of my business? She's the daughter of my best friend, the ex–police chief of this town. Not to mention an assistant D.A."

"Still don't see where it's your business," Cole said, then mentally counted to ten to calm his temper. "Do you think I planned this? And before you ask, of course I used protection, so don't go there."

"You're still a goddamned moron. Who do you think you are, touching a girl like her?"

Cole set his jaw. "She's a woman, Dad. It was mutual."

"She's a damned nice *woman,*" Jed barked at him. "You should have known better than to lay a hand on her. You're just going to hurt her when you leave her high and dry."

"That's between Cole and me, don't you think?" Erin walked down the stairs, dressed for a day at his cousin Nick's cabin on the lake. "Sorry, Cole, but I couldn't help overhearing, and there's no way I'm going to let him pin all this on you."

Cole's head began to throb. "Erin, go back upstairs." She didn't need to hear his father beat up on him once again. And he didn't need her sticking up for him or attempting to fight a battle he'd long since learned he couldn't win.

She shook her head. "It's my house; that gives me some rights. Jed, if you'd like to stay and congratulate us on having a baby, that's great. If you came to cause trouble, I'm going to have to ask you to leave."

Cole was torn between admiration and frustration.

"Erin, I've known you since you were a little girl. What were you thinking?"

She tipped her head to one side, eyeing his father as she would a defendant in a courtroom — much like he envisioned her going after a bug she wanted to squash. Cole decided his father deserved whatever he was about to get.

"I was thinking I couldn't find a better

man than your son to sleep with when I was lonely."

Cole didn't know which admission hit him harder, that she found him a good man even then, or that she'd gone to Joe's that night because she'd been looking for company.

He didn't have time to chew on either, because she wasn't finished with Jed. "And until you can find it in yourself to see Cole the way I do, you aren't welcome here." She stepped around Jed and opened her front door, making it perfectly clear she wanted the older man gone.

"I see my son's manners are rubbing off on you. Your mama would be disappointed."

"Actually, I think she'd applaud," Erin muttered as Jed made his way to the door.

"Now you've got a woman fighting your battles," Jed said, getting in his parting shot at Cole.

"Go home, Dad."

"He'll break your heart just like his mother broke mine, mark my words."

"But I'll be a better father than you ever were," Cole said, getting face-to-face with the man who'd fathered and raised him but had never ever liked him. "And I'll have Brody to thank." Cole slammed the door behind Jed before Erin could take the pleasure away from him.

A few intense, quiet seconds passed, in which Cole took a few moments to compose himself, breathing in and out, letting his heart rate return to normal.

"Cole?" Erin asked softly, placing a hand on his shoulder.

He didn't want to have this conversation. If he could change anything about his relationship with Jed, it would be so he didn't have to suffer the humiliation of confrontations like these in front of a woman like her. Because if anything Jed said had been right, it was that Erin was a damned nice woman, one whom he'd hurt in the end.

But not only was he tied to her through his child; he couldn't bring himself to walk away from her — from this relationship she was attempting to build with him — yet.

He turned. "Sorry about that."

She raised an eyebrow, a defiant look on her face. "Don't you dare apologize for his behavior. The one thing you should learn? How Jed acts is no reflection on you. Now, I'm hungry." She spun around and started for the kitchen.

"It's cold by now," he informed her.

"That's what microwaves are for." She strode into the cheery kitchen with lavender purple accents and picked up both their dishes. "Luckily for you, that's my specialty in the kitchen." She shot him a cheeky grin and proceeded to heat their breakfast.

Conversation about Jed seemingly over.

But was it?

Didn't she want to dig deeper? To poke into his and Jed's unhealthy and definitely ugly relationship? Wasn't she worried that Jed's view of him was somehow right? That maybe their kid would inherit his behavioral flaws? Because Jed might be an emotionally abusive jerk, but he hadn't made up the fact that during his childhood, Cole was one hundred percent an out-of-control pain in the ass. But since Erin wasn't bringing it up, Cole didn't have the stomach to either.

A few hours later, after a stop at The Family Restaurant to pick up the cake Erin had promised Nick she'd bring with her today, they pulled up to Nick and Kate's cabin on the lake. Serendipity Lake was located on the edge of town. Many of the wealthier residents owned summer cabins, and some had been renovated.

Erin was surprised when she'd heard Nick had built his permanent home here, but she knew he was a builder, having inherited his father's business when he passed away. She'd figured he'd bought a rundown place at a good price and fixed it up.

Except that as they approached, it became clear Nick's home wasn't a renovated cabin — this was more like a state-of-the-art luxury home.

"Wow," Erin murmured as they pulled up the paved drive. The other homes they'd passed had gravel-lined paths for cars to take.

"It's something, right?"

"Amazing!" Erin loved the house on sight. Nick had maintained the rustic feel, so the house wasn't completely out of place in the area, but it had a newer, more modern look on way more than one lot of land.

"Nick put his heart and soul into building this house. He planned it for years and worked during slow times, when he could get his crew here." Cole parked behind a Ford F-150. "Inside and out. He even carved a lot of the furniture."

"Impressive," she murmured.

"Nick doesn't like to brag, though. He doesn't show off."

Erin nodded. "Kate's not like that either. I've always liked her."

Cole met her on her side of the car. She took a few steps forward, only to realize he wasn't beside her.

"Cole?" She turned back to face him.

"What's wrong?"

"Nothing." He took two steps forward and she stopped him, putting a hand on his arm.

"Tell me."

He raised an eyebrow. "How do you read me so damned well? I'm an undercover agent, for God's sake. I'm good at hiding things."

She grinned, pleased he thought she could get past any facade he tried to erect. "I'm just good at knowing *you.* Now talk."

He let out a groan. "I don't do this. See family. Hang out with friends. Just . . . be."

Her heart twisted at his hesitantly admitted words. "I know. Just try it. If, after a little while, you want to leave, just get my attention and tug on your ear. I'll take the hint and make an excuse to go. Fair?"

"More than fair." He slid his hand over her cheek, cupping her face and holding her in place for a kiss that was rich for all he didn't say, but there was a wealth of feeling behind it.

He knew she got him in a way no one else ever had, or he wouldn't be so surprised. Or touched. Progress, she thought, was a heady feeling.

Friends and family. Cole might not know from them, but he spent the day surrounded by both. Nick had invited everyone from his mother and sister, April, to people Cole hadn't seen or spoken to in years. There were the three Barron brothers: Ethan, whom Nick remembered from high school, his brothers Nash and Dare, and their wives. Cole recognized some of the women too, including Ethan's wife, Faith, who'd grown up in that mansion on the hill, and whose father was spending life in prison for a monster Ponzi scheme rivaling Madoff's. Others were new to town, like Nash's wife, Kelly, whose smart-mouthed teenage sister, Tess, joined them midway through the day. Dare, another cop and a friend of Erin's, had married Liza McKnight, an architect.

Then there were the babies and toddlers running around, whose ages Cole couldn't remember, never mind which kid belonged to which parent. Nick and Kate opened their home, happy to have everyone hanging out together, neither seeming the least bit overwhelmed by the sheer number of people or the noise level of the screaming, laughing, sometimes crying kids.

Cole expected to feel so far out of his element, his skin would itch with the need to get back to what he knew — pretending to be someone else, living a lie, the pretense manageable because he was doing what he did best, doing his job for the greater good. And because he didn't know how to do things any differently.

Today was giving him a glimpse of what he was missing. Hell, the last few weeks with Erin had been doing that too. And despite everything he'd once believed about himself, he couldn't deny the appeal of his cousin's type of life. The same one he was currently living. Except Cole's current situation, just like his undercover one, was a pretense built on necessity. As soon as Erin didn't need his protection anymore, Cole could go back to his old existence, which suddenly didn't hold as much interest as it used to.

"Hey, you okay?" Nick asked, joining him on a lounge chair beside his, overlooking the lake.

"Fine. Just taking a breather."

"Yeah, it can all be a bit much," the other man said, laughing. "Where's Erin?"

Cole tipped his head toward the pier Nick had built near the shallow part of the water. She, along with some of her friends — Macy included — were with the toddler-aged kids. Erin was holding one child beneath her little arms, despite the round tube encircling the girl's stomach. Shrieks and laughter would occasionally reach his ears.

One thing was for sure — she looked . . .

happy. No stress of a stalker anywhere in her beautiful face. Cole couldn't tear his gaze from her bathing-suit-clad body. Though she'd chosen a one-piece that covered her stomach, it was cut high enough on her thighs and low enough on her cleavage to entice him and make his mouth water. Her long legs beckoned, reminding him of how they felt wrapped around his back as he slid into her hot, wet body. *Shit,* he thought, shifting in his chair to conceal what that thought did to him.

"Someone's got it bad." Laughing, Nick handed Cole a cold bottle of beer. "You two seem to have come to an understanding."

Cole shrugged, still not used to personal conversations like these. Still, this was Nick. "Erin figures if we're together right now, there's no reason to hide it. Once her pregnancy becomes obvious, people are going to know I'm the father anyway." He took a long pull of brew, which tasted good in the summer heat.

"Why do I hear a *but* coming?"

Cole groaned. Wasn't it obvious? "But my job hasn't changed and I'm not here to build white picket fences. I'm not built for that life."

Nick raised an eyebrow. "You're looking pretty comfortable surrounded by the proverbial one right now," his cousin pointed out.

"It's temporary. She knows that. So do you, asshole."

Nick snorted. "Yeah, like Erin's going to be easy to walk away from." He gestured to the water, where Erin lifted her little charge up high and pressed her lips to the girl's cheek, causing her to shriek with delight and kick her little legs in excitement.

Something warm unfurled in Cole's chest. He told himself it was that she'd be a great mother to their kid, nothing more. "I do what I do. I'm not going to leave her here wondering when my cover's over, when she'll hear from me. Or if she'll get a call that says my cover was blown and I'm not ever coming back."

Cole shook his head, remembering the last guy whose wife had to receive that kind of news. No way would he put Erin through that hell.

"I still say it's her call to make," Nick insisted.

Cole exhaled hard. "That's not how it is between us. It's forced proximity and just sex." He winced as he spoke the words that felt like a lie coming from his lips and a betrayal to everything Erin stood for.

Nothing about Erin was *just* anything.

Still, *Whatever it is, for as long as it lasts,* she'd said, and he'd agreed. If she'd developed deeper feelngs for him, she was smart enough to keep them to herself, because he'd made his future plans clear.

Nick tipped the bottle back and drank before addressing Cole. "Keep telling yourself that. I'm sure it'll keep you warm when you're undercover. I'm through hitting my head against a wall. Did I tell you I bought property on the edge of the lake and built a house on spec?"

Grateful for the subject change because it meant he could ignore the knot that felt like a ball stuck in his chest, Cole shook his head. "I'm waiting for housing sales to pick up a little before I list it."

"That's great."

"Want to take a quick look? I've got some time before I have to start grilling burgers."

"Sure thing." Nick was always proud of his finished projects and Cole enjoyed looking at his cousin's talent.

He stood and, along with Nick, walked to the water to tell Kate and Erin where they were going.

Erin met his gaze and lifted a hand to her ear in question.

He grinned, knowing she was asking if he was feeling closed in and ready to go home.

Worrying about him and looking out for him.

Cole pushed those thoughts away and shook his head. "Nick is going to drive me around the lake and show me the house he built and is ready to put on the market."

Her eyes lit up. "Ooh, another Nick Mancini masterpiece? Can I come?"

"Sure thing," Nick said, pride in his voice.

Faith took her wriggling daughter from Erin's arms. "I told you that's the good thing about being a friend or relative. You can enjoy the baby and give them back!"

Erin laughed. "Soon enough I'll be looking for people to relieve me," she said, and everyone around them slid into stunned silence.

"What?!" Kate asked, her voice rising in pitch.

Cole froze.

Erin's eyes opened wide and her cheeks turned bright red as she realized her slip of the tongue. "Umm . . . I —"

Cole met her gaze. Gave her permission with a slight tip of his head. It was her call if she wanted to cover or reveal. But he couldn't deny his stomach was in knots as she pondered her decision.

"Erin?" Faith asked softly.

Meeting Cole's gaze, Erin gave him a tiny

nod back.

But he saw how awkward things had become and he didn't want her to think he was dumping it all on her. "Erin's pregnant. You all would've figured it out soon enough," Cole said, reaching out a hand toward the water.

The tightness in her face gave way to relief. She clasped his hand and climbed out to stand next to him. "We're having a baby," she told them.

There. It was out, Cole thought. Dizziness that had nothing to do with the heat assaulted him as the women around them shrieked. The other guys came running to see what the commotion was all about. As they found themselves the center of attention, they were separated by the surprised well-wishers patting Cole on the back and kissing Erin's cheeks.

He accepted the congratulations, ducked most of the questions, and finally managed to catch Erin's gaze. She appeared flustered and overwhelmed by the attention and when she lifted a hand and tugged on her ear, he knew he'd read her correctly.

"Hey, Nick, you going to show Erin and me that house sometime this century?" Cole called out to his cousin.

Nick caught on quick. "Yeah. Let's go

through the house so I can grab my keys. Everyone go back to your regularly scheduled programming," Nick ordered.

Cole grabbed Erin's hand and pulled her away from her well-meaning, question-hungry friends.

"Hurry back," Kate called to their retreating backs. "The natives will be getting hungry soon."

"Yeah, yeah," Nick grumbled, but even Cole could hear the good-natured chuckle behind the words.

With Cole's hand on Erin's back, they followed Nick to the house.

Erin didn't say a word but Cole sensed her need for peace, quiet, and space. If she didn't get better after the house tour, he'd make their excuses and get her home. Ironic, that she was the one who'd needed to get away from the crush of people, not him.

Surprisingly, even between Nick's pushing Cole on personal issues and the public reveal of Erin's pregnancy, Cole didn't feel a hint of the anxiety he'd anticipated. They drove to his cousin's place and walked around the massive house, which Erin loved, and the tour seemed to draw her out of her shock. Nick had even had a decorator come in and furnish it, so selling the house really would be like selling a model home.

While Nick explained each room and the extras he'd built in, Cole's mind drifted and he contemplated the day further. Cole hadn't been the outsider he'd expected to be. Everyone talked to him, wanting to catch up and make friendly conversation. Shockingly, Cole had been not just receptive but he'd also enjoyed hearing what was going on in old acquaintances' lives. In return, some of the guys suggested they meet up for drinks at Joe's or that Cole join them for poker one night soon.

Cole's conclusion was startling. When he didn't withdraw into himself or put himself on the fringe of the crowd, he seemed to be accepted readily enough. Which made him wonder if his reception on his return was more about his own behavior toward everyone else rather than their feelings about him.

It would be something to think about if he'd planned on sticking around. But he didn't. He ignored the sudden uncomfortable feeling that arose at the thought of leaving Serendipity.

TWELVE

Erin was exhausted. She lay her head back against the seat while Cole drove them home. Boy, would she miss this chauffeur service when his time was done. She couldn't believe how quickly she'd gotten used to being taken care of. Such a dangerous proposition, but at this moment, as she kicked off her shoes and curled into the seat, she couldn't bring herself to care.

Although she'd long since accepted being pregnant, she hadn't thought about the world knowing. The exposure had taken everything out of her. So had watching the happy couples. *Families,* she amended. A melancholy sadness washed over her for what she'd never have with the father of her child. But Erin knew once the exhaustion went away, the sadness would go with it, to be replaced by her determination to make the most of their time together and see where things led.

After all, Erin had always prided herself on being a go-with-the-flow kind of person. All things considered, she'd dealt with the pregnancy news, the shooting, and the stalking, and she hadn't fallen apart. Yay her. Maybe it came from having such a stable family behind her, something Cole didn't, and which he'd admitted had affected how he viewed life.

She sighed and closed her eyes, determined to let sleep overtake her, at least for the ride home. Better than talking about what was bothering her, something Cole, with his perceptive personality, was sure to notice.

Unfortunately, her mind was too worked up to slow down and just be, even for a few short minutes, but she kept her eyes closed. Just in case.

Of course, her thoughts went to Cole and that moment before they walked into Nick's, when she'd caught the hint of vulnerability in his expression. She was as attuned to him as he was to her. She hadn't expected him to admit why the day would be difficult for him, but he had. He'd let her in a little more.

And in the end, he'd not just survived the day, but he'd found a place with these people — if he wanted one.

Please let him want that place with them, but most of all, with me, she thought. Because though she wouldn't let herself use the word, not even in the most private recesses of her own mind, she was falling in . . . *everything* with Cole Sanders.

Even if she couldn't sleep, she let the lull of the truck soothe her wayward thoughts until she felt the familiar set of turns into the condo complex and, finally, into her driveway.

"Stay here."

Cole's voice pulled her out of her stupor, and she forced her heavy eyelids open to see two police cars in front of her house, lights flashing. Her neighbors had congregated on their lawns. Cara and Sam, who'd left Nick's before Cole and Erin had arrived for their evening shift, stood on her front porch.

Erin threw open her car door and headed for her brother.

"I said wait in the car," Cole called after her.

She still ignored him. "What's going on?"

Sam eyed her with concern. "Break-in."

"Why didn't you call me? Why didn't the alarm company call me?"

Cara answered, her voice calm, but her blue eyes warm and sympathetic. "Someone

252

cut the phone line. The alarm went off but the call never went to Central Station. The old woman on the right is almost deaf, and the ones on the left are on vacation. At least, according to Mrs. Flynn."

The nearly deaf neighbor, Erin thought.

"Someone nearby must have finally realized the noise meant something and called it in," Sam said. "You arrived before we could call you."

"What happened?" Cole asked.

Sam tipped his head toward her condo. "Went in through the side window. Broad daylight, brazen as you please," he muttered.

"*She* was in my house?" Erin asked, feeling a very unusual bout of hysteria coming on.

Cole's hand clamped down on her shoulder.

"What did she do in there?" Erin started forward, but he held on fast.

Sam met Cole's gaze over Erin's head.

She stiffened, unwilling to be left out of the loop this time. "Oh no. None of that silent male communication crap. Talk to me."

"There's some damage," Cara said to her. "Erin, look. Assuming it's the same person behind everything else, and assuming we're

253

right that it's a woman, she went for your personal things."

Nausea, which came so easily these days, rose in Erin's throat. "I want to see."

"No!" Cole and Sam said at the same time.

Erin froze at the unilateral command. "Do not tell me what I can and can't do. Not now." She shook Cole's hand off her arm and stomped toward her home.

"Let me," Cara said, catching up to Erin as she approached the front door. She touched Erin's arm. "It's more the emotional aspect of what this person did that will affect you," she said softly, more as a friend than a cop. "It's a violation, sweetie. And you're going to feel it. Are you sure you're ready?"

Erin nodded, certain no matter how shaky her insides had become.

"Then I'm right there with you. Let's go. Just remember —"

"Don't touch anything. I'm still an ADA. I know the drill."

Cara sighed. "Sometimes it's easy to forget when you're also the victim."

Victim. Erin hated that word, had avoided using it or thinking of herself in those terms since all this had started. But as she entered her house, which now smelled of another woman's strong perfume, she felt every inch the injured party. The same people whose rights Erin usually fought *for.*

"Upstairs," Cara said.

Erin pushed forward and headed for her bedroom without having to be told. She knew Cole and Sam had joined them, felt their presence behind her, silently following Erin and Cara.

She stepped into her room and came to a halt, taking in the carnage with her own eyes, yet unable to comprehend what she was actually seeing. Her clothes — her new maternity clothes that she'd spent so much money on — were scattered around her bed and floor, shredded, cut, torn in pieces.

"Son of a bitch," Cole muttered.

Ignoring him, Erin forced herself to take in each item, until her gaze fell on the distinctive lapis blue dress she'd worn Saturday night, cut in pieces. From there, she was compelled to shift her gaze to her dresser, where she'd proudly put her award. Sure enough, the star had been snapped off the base. But that wasn't what caused the lurch in her heart.

Her large mirror had a message scrawled across the glass with red lipstick: *HE'S MINE.*

Erin's gaze flew to Cole's in question, because who else could *he* be referring to?

Why go after Erin's maternity clothes and nothing else unless she felt possessive of him? There was no other *he* in her life, none that would elicit this kind of reaction, anyway.

Color highlighted his cheekbones, anger and a hint of regret in his expression. Clearly they'd come to the same conclusion.

"Who is she?" Erin asked him directly, ignoring the dizziness flooding through her.

He didn't answer immediately, but Erin could see the wheels turning in his mind as he ran through possibilities.

"Let's get you out of here," Cara suggested, wrapping an arm around her shoulders. "Sam and Cole can talk some more."

Erin shook her head. "I want to hear what they say."

"I'm not hiding anything. Hell, I don't know anything." Frustration laced Cole's tone. He met and held her gaze, his expression angry but open.

She believed him.

"Go downstairs with Cara. Sit down. You're pale and look like you're about to collapse."

Erin didn't want to admit it, but Cole was right. She was shaky, and it wouldn't hurt to get off her feet for a little while.

"Go," he said firmly. "I'll talk to your brother and make some phone calls, see if there's something going on with any old cases that I don't know about."

"Fine." She spun around and walked out.

Cole's head pounded as he turned to Sam. Usually considered the mild-mannered Marsden brother, but no less intimidating than Mike, Sam glared at Cole, full-on fury in his expression.

"If there's another woman, if you're fucking with my sister, I will kill you."

If Cole had been hiding anything from this cop, he might be worried. "I'm as in the dark as you are." Ignoring Sam's snort of disbelief, Cole grabbed for his phone and called his boss on his home number. No more screwing around.

The man answered on the first ring. "Rockford? It's me."

Cole listened as the older man reamed him for not returning his calls, for falling off the grid, and immediately jumped to wanting to know when he'd be ready to return.

"No time soon. I've got a situation." He spelled out the entire deal with Erin, from her being pregnant with his kid to the shredding of clothes in her room.

No time to hide the truth from his boss, not if Cole wanted to call in favors and help. Besides, much as he tried to ignore the truth, Erin and this baby would change his life. *How* remained to be seen. But Cole owed the other man the truth if it affected his job, and it did. Already Cole was operating differently, ignoring calls and remaining on leave longer than ever before.

"Pull recent cases, names of people who had a hard-on for me, and women who've indicated interest." As Cole spoke, a vision of the one female he'd done his best to forget about came back to him in vivid detail.

Victoria Maroni wanted Cole for herself. And that was her scent he'd smelled downstairs. She'd always had a heavy hand with the perfume.

Son of a bitch.

"Call Witsec. Check on Victoria Maroni," Cole added.

Sam's eyebrows rose at the mention of a specific name.

Cole held up a hand. "Right. They were holding her to testify in another case involving her husband's associates." Last time Cole saw Victoria, it was right after he'd shot her husband during the raid that took down his operation.

His boss said he'd get back to him when he had something. Cole ended the call and turned to Sam. "Before you say a word, she's the wife of the last guy whose organization I infiltrated. He treated her like dirt and as I moved up in his inner circle, I befriended her. When things went down, I made sure she was protected. She misread the situation."

She'd looked to Cole as her savior, her white knight, a man who'd rescued her from a life of hell for no other reason than his love for her. He'd just been doing his job. He remembered how he'd thought of her as a poor deluded woman, one deprived of love and affection.

"She mistook my friendship and protection as something more than it was. I felt sorry for her, but I never perceived her as a threat."

"Maybe you were wrong," Sam said in disgust.

The way Cole's stomach was churning, he agreed. "And that mistake put Erin in harm's way." Nothing he could do about the past, but he could do something now. "I need to get her out of here while you do your jobs."

Sam nodded. "Where?"

Cole remembered the look on her face

259

when she'd walked through Nick's spec home. "I'll talk to Nick." He explained his idea and Sam agreed.

"How are you going to get Erin to go along quietly? And miss work until this is over?"

"She'll go if I have to tie her up for a goddamned month," Cole muttered.

Sam barked out a laugh. "I don't like one thing about this mess, but I have to admit I'd pay to see that."

Cole didn't reply, because if he had Erin tied up anywhere, her brother was the last person he'd want around to see what he did with her.

"I need you to help me get her out of here unnoticed," Cole told Sam. "And I need you to talk to your mother. Whatever clothes Erin bought when they were together? Tell her to replace them and have them sent to you. On me. I'll make arrangements to get them from you."

Sam's expression turned from wary to something more akin to respect. Cole didn't deserve it. As far as he was concerned, Jed finally had a point. All Cole had done was mess up Erin's life from the second he'd come into it. The best he could do now was to make sure she remained safe.

■ ■ ■ ■

This is what her life had come to. Hiding under a blanket in a car as Cole drove her away from her house. Seriously? Where was the dignity?

She groaned.

"I'll make it up to you," Cole said from the driver's seat.

She wanted to tell him to go to hell, but rationally she knew this wasn't his fault. At least, it had better not be his fault. Whoever this woman was, he better not have led her on. She bit the inside of her cheek and thought about what she knew of Cole. He'd never pretended with Erin. She knew exactly where she stood with him from day one. But he'd been undercover. Who knew what he'd had to do . . .

The car came to a stop.

Erin didn't know where they were headed. Cole said it was a surprise, and since she'd had to pack what she could of her personal things and toiletries, she hadn't been privy to his phone conversations to set up a place for them to go. Sam stayed behind at her house, supervising the forensics team that was dusting for prints and making sure everything was bagged and tagged. So to speak.

"Hang on," Cole said.

She heard the sounds of him opening the car door, getting out, then returning and shutting the door again. Soon the car moved another few feet. Not long after, he rescued her from her hiding place in the back seat.

She stepped out of the car and into a darkened garage. "Where are we?"

"Guess." A dimple flashed in his cheek.

She loved it when he got playful. He didn't do it that often, but when he did, it was downright adorable. Not that Mr. Tough Guy would want to hear that about himself, so she remained silent.

She let her eyes adjust and he opened the unlocked door to the house. The minute she stepped inside, she knew. "We're at Nick's spec house!" she said, excitedly. She'd fallen in love at first sight.

Their bags in hand, he gestured for her to go upstairs. "I called Nick and explained the situation. It's ours as long as we need it."

"Oh my God." It would be even more like living her dream. A big house, the perfect man, Erin pregnant . . . but it wasn't. Her balloon of excitement popped as she reminded herself she needed to keep reality firmly in mind. She was here because she was being stalked, and Cole was only with her for that same reason.

Suddenly, she didn't want to think anymore. "I'm wiped out."

Understanding lit his heavy-lidded gaze. "Go up to the master bedroom and lie down. Nick left the house open for me, so I want to walk through and make sure everything's secure." He hesitated before continuing. "I'll meet you up there?"

She was surprised he'd phrased it as a question. After all the bossing around, suddenly he was hesitant?

"Sure." Hadn't she told him she wanted to be in his bed? Unless . . . "If you want to."

"I just thought maybe you were pissed. You wouldn't be in this mess if it weren't for me."

She rolled her eyes. "It's not like you asked this crazy lady to stalk me. Assuming it's her, anyway. But I do have a question," she said before she lost her nerve.

"Shoot."

"Maybe I don't have the right to ask this, but . . . did you sleep with her? Is that why she got the wrong idea about the two of you?" she asked.

"No!" The word exploded from him, his

expression horrified. "Is that what you think? That I led her on during the assignment and then dumped her as soon as it was over?"

She bit the inside of her cheek. "Not really."

He folded his arms across his chest. "But the thought crossed your mind."

"For a minute," she admitted. "I mean, it's pretty extreme for a woman to go psycho. Although I have prosecuted cases where it's happened." She raised her hands, then let them drop, knowing she was rambling, not making sense. "Just chalk it up to me being hormonal."

And wanting to be special to this man and so very afraid she was just another body in his bed. Her pulse set a rapid beat in her throat.

He studied her for a long moment. She stared back, taking in his exhausted features, the tension in his taut cheekbones, his eyes dark, mouth pulled tight. This was getting to him every bit as much as it was her, and she felt bad getting into arguments with him over nothing.

"Go lock up. I'll see you in a few minutes," she told him. They were both tortured by their own thoughts, and maybe space would help.

She just wished she knew what his thoughts were.

Despite wanting to stay awake, Erin passed out the minute she laid down on the comfortable bed and slept straight through until sunlight streamed through the windows the next morning. She wasn't usually such a heavy sleeper, but this pregnancy was totally changing so much about her normal habits.

She blinked, taking in her surroundings. Windows with large plantation shutters wrapped around one side of the room. The decor was neutral, a warm cream color scheme, allowing for whoever moved in to the house to add their own touches.

Not letting herself dwell on the thought of another owner of this beautiful home, she stretched, and suddenly noticed she was alone in the bed. Cole must have gotten up much earlier.

She went to the bathroom, surprised to find all her toiletries laid out for her already. This sweet, caring side of him never ceased to amaze her, and to keep her addicted to hope — the very thing that might destroy her in the end. Ignoring her wayward thoughts, she brushed her teeth, washed her face, and walked out in time to see Cole step into the room.

His hair was still mussed from sleep, but he'd pulled on an old pair of jeans, leaving them unbuttoned. His feet were bare, as was his chest, and Erin's mouth watered at the sight of him.

"Morning," she said, not surprised the word came out a husky croak.

"Hey. Sleep okay?"

She nodded. "Like a dead person."

His mouth turned down. "Don't even joke like that."

She settled on the bed, tucking one leg beneath her. "If I don't joke, I'll cry, and I refuse to go there."

His eyes darkened and he joined her on the bed. "I hate that any part of my life has touched yours. Jed was right when he said I'd be no good for you."

"Jed's an ass," Erin muttered. "Are you seriously telling me you feel responsible for a crazy woman's actions?" It wasn't the first time he'd let himself feel responsible for someone else's behavior. First his father, now this woman.

He let out a snort of disbelief. "A crazy woman whose radar you wouldn't even be on if not for me."

"It could just have easily been someone I prosecuted and who got out and wanted revenge. We aren't responsible for other

266

people's actions."

Cole eyed her warily. As usual, he found himself disarmed by her practical nature and her ability to let life just go on around her. "It's not the same thing."

"Why? Because you don't like it when your solitary world touches anyone else's?" she asked, challenging him in a way no one else ever dared to.

Her eyes, more green today in the sun-drenched room, flashed angry sparks. Her spunk, her ability to bounce back, to go up against him, aroused him like crazy. Made it impossible to keep his distance, when distance would be in her best interest.

"Well?" she asked, straightening her shoulders.

Her soft, silky tank fell lower, exposing mouthwatering cleavage.

"Well what?" He'd totally lost the thread of conversation.

Erin's gaze fell to her chest before she raised her gaze to his once more. "You're such a man," she muttered, but with cheeky laughter, not anger, in her voice.

That's all she needed to do in order to completely disarm him and make him putty in her hands. "Something wrong with that?" he asked, suddenly feeling equally playful.

She raked her gaze over him, the same

awareness he'd seen when she walked out of the bathroom flaring there now. "Nope, nothing wrong at all."

Her words and teasing tone poked at him, and with a low growl he pulled her beneath him on the bed. She stared up at him with those eyes he could drown in.

"You're dangerous, Cole Sanders," she said, reaching up and brushing his hair off his forehead.

She didn't know the half of it. "Never intentionally, not to you."

Before she could reply or he could get himself in any more trouble, he sealed his mouth over hers, effectively ending all conversation.

She moaned and slid her fingers into his hair, holding him in place. Another surprise. This woman who clearly didn't know from one-night stands four months ago was now his equal in the bedroom. Damned if that didn't turn him on even more.

And when she hooked a leg around his, locking him in place, he let her, but by no means did he intend to be passive in this exchange. He ground his hips into hers, as he thrust his tongue in and around her mouth, working her into a writhing frenzy of want.

She turned her head to the side and

nipped his earlobe. "I need you inside me," she said, following the small bite with a loving lap of her tongue.

His cock swelled and hardened. "Jesus," he muttered, his entire body shaking too.

It didn't take long to strip her of her flimsy top and shorts, discovering she was bare beneath. "You're going to be the death of me."

With a laugh, she went to unzip his fly, but he stilled her hand. "I've got it." If he let her try to pull the zipper over him now, he'd lose it for sure.

He rose and stripped fast, returning to the bed and coming over her in one swift move. She reached for his erection but he grabbed her wrist, pinning it over her head. "No touching," he said through clenched teeth. "Not if you meant it when you said you need me inside you."

At his words, a soft moan escaped her lips and she arched her hips upward, her damp heat coming into direct contact with his aching shaft.

He met her clouded gaze, enjoying the depth of need reflected there. "Other hand over your head too," he said.

Eyes wide, she obeyed.

"Now keep them there so I can focus on not coming until you do." He slid his cock over her clit and her eyelids fluttered closed.

Happy to have her break that emotional connection threatening to pull him under, he chose that moment to plunge deep into her hot channel.

"Oh, Cole."

She moaned his name, and as her body throbbed and clenched around him, he felt more than the physical connection of their bodies. Emotion welled in his chest, a thick, heavy, and unfamiliar sensation beating at him from inside out. He knew the feeling, recognized it despite it being both unfamiliar and unwanted.

And he refused to give *it* a name.

Instead he concentrated on the movement of their bodies, the singular act of seeking release. That was easy — but Erin wasn't.

And being Erin, she took him out of his comfort zone, by burying her face between his neck and shoulder, where he felt her hot breath against his skin, her lips pressing warm, wet kisses to his flesh.

Her softness called to him, beckoned to that part of him he kept cold and encased in ice. She stole his ability to remain detached by keeping his focus not on the pounding thrusting of their bodies but on *them.* He wanted more of her. All of her. He was driven to own, to possess. His cock full to bursting, he pressed harder, plunged deeper, and must have hit her sweet spot because she threw her head back and moaned.

"God, do that again." Her hips shifted and urged him on.

He forced his eyes open. Her arms remained above her head, her skin was flushed a pretty pink, eyes dilated, lips swollen, and he couldn't resist her plea.

Holding back his own orgasm, Lord only knew how, he braced his hands on either side of her head and focused on his thrust and grind, making sure to hit the same spot over and over. Her eyes rolled back and he swore her breathing stopped for a split second before she came — long and hard, shaking, shuddering, her body clamping around him — screaming his name.

Cole waited until every last mini-shudder subsided before letting himself go and taking his own pleasure, losing himself completely inside her in a way he never had before.

It took him a hell of a long time to come back to reality, and when he did, his sweat-slickened body covered hers, the only sound in the room their commingled heavy breathing. First thing he realized? The silence surrounding them was comfortable. Next after

271

that? He was still partially inside her.

And he liked it.

He pulled out quickly and she groaned. "Don't go."

"I'm heavy." And he needed space. "I'll be back," he said, and slipped into the bathroom to regroup.

THIRTEEN

When the shower water ran in the bathroom, Erin knew Cole wasn't coming back
to bed. She pulled her top and shorts back
on and walked to the windows, adjusting
the shutter so she could see out. Below her
was a blue-stone-covered patio, with a brick
built-in barbeque and wall surrounded by
an array of colorful flowers. It was so beautiful, she thought. So real.

So out of her reach, just like Cole.

Suddenly chilled, she wrapped her arms
around herself in search of comfort. Each
time they came together, Erin *felt* more, and
by the way he reacted to her touch, she was
convinced he'd experienced the emotional
connection too. But considering how
quickly he'd pulled back, those feelings
frightened him, because she refused to
believe the alternative — that she was just
another woman he slept with. One he'd got-

ten pregnant and was now stuck with in his life.

Erin came from a family of cops who prided themselves on their instincts in life and in dealing with people. And hers were screaming at her not to give up on Cole. But damn, he didn't make it easy.

She was lost in thought when the bathroom door opened with a squeak. "Needs WD-40," she muttered, spinning around to see Cole step out of the steam-filled room.

A towel wrapped low on his waist, he dried his hair with a hand towel and one hand. Sexy didn't begin to describe him, while she looked like a disheveled pregnant woman who'd woken up, had sex, and hadn't taken a shower.

She straightened her shoulders, intending to tell him they were due for a talk.

"We need to talk," he said first.

Oh. "We do," she agreed.

"About work. You can't go in today."

"Oh my God, it's Monday!" How had she forgotten? She glanced at the clock on the nightstand.

Eight thirty. She did a quick mental calculation. "I'll be late, but I can still get there at a decent hour." Heart racing, she started for the bathroom, only to have Cole stop her with a touch on her shoulder.

"Whoa. Didn't you hear me? You can't go in today. Or any other day this week." Before she could argue or ask questions, he held up one hand. "Until this psycho is off the streets, it's too dangerous for you — and the baby — to follow your normal routine and make yourself an easy target."

Erin exhaled a long, slow breath and let his words sink in. She didn't know what disturbed her more, the fact that despite her hating it with every fiber of her being, Cole had a point, or that she'd completely forgotten today was Monday and a workday.

"Okay," she said at last.

He narrowed his gaze. "You aren't going to fight me on this?" he asked, sounding stupefied.

This stalker woman, whoever she was, had gotten into Erin's home. Cut up her things. Had her shot at. Even if she wanted to go about her business and not give in to fear, she'd never ever put the child she was carrying at risk.

"I'm not a fool. I understand how dangerous this woman is. And despite what you think, I don't argue for the sake of arguing. I only do it when the men in my life think they know what's best for me. I just want the right to make those decisions for myself." Her throat ached from holding back unexpected, sudden tears.

"Dammit," she swore, and stormed into the bathroom and slammed the door behind her.

She splashed cold water on her face, embarrassed and frustrated at the same time. She'd had it with the pregnancy hormones, the ups and downs, the stalker, and she'd had it with Cole blowing hot and cold. But she didn't want to cry in front of him, and just because she'd shut herself in the bathroom didn't mean he hadn't figured out she was upset.

As evidenced by the barrage of knocking on the door. "Erin, let me in."

Not wanting to be any more dramatic than she'd been, she opened the door. "Go away. I need to shower."

He raised an eyebrow. "First tell me you're okay."

"I'm okay," she said, deadpan.

A muscle ticked in his jaw. "I'm not joking."

"Hormones suck. Is that what you want to hear? Being stalked by some freaky female that wants you to herself sucks." She drew a deep breath, knowing what was coming and unable to stop herself. "And while we're being honest, your freaking changing moods suck! Now go away and let me shower." She grabbed for the door but he blocked her from closing it with his body.

His eyes softened. "You're right. Everything's been dumped on your shoulders and it's not fair."

She blinked, first in surprise, then in an effort to push back oncoming tears. She didn't want him feeling sorry for her. "Don't be nice. It'll just make me cry."

She tried to turn but he grasped her shoulders. "Erin."

"What?"

"You deserve to have me be nice to you. You deserve a hell of a lot of things —"

"That you can't give. Blah, blah, blah. I. Know. Do you hear me asking you for anything? Hmm?" No matter what she wanted, she'd never once expressed her private hopes or wishes.

He opened his mouth, then closed it again.

"Well, other than asking you not to get out of bed two seconds after we made —" She caught her mistake before the words were out, and paused to cleared her throat. "After we fucked, then no, I don't believe I've requested a damned thing."

Fire flashed behind his dark eyes. "Erin," he said, his voice sounding in a warning growl.

"Now what?" She set her jaw, not wanting

to have this — or any — conversation with him right now.

"I don't care how big of an ass I've been, don't say we fucked. It's demeaning both to you and to —"

"To what? To us? To everything we share?" she asked, her voice rising. "Well, do me a favor. Unless and until you're ready to commit to an *us,* don't you dare ask me to call it anything else. Because you're right about one thing. The way you're behaving right now? I do deserve better." She pointed through the doorway. "Now out. I'm taking a shower. Alone."

Cole looked like he wanted to say something, but just as Erin expected, he turned and walked out, leaving her alone.

For the rest of the morning and into the afternoon, Cole kept himself busy. He made phone calls to people she didn't know, asking questions about old cases. He called Nick and informed him that he wanted a better security system here, which Erin tried to say was ridiculous, since for all she knew they could be gone tomorrow. But Nick apparently had no problem with the idea, and a crew was coming out later in the day to work.

Erin called Evan and explained the situation as best she could, leaving out the connection to Cole. She didn't need the man riled up any more on her behalf. As it was, she had to refuse to tell him where she was *in hiding,* not wanting a confrontation between the two men. She promised Evan she'd keep in touch, while he assured her he'd take care of redistributing her caseload. Erin winced at the thought of the extra work others in the office would have to take on because of her. Between her pregnancy-related days off and now this, she felt like she was abusing her position and her colleagues.

Then she'd have the baby and be entitled to maternity leave, and who knew how she'd handle things after that. Her head began to swim with all the implications, and Erin deliberately pushed those thoughts aside. There was time enough to deal with her future once her present was settled. And until her brothers found psycho-lady, as Erin had begun to think of her stalker, she was stuck in limbo.

With Cole.

And who knew where he'd disappeared to, but she had heard the alarm beeps, informing her he'd opened one of the exit doors and gone outside.

She was surprised a few minutes later

when her mother walked into the kitchen with bags of groceries in her hands. "Mom! I can't believe you're here." Erin hugged her mother, so happy to see her.

Ella put the supermarket bags on the counter and turned to Erin. "Give your mother a hug." She held out her arms, and just like when she was little, in Erin went.

Her mother's familiar scent wrapped around her, easing the ache in her chest "So?" Erin asked. "How'd you know?"

"Sam called and told me what happened. He said Cole asked him to have me run a few errands and come by, so here I am."

Erin looked over her shoulder, but saw no sign of Cole. "Where is he?"

"Bringing all your new clothes in from the car, I'd imagine."

"What?"

Her mother's attractive face wrinkled in confusion. "He didn't tell you? Cole asked Sam to have me go to the store where we went maternity shopping and replace everything that was *destroyed,*" her mom said, a diplomatic description if Erin had ever heard one. "He said to buy whatever we chose that day, and whatever else I found that you'd like." With a twinkle in her eye, one that indicated how pleased Ella was with Cole's behavior, she turned away and began unpacking the groceries.

Erin stood stunned, unable to process what she'd heard. "Cole said *that*?"

Her mother nodded. "And he took the bill from me when I pulled in. He's paying for it all. Now close your mouth, you're catching flies."

Erin lowered herself into the nearest chair, needing to think about Cole's actions. On the one hand, they made sense. It was obvious she had nothing to wear — right now she was in a pair of her biggest drawstring sweats and one of his old T-shirts, which he'd left out for her on the bed. But the easiest thing would have been to have her mother pick up a couple of items until Erin could shop for herself again.

But to replace everything? And add more? And pay for it all himself?

"Guilt," Erin said out loud. "He feels responsible that my life has been turned upside down and my clothes ruined, probably by some psycho stalker, and he blames himself."

"Maybe." Ella's eyes narrowed at Erin's conclusion. "Or maybe he wants to take care of you and this is the way he thought to do it."

Erin wrinkled her nose at the notion. "Doubtful."

"Oh ye of little faith. Even your brother seemed impressed," her mother said.

"Sam?"

"Yep. He said he doubted he would have done something that thoughtful. Then Mike said —"

Erin jumped up from her seat. "I don't want to hear Mike's negative comments." She stuck her hand in the nearest bag and began helping her mother put away the groceries.

"You'll want to hear this," Ella said. "Mike actually told Sam that *no* man would think that way unless he cared about the woman in question."

Erin froze in the process of putting eggs in the refrigerator and turned to her mom. "Mike took Cole's side? He said he thinks Cole cares about me . . . *that* way?" Shock and disbelief reverberated through her.

Erin knew Mike paid lip service to cutting Cole slack, but she didn't believe her protective older brother would actually do it.

Ella nodded. "Of course, then Mike ribbed Sam about his single status and ended by informing him that only when Sam fell that hard would he understand."

"I think I might faint," Erin muttered.

Her mother chuckled, shutting the fridge door behind Erin. "Over which part? Mike taking Cole's side? Or the possibility that he might be right and that man might really be falling for you?"

Erin closed her eyes, wishing with everything in her that Mike had a point, that Cole could care about her — as deeply as Mike loved Cara.

"I know how I feel, what I want — and sometimes I think I'm on the verge of breaking through to him. But then something clicks in his male brain and he withdraws. It's like he's feeling too much and it scares him."

"Maybe that's true. Remember, he doesn't have two parents who are still together like yours are. By the time his mother married her second husband, Cole was older. Cynical. With his negative views about himself already formed by Jed. You know how young and impressionable children can be damaged by bad parenting."

"Cole said the same thing to me once. When I asked him why his stepfather's positive views of him didn't override his father's negative ones."

There's only so many times you can hear negative shit before you start believing it yourself. By the time we got out, I'd had sixteen years of disappointing Jed under my belt.

She shivered at the memory. "Every time he pushes me away, I promise myself I won't react. But it hurts, and I push back." This time, she had done worse than that.

Unless and until you're ready to commit to an us, *don't you dare ask me to call it anything else. Because you're right about one thing. The way you're behaving right now? I do deserve better.*

She'd reacted with hurt and anger, hormones and frustration, and by doing so she'd validated his worst fears about himself. She rubbed her hands over her eyes.

"You're human, Erin. You can't blame yourself for acting like it."

She forced a smile for her mother's sake. "You're the best, you know that?"

"So are you, honey. And so is that man of yours."

Erin nodded in agreement. She knew that. *Now.* "I just wish he believed it too."

Her mother patted her shoulder. "If anyone can show him the error of his ways, it's you."

Erin shook her head, not as certain as her mother in her abilities. Sure, it was easy to see things clearly when not overwhelmed with him. By him.

Now to somehow remember that when dealing with the hardheaded but warm-blooded man she desperately wanted for herself.

Cole stared at the ceiling in the bedroom, wondering how his life went from the solitary living being undercover entailed, to . . . this completely complicated fuckup. Didn't matter, anyway. One thing he knew for sure — this ended. Now.

Erin's outburst merely cemented what he should have known all along. She wasn't cut out for his kind of life or affair. Every time he was with her, he gave her false hope, only to pull it away again when he withdrew. No more.

The way you're behaving right now? I do deserve better.

And he intended to make sure she got it, by getting her through this stalker mess with what was left of her emotions and pride intact, then walking away. Just like he should have done all along.

Cole's cell phone rang, interrupting him from his painful thoughts. "Sanders," he said, happy to talk to someone, anyone, to take him out of his own head.

"It's Rockford."

"What do you have for me?" Cole asked, eager for any news that would end Erin's nightmare faster.

"When do I get you back?" the other man asked.

Cole wasn't in the mood for games. "Never, if I don't get some answers."

Rockford cursed.

Cole braced his free hand beneath his head. "Not joking."

"I can't believe you're threatening to sacrifice everything for a piece of ass."

Cole clenched his jaw tight and he actually thought he might burst a blood vessel. "Talk about her like that again, and I'll offer my services to the federal government instead."

His boss let out a low groan. "She's not just your baby's mother." Another round of cursing commenced. "And I'll be losing you anyway."

"No, you won't. Give me what I need and I'll be back before you know it."

He could hear the sound of shuffling papers in the background. "Victoria Maroni went AWOL on Witness Protection after she testified."

Cole bolted upright in bed. But instead of swearing up a storm or going crazy, everything inside him went silent, much as it did when he was undercover and things were about to come to a head. "The Feds didn't follow up on her?"

"Why should they? She did her job, testified, and the guy was convicted. They won't spend man power or money to keep track. She's not their problem anymore."

But she was his, and Cole had just gotten proof that Victoria had dropped off the grid.

He ran a hand through his hair. The crazy woman could be anywhere, including Serendipity. But how the hell could she have been in such a small town all this time and not have drawn attention to herself? Unless she just came and went, slipping in and out unnoticed.

"You there?" Rockford asked into the silence.

"I've got to follow up on something. I'll be in touch."

"Hey! I got you your information. You owe me —"

"Talk to you later," Cole said, disconnecting the call. He immediately dialed Mike. "Pull photos of Victoria Maroni. Show them to John Brass, see if she's the brunette who hired him." Cole felt certain she was behind the shooting and was now stalking Erin, but he wanted to build an airtight case.

"Who was that?" Erin asked, joining him in the bedroom.

"Where's your mom?"

"She left." Erin pointed to the phone,

indicating she expected an answer.

"That was Mike." He explained everything he'd learned up to that point.

"So basically all we have now is confirmation."

He nodded.

"That and a buck fifty will get me a bus ticket." She began pacing back and forth on the plush cream carpet.

"But now we have a face. Your brothers know who to look out for. It's a small town and if they show her photograph often enough, someone's bound to have seen her."

Erin paused. "Okay, I'll think positive," she said, correctly interpreting his unspoken message.

"Good."

"Cole?"

"Yes?" he asked.

She stepped to the bed, settling next to him. His T-shirt was huge on her leaner frame, but he liked her in his clothing. It was a damn fine view, especially since he wouldn't be seeing her undressed anymore.

"My mother told me about the clothes you had her buy."

"They're hanging in your closet. I brought a few shopping bags of things in too." He hadn't wanted to go through the more personal items.

"I'm . . . well, thank you. It was beyond sweet of you to have her replace everything and —"

"You lost everything. It was the least I could do." He really didn't want her making him out to be some sort of nice-guy hero. Just because he replaced her clothes didn't mean he could give her what she expressly said she wanted.

His head pounding, he rose to his feet.

"Where are you going?" she asked.

This was it. "Moving my stuff into another room."

Erin reared back as if he'd slapped her. Exactly how he'd felt on hearing her words, knowing that each time he indulged in her sweetness, he was hurting her more and more. Yet he wasn't doing this for payback. He really was trying to be a decent guy. Sleeping with her when she wanted more? That would be more cruel than pulling back now.

She folded her arms across her chest. "That night at Joe's, you agreed. Whatever it is, for as long as it lasts. Isn't that what we said?" Her voice quivered, but she kept it together.

"That was before I realized how much I'm hurting you. I'm in, we sleep together, you hope for more, I pull away . . . it's a vicious cycle. You deserve better. At least now we both agree on that."

She looked down, ran her tongue over her lips, clearly collecting her thoughts before speaking. Finally she raised her head and looked at him head-on. "You know I said that out of frustration. I'm pregnant and hormonal. This whole enforced confinement thing is getting to me and it hasn't even started yet. Don't use my stupid words, said in the heat of the moment, as any kind of agreement. I told you all along, you're not the man Jed says you are."

"But I told you all along, I'm not the man for you. As soon as this stalker situation ends and you're safe, I'm expected back in Manhattan. They'll brief me and send me back undercover for who knows how long. I can't call. Text. Check in at all. It's not any kind of life you'd want."

"Says you." Anger shimmered in her eyes, which narrowed.

"Someone has to be rational."

"And you telling me what I can or can't handle, or better yet, what I do or don't want in my life, that's rational?"

"Yes."

She blew out a long, clearly pissed-off breath. He waited for the explosion he felt sure was coming. Instead she turned and in silence started for the door.

"Where are you going?"

She swung back around. "I don't know. But I have thirty-five hundred square feet to find a place far away from you." With that, she walked out.

And Cole's headache turned into a full-blown pounding in his temples.

Cole didn't know how much more of this he could take. Two days had passed since he moved out of the master bedroom. By dinnertime on Monday, Erin had gotten over her fit of anger, but as the next couple days passed, Cole realized she'd changed the rules between them drastically.

Whereas she'd been letting him cook for them both when they were at her house, insisting she clean up in exchange, now she was taking care of herself. She beat him to the kitchen for every meal, heating up her mother's food, adding a premade salad for dinner, also courtesy of her mother, and leaving him to figure out his own breakfast, lunch, and dinner. Of course, he was free to join her, she'd told him, and to eat whatever she was having if he wasn't in the mood to cook. But she wasn't doing anything *for* him.

She handled her own laundry but didn't

touch his. Straightened up the master bedroom and bathroom, along with anything she used in the kitchen, but left him to clean up after himself. She was perfectly pleasant and completely aloof, treating him like . . . she'd treat any bodyguard who'd been hired for the job.

No, he realized. Knowing Erin, she'd be nicer to someone hired to watch over her than she was to him. In fact, he felt sure she'd offer to heat up a second slice of lasagna along with her own, or pour a salad into an extra bowl.

He'd thought she wasn't angry at him anymore, and maybe she wasn't — but she clearly had an agenda. One he'd yet to figure out. All he knew was that they were in the same house, living even more separate lives than before they'd started sleeping together again.

She was back in independent Erin mode, and as much as he respected it, he hated it at the same time.

He stalked to the sliding glass doors of the kitchen and looked out, only to see her sitting in a lounge chair, a glass of water on the table, along with an e-reader of some sort beside it. She talked on her cell phone, waving an animated hand in the air.

But what struck him hardest was the bathing suit she'd chosen. Alone and away from friends, family, and prying eyes, Erin had chosen a purple bikini. A two-piece number that left nothing to the imagination.

The all-purple top exposed her now even more generous cleavage, while the bottom was the same color, cut high on the thigh, but a white band cut across her belly, and she'd rolled it down lower than necessary, enabling her to tan. He took in her generous curves and her softly rounded stomach and ground his teeth so hard, he wondered if he'd crack a molar.

Torturing himself wasn't his style, and he'd just turned away when the doorbell rang.

Grateful for any reprieve, he went downstairs to answer it, surprised to see Mike and Cara waiting on the front porch.

He let the couple inside. "What's up?" Cole asked, hoping like hell he wasn't in for any kind of brotherly lecture.

"Cara wanted to see how Erin was doing and I figured I'd tag along."

"Erin's out back. I'm sure she'll be happy to have company." Since she wasn't including him in her daily interactions and plans.

"Let's all go out back. It's nice out."

"This way." Cole led them to the kitchen and the sliding doors, taking them out back.

Erin didn't seem all that surprised to see them, and when Cara stripped off her top, revealing a bikini that Mike couldn't stop ogling, Cole wondered if Erin hadn't invited the couple over without his knowledge.

At this point, nothing Erin did should surprise him. Acting like the host of the house, he offered everyone a drink, brought sodas out back, and finally got himself settled in a chair next to Mike.

"You look like hell," Mike said, stretching his legs out in front of him.

"Thanks. Aren't you two supposed to be at work?"

Mike grinned. "It's Cara's day off and I'm the boss."

"Any news?" Cole wanted Victoria caught already.

Mike shook his head. "Positive ID on Victoria Maroni as the one who paid Brass to shoot Erin, but that's all. In the meantime, I've got people watching Erin's house and your apartment. We've both got people in Manhattan covering Maroni's favorite places before she went into Witsec. And we're discreetly showing her picture around Serendipity at places like the supermarket or Joe's. Nothing."

Cole exhaled low and hard. "I'm losing it," he muttered.

"I noticed there's been no looks between you two, no little touches, what gives?" Mike eyed him warily.

Cole didn't have much to lose by telling the truth. "You'll be happy to know I've come to my senses. I'm giving Erin space until this is over and I'm gone."

Mike raised an eyebrow. "You are one stupid fuck. Almost as dumb as I was," he said, laughing.

"What's so funny over there?" Cara called out.

"Mind your own business, baby."

"You'll pay for that later," she promised, blowing him a kiss.

Erin let out a gleeful laugh, obviously appreciating her brother being put in his place by his wife.

Cole merely rolled his eyes.

"Hey, don't knock it till you've tried it," Mike told him. "So what happened between you two? Why aren't you still behaving more like a couple?"

Cole adjusted the frames of his sunglasses and looked over the freshly manicured lawn. "There's nothing going on between us anymore."

Mike rocked forward in his chair, resting his elbows on his knees, staring at Cole like he could see inside his skin. "When my sister's happy, that makes me happy. So when she convinced me she could get that from you, I backed off. What's changed?"

Cole didn't do the buddy-buddy talk thing, but with Mike pressing him, he had no choice. "Once she's safe, I'm back to work. You tell me if it makes any sense to keep up something that has to end. Especially when she's admitted she wants more than I can give her. Being with her only hurts her and that's not something I ever wanted to do, no matter what you might think."

Mike studied him, assessing him in silence. "How about this," he finally said. "You play things your way . . . for now. But when you're losing your mind over losing her and you don't know which end is up? Call me. I'll kick your ass the way Sam kicked mine."

Cole didn't know what Mike meant, and before he had a chance to ask, both his and Mike's cell phones rang.

His gut screaming, he answered. Mike did the same. Both men had brief conversations, then, hanging up at the same time, met each other's gaze.

Mike merely nodded, giving Cole permission, not that he needed it.

Cole turned to the women. "Erin?"

Mid-laughter over something Cara said, Erin turned, her beautiful face void of expression when she looked at him. *Intentional, no doubt,* he thought, his heart lurching. He ignored the sensation.

"What is it?" she asked.

Though he wished he could handle this without involving her, he knew she'd never forgive him for keeping her in the dark. "Enforced confinement has just come to an end. Sam just arrested a woman lurking outside your back windows."

FOURTEEN

Cole and Mike headed to the precinct, leaving an angry Erin behind with Cara. Although she wanted to be there, and Cole respected the desire, both he, Mike, and Cara thought it was a bad idea to put her in the same vicinity as the woman stalking her.

Now, at the precinct and knowing Victoria was a room away, Cole wanted to burst in and question her himself, but Mike refused. "Let us do our jobs. Sam's in with her now."

"Then let me watch."

Silence settled around them in Mike's office as the other man studied Cole. "You look ready to explode."

"You're damn right. But I know how to keep it together."

Mike inclined his head. "Let's go, but don't make me regret this."

A few minutes later, Cole found himself on the opposite side of the glass, watching

Sam and Victoria, knowing she couldn't see him.

He shoved his hands in the back pockets of his jeans and studied the scene in front of him.

Sam sat with his back to the mirrored window. Victoria stared at him, while Mike studied her. Granted, it had been a while since he'd seen her last, but she looked . . . different.

He braced his arm on the wall and leaned in closer, trying to figure out what was off. "I want to hear."

"You promise to stay calm?" Mike asked.

Cole nodded.

Mike flipped the switch, turning on the sound.

"Let's try this again," Sam said. "What's your name?"

"Is he kidding?" The muscles in Cole's arm strained from holding back his anger.

Mike placed a restraining hand on his shoulder. "Listen."

"How many times do we have to go over this? No matter how often you ask me, the answer's the same. Nicole Farnsworth."

"Victoria's maiden name is Farnsworth. Parents are rich. Disapproved of their daughter getting involved with a known mob guy. She ran off with him anyway,"

Cole said.

But why wasn't she owning up to who she was?

"Did you fingerprint her?" Cole asked.

"I checked when we arrived. She was printed and booked for trespassing as soon as she came in. We're running her prints."

Cole set his jaw. "What about the rest of the charges? Attempted murder, stalking . . ."

"We'll get there. For now, we just need enough to hold her."

Cole studied the woman carefully. Same dark hair, longer than he remembered, but again, time had passed. She dressed differently than Victoria. More casual. Victoria was always well-groomed, to perfection, in fact. Full face of makeup, dark lipstick, hair teased. This Victoria was . . . softer.

That was the word he'd been searching for. Softer. More gentle. And she said her name was Nicole.

Cole narrowed his gaze, then pulled out his cell and dialed. "I need information on Victoria Maroni's siblings. ASAP," Cole said into the phone, then hung up without waiting for a response.

"You think she's telling the truth?" Mike asked.

Cole nodded, hating what that meant.

"The woman in there with Sam? She couldn't spend five minutes with Vincent Maroni and not get eaten alive."

Mike swore. Cole understood, because it meant Victoria was still out there. At least Erin was with Cara, a trained police officer, which soothed him — just barely.

Mike picked up the phone in the room and dialed. "Put a rush on those prints."

"Let's go with my gut on this and assume she's telling the truth. I can get more out of her than Sam, so will you let me in there now?" Cole asked.

"You can't interrogate her like a cop."

"I am a cop," he reminded the other man.

"Out of your jurisdiction. But I agree. Your personal stake in this might get her talking — assuming she feels bad when she finds out what her sister's done."

Cole nodded. "Let's go."

Before they could walk in, an out-of-breath rookie burst into the room. "Prints you requested, boss." He handed a file to Mike, who opened the folder, scanned the results, and nodded at Cole.

"Let's do this thing." Mike opened the door.

Sam and the woman across from him turned their way, as Mike, followed by Cole, stepped into the small room. A table, the two chairs, dingy walls, and not much else.

"What's up?" Sam asked, rising from his chair.

"Seems she's telling the truth." He slapped the folder onto the table.

The other woman jumped at the loud sound. Cole would have felt sorry for her if this mess weren't so serious.

"I *told* you I'm not Victoria," she said, pinning Sam with a triumphant look that had her cheeks flushed pink with victory. The other man actually squirmed.

She surprised them by rising from her seat.

Mike stepped in front of the door. "Where do you think you're going?"

She blinked, startled that the answer wasn't obvious to them. "I'm not the person you're looking for, so I'm leaving."

The hell she was. "Not so fast." Cole braced his hands on the table. "You were still found trespassing, and we have questions about your sister, so *sit. Down.*" His voice rose and the woman flinched.

Cole realized his initial impression was right. She was nothing like her sister.

Before he could moderate his tone, Sam jumped from his seat so fast his chair hit the wall behind him.

"Back off," the younger Marsden snapped

at Cole. "This isn't your interrogation." The easier brother was suddenly every inch the defender, the in-charge cop Cole knew him to be.

"Everyone calm down." Mike stepped to the table as Sam righted his chair. "Miss Farnsworth? This is Detective Cole Sanders. He's NYPD and he has a —"

"You're Cole? The same Cole my sister's gone crazy over?" Her light blue eyes settled on his.

"What do you know?" Cole asked, controlling his frustration with her lack of answers. Sam was right. Scaring her wouldn't accomplish his goal of getting her to talk.

"Why don't you sit back down?" Sam asked, gesturing to her chair.

She lowered herself into her seat.

"Drink?" Sam asked.

Mike whipped his head around to stare at his brother.

"No, thank you. I'm fine." She shot Sam a grateful look before glancing at Cole. "Before I answer your questions, I want to know what my sister's been up to. You tell me that, and I'll tell you whatever you want to know."

Cole glanced at Mike, then Sam. "You don't know? You haven't been in touch with her?"

She folded her arms across her chest and waited. Apparently she was serious. They answered her first. Maybe there was more steel in Nicole's spine than Cole had previously thought.

Knowing whose jurisdiction he was in, Cole deferred to Mike. "Well?"

The other man shrugged. "Tell her what she wants to know."

Cole did. From the shooting to disabling Erin's security, breaking into her home and destroying her clothes, he ran down a laundry list of what they believed Victoria had done to Erin.

Nicole Farnsworth's face paled. "It's worse than I thought," she said, more to herself than to him.

"Now will you tell us what's going on with your sister? When you last spoke to her, what you know, and why you were at Erin Marsden's, looking into her side window?" Sam asked, his voice gentler than Cole had ever heard him.

Cole shook his head, hoping the other man knew what he was doing.

"First drop the charges against me," she said, taking all three of them by surprise.

Cole stiffened. "That wasn't the agreement. You asked what your sister had done and we told you."

"Well, forgive me for not thinking about everything important all at once. It's not like I've been arrested before! Cuffed, printed, humiliated —" She scowled at Sam. "I'll tell you this. I was trying to find out what was going on with my sister, if she'd gone looking for this Erin. And I was going to warn Erin, if I saw her."

"By lurking at her windows and scaring her?" Cole asked in disbelief.

"If I rang the doorbell and either one of you saw my face, would you have let me in for conversation and coffee?" she asked, her sarcasm thick.

Sam let out an unexpected chuckle. "She's got a point."

"Shut up," Cole muttered.

"Drop the charges or I want my lawyer." Ignoring Cole and Mike, Nicole's gaze settled on Sam, as if she'd already figured out he was the key to getting what she wanted.

Or she was just responding to the same mental deficiency that had hit Sam.

Mike groaned. "I'll take care of it. Meanwhile, *you*." He pointed to Nicole. "Talk. This is my sister's life we're talking about." Mike stormed out and slammed the door without looking back.

Silence surrounded them, until Sam

cleared his throat. "We've all got a personal interest in this case. Erin's my sister too. We need whatever information you can give us about your sister and her plans. Start from the last time you heard from her."

Nicole ran a shaking hand through her hair. "It's not that simple. Vicky's always been . . . *unstable* is the best word I can give you. She has emotional issues." She hesitated, as if debating how much to reveal.

Cole decided to let her do this her own way in the hope of slowly gaining her trust, and with it, more details.

"To start with, she's always been needy, and transferred that need from man to man."

"Her husband treated her like dirt," Cole said bluntly.

Nicole swallowed hard. "Well, she didn't get much attention from our parents, but going out with Vincent got them to notice her enough to forbid the relationship. She ran off with him anyway. I didn't hear from her often over the years, but after the raid and Vincent's death, we had the first long talk we'd had in ages."

"What did she say?" Sam asked.

Nicole clasped her hands tightly together on the table. "She called against orders, I'm guessing, to tell me she was going into Witness Protection because she had to testify in a federal case against some of Vincent's business associates. But once it was over, she was going after the one man who really loved her and treated her like a queen." Her blue eyes leveled Cole with an icy glare. "I'm not saying she's rational, but if you led her on in any way, so help me —"

Damn, Cole was tired of that accusation. "I was nice to her," he said through gritted teeth. "I talked to her like she was a lady, something she didn't find much in her husband's crowd. I felt sorry for her, if you want to know the truth, but no sane person would mistake my behavior for anything more than simple human kindness or friendship. And once she learned I was there undercover, it should have been perfectly obvious why I befriended her in any way."

"You needed information from her." She scowled.

"That, and frankly, once I realized she wasn't in on anything within the organization, I thought I could protect her when things went down. That's it." Cole spread his hands wide, indicating he'd done what he could to help her sister.

She stared at her intertwined hands for a while. Finally she looked up at Cole, but let her gaze settle on Sam when she spoke next.

"He just said no sane person would mistake his behavior as genuine interest. Well, Vicky's bipolar." She choked over the word.

And there it was, Cole thought as he leaned against the wall. Finally they'd gotten the truth. Now to find out whether, beyond wanting to help her sister, Nicole would be willing to help them too.

"Thank you for that," Sam said, his hand covering hers. "Is she on medication?"

Nicole swallowed hard. "Supposed to be. But she has a history of stopping when she's feeling good, of refusing to believe she needs to live on them in order to function in the same world as the rest of us."

So they were dealing with a sick woman. Cole hoped that was better than her being purely delusional. Maybe there were threads of humanity in there that they could work with.

"Did she tell you where she was going when she left the program?" Cole asked.

Nicole shook her head. "I asked, and she said that Cole was meant to be hers and she was going after him. That's when I knew she was probably off her medication and I tried to keep closer tabs on her, but she never answered her phone, and her contact was sporadic." She twisted her hands together in a way that had to be painful.

"Then, a few days ago, she called in the middle of the night, hysterical. She was rambling about how this Erin Marsden was ruining all her plans. She said something about watching Cole, waiting for the right time to approach him, but Erin was in the way."

"That's another thing that doesn't make sense. Why didn't she just come find me right away?" Cole asked.

"From what I could understand of her rambling, when she first came to town, she watched. She wanted to get an idea of your life. And she saw Erin leaving your apartment."

"That was over four months ago!" Cole's head nearly exploded.

"I know. Like I said . . . bipolar. She's always spent more time plotting and planning than doing. But when she makes a move, it's big."

"Like running away with Vincent," Sam said.

Nicole nodded.

"When did you hear from her again?"

"The day she saw Cole and Erin talking at some coffee shop. She went ballistic. I guess that's when she started targeting Erin specifically, but I didn't know she'd hired someone to shoot her! I didn't think she was violent." Nicole lay her head in her hands and moaned. "I don't know what to say." She lifted her pain-filled eyes to Sam's.

The way she kept focusing on Sam and not Cole, despite Cole's connection to her sister, he knew he hadn't imagined the connection there. Interesting.

"Do you know where she's hiding out? Because this is a small enough town that we'd have had a sighting by now if she was living here," Sam said gently.

Her eyes shimmered with tears. "I don't even know how to tell you this."

Cole's nerves jangled. "What is it?"

"Last time Vicky called me, it was right before the weekend. She was hysterical because she'd been setting up a special place for the two of you to live and she found out Erin was pregnant."

"Where is this place?" Cole asked.

Nicole spread her hands wide. "I don't know."

"Who would?" Cole asked.

She shrugged, looking helplessly at Sam.

Sam cleared his throat. "We just need you to think. You said she's setting up a special place. Would she use a Realtor? Does she have any friends she'd confide in?"

She pressed her fingers against her forehead. "Umm . . ."

"Anyone you can think of," he encouraged her.

"No friends. She's not good at keeping them," she muttered.

"Real estate agent?" Cole asked.

She shook her head.

"Decorator?" Sam said, obviously grasping. "Someone who'd have the address for deliveries."

"Well . . . there's this antiques dealer she's used for unique items in the one apartment she had on her own and both houses Victor owned."

Cole exhaled a long breath. "Call him."

"I don't remember his name and I certainly don't have his phone number memorized. I need to think, and I can't do that with all of you pressuring me."

Cole nodded and took a step toward the door. "Fine. I'll go." This woman represented the only shot they had at finding Victoria before she went after Erin again. She wouldn't cooperate if he suffocated her. "Just answer one question for me?"

She turned in her seat. "What is it?"

"How dangerous do you think your sister is? How big a threat?"

She bit down on her lower lip. "Truth? I've never heard her so out of control before. That's why I came here. To find her

311

and try to make her see that she's behaving this way because she's off her meds. And to warn Erin."

Son of a bitch. "Thank you for being honest."

Nicole inclined her head. "She's my sister. I want her to get help."

Cole wanted her behind bars or, at the very least, padded walls, far away from Erin and his unborn child, but he couldn't tell her sister that. They needed Nicole to keep them in the loop.

She didn't trust Cole. Sam was another story.

Cole leaned his head against the wall, trying to think clearly. "Sam. A word?" Cole tipped his head to the outer room.

Sam placed a hand over Nicole's. "Sit tight. I'll be right back."

Erin and Cara remained out back at the house while Cole and Mike went to the station. Erin was not happy they all insisted she remain behind. She wanted to see this woman firsthand. Confront the threat. But she also understood the wisdom of being smart and protecting herself and the baby. Which didn't mean she had to like it.

The only good news was that the day had remained full-on gorgeous, with bright sunshine and warm temperatures, allowing Cara and her to sit on the patio and soak up the rays.

Cara's cell rang suddenly, interrupting the serene peace Erin had almost begun to find.

"Hello?" Cara answered. She waited a couple of beats, then . . . "Yes, I understand. I'll tell her. Thanks. Tell Sam to be careful."

Erin sat up straighter. "Tell Sam to be careful about what?" Her heart rate picked up speed.

Cara met her gaze. "Apparently the woman Sam arrested wasn't Victoria, but her twin sister, Nicole. It seems Victoria is bipolar and off her meds, which goes a ways toward making sense of her irrational, impulsive behavior."

"I'd feel bad if my whole life weren't turned upside down," Erin said. "Okay, I do feel bad. But she's still a threat to me."

Cara nodded. "But Nicole isn't. Mike said she was at your house trying to find her twin and to warn you."

Erin narrowed her gaze. "Why does Mike believe her?"

"I don't know yet. We'll have to see what he has to say when he gets here, but I'm guessing he's not one hundred percent convinced, because Sam's going to stick close in case her sister makes contact."

Erin frowned. "So that psycho's still out there."

"I'm sorry," Cara said.

Erin rose from her seat. "I have to do something." She paced the back patio. "We need to draw her out. She wants me — let her think she can have me."

"Over my dead body." Cole approached from the side of the house. Faded jeans molded to his well-defined body and a white T-shirt hugged his chest and muscular forearms. His expression was dark, frustration emanating from him.

"Why are you coming up that way?" Erin asked.

"I wanted to walk the property, check the perimeter. Just in case."

"Okay."

"You are not making yourself a target. If Victoria wants anyone, it's me."

Erin nodded, an idea slowly forming. "Then let's give her what she wants."

"What?" Cara touched Erin's arm. "What are you talking about?"

Erin swallowed hard, hating her idea, as much as she thought it made perfect sense. "A public breakup. A loud, ugly public breakup where you make it clear we will never be a couple."

Cole stared at her long and hard. "That

won't remove you as a threat to her. You're still the mother of my child."

Oh, Erin knew that all too well. One he wouldn't or couldn't commit to, and she wasn't so sure the distinction mattered anymore.

"I know. I'm just thinking about the psychological profile of this woman. She's clearly in a manic state. She wants a man who will take care of her, love her. A man who needs her. She's going to respond to any opening she sees. By this point I'm sure she's itching to talk to you face-to-face. So you're going to make sure she thinks you'll be happy to see her."

Cole tipped his head. "How?"

Cara watched them both carefully, as if looking for hidden meaning in Erin's words. Considering her sister-in-law knew just what had transpired between Erin and Cole, Erin didn't blame her. But this plan really was intended to play into Victoria's needs, not Erin's insecurities — although in the end, Cole's words would indeed slice open her heart.

"You'll let me know, in public, that just because I'm having your baby, I shouldn't expect us to be a family. But that you know firsthand a kid needs two loving parents, like your mother and Brody, so I'm free to find someone else. And you'll do the same."

Cole's eyes darkened. "What the hell do you expect to accomplish with that?"

Cara blinked. "As warped as it sounds, that makes sense. She'll know you're open to being with someone else. That Erin's no threat to her."

Erin nodded. "I'll move back home, and you'll leave, taking all your things with you. When you're on your own again, she'll know you meant what you said. That gives her a chance to come to you." Erin finished with what she thought was a flourish.

Inside, she was sick to her stomach. She might have known her time with Cole would come to an end, but she wasn't ready now. And she had no desire to play this scene out in public. Still, it would give Cole a chance to arrest Victoria, once and for all.

Cole's expression was as dark as she'd ever seen it. "If I go along with this, I want Cara taking over for me until Victoria's caught. You have a full-time bodyguard or this doesn't happen," Cole said.

"Done." Cara agreed immediately, not giving Erin a chance to argue. "I'll take time off. I happen to have an in with the boss." She smirked at that. "Not to mention that he'll want his sister protected too."

"But —"

Cole silenced Erin's complaints with a glare. "If you want to play things your way, you'll give me this."

She clenched her teeth, wanting to scream at his bossy tone. Still, he'd granted her a concession by giving in to her plan, and she knew it. So she remained silent.

"Good." He folded his arms across his chest, his eyes still stormy.

Cara stepped between them. "So how about this for a plan? You stay here until Wednesday night. Then, at Joe's, you play out the breakup thing." Her excitement grew as she described the plan. "I'll be there for you, Erin, when you're *upset,* and I'll take you back here. Meanwhile, Cole will head on upstairs alone. If Victoria doesn't come to Cole that night, we move you home in the morning and wait."

Cole exhaled hard. "Yeah. Fine."

"Erin?" Cara asked.

She tossed her hands in the air. "Fine. We wait till Wednesday." What was two more days when all she'd been doing lately was *waiting.*

She wanted her life back. So if she had to live through a public breakup with Cole and humiliate herself to achieve her goal, she'd do it.

FIFTEEN

Wednesday arrived too soon. Cole hated what was about to go down, even if the idea, once he let himself accept it, was brilliant. Remaining in hiding and out of sight had kept Erin safe, but it did nothing to lure Victoria out. Tonight's plan would. He didn't blame Erin for wanting to reclaim her life, but he'd never approve of her making herself a target to do it.

Making himself one was another story.

But once their *show* ended, Cole's entire life would change. He'd go back to the solitary life he hadn't wanted to leave in the first place. So how was it that now he'd rather live with a cool-to-him Erin than move back upstairs to his small apartment over Joe's? He'd gotten used to more space and pleasant company. Sleeping with Erin's warm body by his side — and damn, he missed that already.

Cole shook his head in disgust. Obviously

ending their arrangement before he lost more of his mind made sense after all.

He'd just stepped into the kitchen, where Erin was eating yogurt mixed with granola, having reverted back to her old eating habits. He was still cooking, but she was eating her own food, and nothing he did or said would change her mind.

"I'm making eggs. Do you want some?"

"No thanks. I'm almost full."

He groaned. "How long are you going to punish me for doing the right thing?"

Erin met his gaze with wide, too-innocent eyes. "I'm doing no such thing."

"You're cutting off your nose to spite your face. So to speak."

She shook her head. "Because I don't want your eggs?"

"Because you don't want anything from me, including my company." Had he really just said that?

A whisper of a smile crossed her lips. "Still sending those mixed messages." She rose and cleaned up her breakfast without saying another word.

He muttered a curse. Just then, his cell rang. A glance told him he had Mike on the line. "Hey." He turned away from Erin.

"Nicole got in touch with Sam. Said she called her mother, who did know the antiques dealer, and she gave Sam an address where she thinks her sister set up house. It's about twenty minutes from here," Mike said.

"You going to check it out?"

"Yeah. I'll wait to hear if you find Victoria."

Mike clicked off and Cole returned to where Erin stood. "Mike thinks he has a lead on where Victoria's hiding out."

"If he finds her, we won't have to go through with tonight?" she asked, stark relief in her voice.

"You don't have to go through with it no matter what. We can still opt to wait her out, hope she shows herself eventually."

And damn if a part of him wished she'd choose that option.

Erin hadn't dressed up nor gone out for fun in so long that despite the circumstances, she put thought and effort into her style. Maternity clothes or not, she wanted to look good. And she wanted to hang out with her friends before all hell broke loose, so she called Trina and Macy to make sure they'd be there for moral support. She hadn't filled them in on the details of the plan. She wanted to do it in person.

She also wanted an outlet for the stress

building inside her. Mike had called earlier, and he'd found Victoria's location, but not the woman herself. He wondered if she'd been tipped off by her sister, but unable to prove it, he said he had to live with Sam keeping an eye out.

But Mike had gone to check out Victoria's place himself, and the house had creeped her brother out. Inside, there were photos of Cole from afar, both framed and laying around, making it look like it had come from an episode of *Criminal Minds*. Or at least *America's Most Obsessed* — not that there was such a thing.

She and Cole were going to Joe's separately, in order to make a statement they'd further reinforce later. Erin knew the plan. She'd crafted it herself, but she hoped she could be as good an actress as it required.

She walked downstairs to see Cole pacing the front hall. "Cara should be here soon to pick me up."

He faced her, looking delicious in faded denim and a soft gray T-shirt that, as usual, hugged him in all the right places. Erin did her best not to drool.

"We'll get her," he promised, obviously focused on the plan and not their imminent parting.

She forced a smile. "We'd better. This hiding out is getting old."

"I can't imagine how bored you'd get on a good old-fashioned stakeout." He paused to glance out the window before facing her again.

She laughed. "I'd probably want to hang myself."

His grin lightened the more somber mood that had been hanging over them for too long. Since she'd opened her big mouth and he'd moved out of the bedroom.

The sound of a car horn broke the silence between them and Erin tore her gaze from his. "I'll see you at Joe's."

Cole raised his hand in farewell.

Erin drew a deep breath and walked out the door.

At Joe's, surrounded by friends, Erin could only focus on one thing. "Where's Cole?" she quietly asked Cara, who sat by her side.

"I don't know. He should have been here by now. Wasn't he ready to leave when I picked you up?"

Erin nodded. "He said he'd be a few minutes behind me."

"Have you called him?"

Erin tipped her head to the side and glared at her sister-in-law.

"Okay, dumb question." Cara laughed.

"Let's talk about something else while we wait for showtime. How are you handling everyone knowing your secret?" She reached out and patted Erin's stomach.

Erin took a sip of her club soda. "Considering I haven't been allowed to leave the house since the news broke, just fine."

Cara winced. "Right. So . . . how's it going being out tonight?"

"You all already know." Erin gestured around the table to Macy, Trina, and most of the same people who were at Nick's. Though Joe's was crowded, Erin had immediately taken a seat. Besides, she was so thin she could still cover . . . mostly.

But there was nothing she could do about the news being public.

"Erin! You're out and about." Evan Carmichael's familiar voice sounded from behind her. He walked around and eyed her warily.

"It's not what it looks like," she assured him. Erin knew that if she wanted to save her job, she needed to explain. "Give me a second and we'll talk, okay?"

He nodded, but his expression showed his confusion and displeasure.

She swiveled in her seat. "Cara, I need a few minutes to talk to my boss. I won't go far. Just to the nearest quiet corner."

The other woman frowned. "Erin —"

"It's about my job," she said, rising from her seat before Cara could stop her. "I have to do this," Erin insisted.

Cara let out a groan. "Fine. I'll call Cole in the meantime. And you keep me in sight. Your brother's at the bar with an eye out too. Any problems, just let us know," she said, tipping her head toward Mike, who leaned against the bar, talking with some guys from the station. But Erin didn't miss that he was alert, his gaze shifting around the room.

"I'll be right back."

She and Evan stepped to the nearest wall, but they were constantly jostled by people walking by, and it was too noisy for a private conversation.

"This is ridiculous," Evan muttered. "Come on." He steered Erin toward the bathroom hallway. She would have argued but he wasn't listening, and since she could still see her brother from her location, she tried to relax.

He faced her, his back to the main room. "What's going on? And I'm asking not as your boss, but as your friend. Because I know you well enough to realize you wouldn't bail on work but come drink at Joe's." He raised an eyebrow, the concern in his chiseled face very real.

Erin opted to explain the stalker part of her situation first and gave Evan the briefest overview of why she was in Joe's Bar tonight and what she hoped to accomplish.

He nodded slowly. "So where's your partner in crime?"

Erin swallowed hard. "I can't imagine what's keeping him."

The other man's scowl told her just what he thought of Cole. "Do you really know what you're getting yourself into with him? You must realize you can do so much better."

Erin stiffened. She disliked being told who or what was good for her, but even more, she hated anyone making assumptions and insulting Cole. He might not be the man for her, but he had reasons she had to respect — though none that warranted Evan putting him down.

"Look, I appreciate that you think you mean well, as a friend and as my boss, but I've told you before, the subject of Cole is off-limits. He's going to be in my life for the foreseeable future and that's the end of it." Her voice sounded harsh, brittle to her own ears.

Evan stepped back and studied her. "For God's sake, why can't you see he's just go-

325

ing to leave you high and dry when he's had his fill?" the man asked.

Erin blinked, unable to believe his nerve. Beyond being uncalled-for, it was just plain rude, with no real care for her feelings. So much for calling himself her friend. His jealousy was showing and it was just plain ugly.

Erin had been carefully choosing her words, but no longer. "Why?" she asked. "You want to know why he's in my life? Because he's the father of my unborn child, that's why!" she yelled at him.

His mouth opened wide but no sound came out. His gaze traveled from her face down to her stomach. Erin knew she was being bitchy and rude but she couldn't stop herself. She flattened the flowing material of her shirt over her stomach, letting him see the tiny bump.

A vein throbbed on one side of his head as he forced himself to look her in the eye once more. "I'm speechless."

"I know. It doesn't happen often. Look, Evan —"

He held up a hand. "Let it go. Obviously I'll have to."

Before he could reply, he turned around and walked away. This time, it was Erin left with her mouth open, no sound coming out.

She pulled in a couple of deep breaths, needing to calm down before going back inside to face other people. She reached a point of rationality and was about to head back, when someone bumped her from behind.

Erin spun around to see a woman with teased blonde hair, staring her down. "Do I know you?" Erin asked.

"No, but you should. I'm the one who matters. Not you."

At the hate-filled look in the woman's eyes, a chill raced through Erin and she shivered. Despite the hair, which had to be a wig, Erin suddenly knew who she was facing. "Victoria."

"So he *has* mentioned me to you!" Her eyes lit up in her face.

"Yes," Erin murmured, realizing what she should do. "He's spoken of you quite often."

"Then you realize that kid of yours won't let you hold on to him when he really wants me."

Her throat dry, Erin forced out the words. "Cole and I aren't together that way. He doesn't want me. I don't want him."

"Liar," the other woman spat.

Erin drew in a deep breath. She could wait for Cara to come looking for her, scream and send Victoria running, or — she reached for Victoria's hand. "Look —"

With a vicious tug, the woman yanked her hand from Erin's so fast, she'd had no time to get a real grip. Erin turned and screamed her brother's name but when she spun back, Victoria was running for the back exit door. By the time Mike pushed his way through the crowd, all Erin could do was point to the half-open door.

Mike sprinted after her, but Victoria had disappeared. Her brother was furious over the entire turn of events. "And where the hell is Cole?" he asked, when he, Cara, Erin, and Sam gathered together once the excitement died down.

"When Cara picked me up, he was supposed to leave to come here right after me." She turned to Cara. "Any luck reaching him?"

The other woman shook her head.

Erin reached for her purse and pulled out her cell phone. She was about to dial him again when she saw the message indicator. She listened to Cole's message in complete disbelief.

"What?" Mike asked, irritation oozing from him.

"His father's in the hospital. Jed had a heart attack." Erin grew light-headed. Her first thoughts were of Cole and how this news would affect him. "He said he knew I was safe with Cara, and he'd be in touch when he knew something."

He hadn't asked her to meet him there. Hadn't said he'd appreciate her company, or support. No, Cole being Cole, he'd chosen to face this alone.

Or so he thought. Because there wasn't a chance in hell Erin would leave him alone at a time like this.

Cole didn't know how to deal with his father on a good day, and today wasn't one of those. No sooner had Cole climbed into his car than his cell rang. A nurse from the hospital had used Jed's cell to find his IN CASE OF EMERGENCY number. Lo and behold, the old man still had Cole listed. He hadn't, however, wanted him called, something he'd made perfectly clear when Cole entered the Cardiac Intensive Care Unit. Another thing Cole didn't know how to deal with? These feelings running through him about his father's heart attack.

He'd never thought of Jed as mortal. In fact, he'd always thought the old man would be around to insult and torture Cole forever. But even he knew the Cardiac Intensive Care Unit — or CICU, as the nurses referred to it — meant things with his father were serious. His throat swelled at the notion.

Good thing he had his father to keep his emotions in check. When Cole walked in, Jed had gotten so worked up, the doctors asked Cole to step out because stress wasn't good for him. Cole moved to the waiting room — a place he'd been before, when Erin had been admitted for the gunshot wound — and stared at the ceiling.

From the minute he'd received word, he'd been torn between wanting to be with Erin and needing to make certain his father would be okay. Erin, he knew, would be fine with her brother and Cara's protection. Jed . . . he was still waiting for word. A little over an hour had passed since he'd arrived and nobody had been out to see him.

He rose, deciding he'd check in at the nurse's station — spare Jed his presence but find out when someone would explain his father's medical condition.

"Cole?"

He turned at the sound of Erin's voice, surprised to see her. To his relief, Cara followed behind her, which meant Erin hadn't run off on her own after receiving his message.

"I didn't mean for you to leave Joe's to come here."

Her soft lips pursed together. "You thought you'd handle your father's heart attack alone?"

He nodded. Of course he had.

"And you assumed I'd let you."

He couldn't help but grin. "Guess I should have known better." He glanced over her shoulder. "Hi, Cara."

"How's Jed?" Erin asked.

"Still don't know anything," Cole said, surprised to hear his voice catch as he spoke. Apparently he was more upset than he wanted to admit to himself. He cleared his throat. "I was just about to go in and push for answers."

Erin faced Cara. "Go on back to Mike. Plan's scrapped for today, and I'll be here as long as Cole is. We'll just go back to the house together."

"No," Cole said. "You go back with Cara and Mike. I don't know how long I'll be here."

"All the more reason for me to stay." Erin waved Cara away.

He should have known she'd pull the stubborn routine. Despite trying to push her away, he was grateful she wasn't listening. He didn't want to deal with doctors by himself, let alone Jed. Hell, he didn't want to deal with the realities inherent with his father being so ill.

Cara glanced back and forth between them. "Well, given the choice between hanging out with you two and all these outdated magazines" — she pointed to the dog-eared glossies on the table — "or going home to my husband . . . easy choice. And you'll be safer with Cole," she muttered.

"What's that mean?" Cole asked.

Cara pulled him into an unexpected hug. "Take care. And I hope your dad's okay," she said, backing away just as quickly.

Cole was glad. Hugs and emotion from Cara were as unfamiliar as the panic coursing through him.

"Okay, you two, I'm gone," Cara said.

He nodded. "Drive safely."

"Will do. And one of you call me when you have news."

"Sure thing," Erin promised. She glanced at Cole. "Well? Let's go find the doctor."

He shook his head. "Hold up." There was something they needed to discuss first.

"What is it?" She looked up at him with guileless hazel eyes that, on top of Cara's cryptic comment, Cole suddenly didn't trust worth a damn. "You tell me."

Erin blinked. "I don't know what you mean."

"Start with what Cara meant by you'll be

safer with me? Did something happen at Joe's?"

"Shouldn't we be checking on Jed?" Erin started for the swinging double doors, but Cole pulled her back.

He caught her around the waist, stilling any jittery movement. "Out with it. What happened?"

"Well, I might have had a run-in with Victoria." She winced as she said the words.

All the blood running in Cole's veins froze. "What?!"

She forced herself to meet his gaze. "Okay, it's like this. I ran into Evan when I was with Cara, and seeing how I haven't been working but he saw me in a bar, I needed to explain. It was crowded and loud, so we stepped into the bathroom hall. Cara and Mike were within shouting distance. It was fine."

Cole cocked an eyebrow. "Somehow, I don't think it was fine," he said through clenched teeth.

"I'm here, aren't I?"

"But she got close to you," he bit out.

Erin ran her hand down his arm in an obvious effort to soothe him, but instead of calm, all he felt was frustration that he hadn't been there to protect her.

"Finish the story."

She sighed. "Evan and I argued —"

"About what? The bastard was annoyed you were out?"

She shook her head. "Not exactly."

He waited in silence.

"Fine. He insulted you — again — so I told him you'd be in my life for the foreseeable future, seeing as how you were the father of my baby. And then I punctuated the point. Like this." She pulled her loose top tight against her tiny baby bump. "See?" She shrugged.

Cole stared at the little spitfire, trying not to laugh at Carmichael's expense. Trying harder not to pull her into a hard kiss for defending him . . . yet again. He didn't bother fighting the overwhelming admiration he felt for this woman, or the gratitude at how easily she stood up for him. Whether he deserved it or not.

"Stop laughing."

He let his grin show. "I'm trying."

She rolled her eyes.

"What'd Carmichael do?" Cole asked.

"He stormed off," she said, wincing at the memory. "And that's when someone bumped me from behind."

Cole sobered. Only Erin could have him so distracted on so many different levels that he'd forget the reason they'd started this conversation to begin with. "What happened?"

"Once she realized I knew her name, she got all excited that you'd obviously mentioned her to me. I tried to convince her we weren't involved in any way, not anymore. She called me a liar. I didn't want her to leave, so I tried to grab her hand, and when she pulled away, I screamed for Mike and Cara. They came immediately, but she'd run out the emergency door, and Mike couldn't find her." Erin spread her hands in front of her. "End of story."

Not by a long shot, Cole thought, his pulse pounding so hard he felt the beat in his left temple. Her brother and sister-in-law should have been a hell of a lot closer to Erin than they'd been, but there was nothing he could do about it now. Obviously that was what Cara meant when she'd said Erin was safer with him.

"It happened fast," Erin said, as if reading his mind. "In seconds, really. I never left anyone's line of sight. I never figured I'd be alone —"

"Because Carmichael was supposed to be right beside you." Cole's anger at the other man only grew. Her boss wasn't her bodyguard, but the other man knew the seriousness of the situation, had been told Erin was in danger, and yet he'd let his ego over Erin's pregnancy get in the way of his common sense.

Erin touched his cheek, capturing his attention. "It's all okay. I'm fine. She's gone, but I'm here with you now, and we can focus on Jed. That's what matters."

He drew in a calming breath. "You have a way of making me insane," he muttered.

She patted him on the shoulder. "Anything to keep you distracted from your problems."

He shook his head. "She shouldn't have gotten close to you. She's crazy. What if she'd had a knife on her?" He didn't know what he'd do if he lost her that way. His hands clenched into fists.

"Mr. Sanders?" A man in a white coat walked through the double doors.

"Yes?" Cole strode over to meet the man, nerves suddenly jangling.

No matter how much conflict existed between him and Jed, the man was his father. The only blood one he had, and dammit, the little boy in Cole still wanted the chance to make peace. Getting the other man's approval might be asking for too much but he'd settle for a cease-fire, a cessation of hostilities and maybe even a permanent truce for the future. Especially since Jed was going to be his kid's grandfather. There was no way Cole wanted his child to experience the kind of constant anticipation of disapproval or rejection from Jed that he had.

As long as Jed had a future, Cole thought, and, heart in his throat, he faced the doctor to hear his father's prognosis. A few minutes later, only one word stuck out in Cole's mind.

"Surgery." Cole said the word out loud, but hearing it didn't make it any more real.

Quadruple bypass surgery, without which, according to the doctor, Jed would have another imminent heart attack, this one probably fatal. The doctor, an older gentleman with sparse gray hair, continued to explain the procedure to Cole and Erin.

Cole vaguely heard him toss a lot of other medical terms around, but he didn't hear everything. He couldn't process all the details of how they'd crack open his father's chest, use a heart and lung machine to keep him breathing during the procedure, without wanting to jump out of his skin. He thought instead about their strained, difficult relationship, and wished things could be different before his father went under the knife.

Erin slipped her hand into Cole's, and her warmth registered against his palm. She not only calmed him but she focused him too.

He was able to concentrate more on what the doctor was saying, including Jed being a higher risk patient. "Your father has high blood pressure and high cholesterol, and has been suffering from anginal pain without reporting it to his doctors until the pain was so severe, he almost couldn't call 911."

Cole sucked in a startled breath. Damn the stubborn man.

The other man continued to run down the risks of the surgery for any patient, causing Cole to shut down again because he couldn't let himself hear all the negative possibilities. Not if he was going to make it through the next however many hours.

"So, all that said, your father's prognosis is decent, once he wakes from surgery," the doctor said, his words, as well as Erin's hand squeeze, bringing him back once more.

"When?" Cole managed to ask.

"First thing tomorrow morning. The surgery lasts four to six hours, could be longer. In other words, tomorrow will be a long day. I suggest you go home tonight and get a good night's sleep."

"I'd like to see him," Cole said. He couldn't imagine living with himself if anything happened on the table and the last words between them were Jed telling him he didn't need him here.

The other man frowned. "The nurses told me your last visit agitated him. He's in a fragile physical state. If he works himself up again, we won't need the OR," the other man said with brutal honesty that Cole respected.

"Fine."

"Wait." Erin spoke up.

"It's okay," he assured her. Whatever was best for Jed, that was what mattered now. Not Cole's feelings.

She shook her head. "Jed and Cole have a difficult relationship, but now Jed knows his condition, right? He knows he's having surgery tomorrow?"

The doctor nodded.

"So ask him if he's up to seeing his son. Better yet, let *me* ask him."

"Erin —" Cole said in a warning tone.

"Shh. I've known him for years. He likes me, or usually does." Neither Cole nor Erin mentioned she'd thrown him out of her house a few weeks ago. Even Jed wouldn't hold that against Erin. But that didn't mean Cole wanted Erin to try to sway Jed on his behalf. He hated the embarrassment caused not just by their dysfunctional relationship but by Jed's assessment of his son's failings.

"Maybe knowing what he's in for, Jed will *want* to talk to you." Erin spoke in her softest, most understanding voice. Then she looked up first at Cole, then the doctor, with a sweet, imploring expression that probably had juries bending over backward to see things her way. Lord knew he couldn't deny her anything. He was pretty sure she'd get Jed to see things her way.

"Please let me go in?"

Dr. Wilson, he'd said his name was, clutched his clipboard and smiled. "You're persistent, Ms. . . ."

"Marsden. Erin Marsden."

The other man's eyes opened wide. "I know your father. His oncologist referred him to me when he was trying to decide on treatments for his cancer last year."

Erin wrinkled her brow. "Really?"

This time Cole squeezed her hand, offering her comfort.

"Some of the chemotherapy drugs can be hard on the heart. We often confer, go over a patient's history and situation before they decide on a course of treatment."

Erin nodded in understanding. "My parents dealt with everything about the treatment and the cancer themselves. They kept us kids in the dark about specifics, but I do know dad's in remission thanks to the care he received, so thank you." She beamed at the other man, obviously recovering from her surprise. "And I'm sure Cole's father will be getting the same type of excellent care."

"We'll do our very best. Now, I'll take you in to Jed so you can work the same magic on him you just did on me. If he agrees to a peaceful, quiet visit with his son, it's fine with me."

Cole, well aware they were talking about him as if he weren't there, knew he owed a debt of gratitude to the amazing woman by his side. No matter what his stubborn father ultimately decided.

SIXTEEN

Erin stopped in the doorway to Jed's room, surprised by how frail the older man suddenly looked. The doctor had paved the way for Erin's visit, so Jed was expecting her. She knocked, and he turned his gaze from the window overlooking the parking lot.

"Hey, there," Jed said. "Doctor said you wanted to see me."

She nodded and walked up to him, pulling a chair beside the bed. "You're still speaking to me after the way I threw you out of my house?" she asked with a quick smile.

"I can't hold a grudge against you, but you knew that or you wouldn't have asked to come in. I take it you're here with that son of mine?"

Erin swallowed hard and nodded. "He's worried about you. He came as soon as the hospital called him. He dropped everything to be here."

"He needn't have bothered. I'm going to be fine."

His voice trembled, and Erin knew his words were more bravado than real belief. "I'm sure you are. But on the off chance we're wrong, do you really want to leave Cole with things left unsaid? Or worse, with his last memory of you telling him you didn't want him here?"

Jed turned his head toward the window.

"I don't know why you feel the way you do about him, and I don't want to know," Erin continued. "That's between the two of you. But I'm having your grandchild, and if you want a relationship with him . . . or her . . . you're going to have to forge one with your son first. Think about that for a minute."

Only when she felt enough time had passed for Jed to use that brain of his, did she speak again. "Cole wants to see you before surgery. Based on your reaction last time, the doctor refused because your body can't handle stress. Think you can manage to have a civil conversation with Cole?" Erin asked him.

Being a stubborn mule, Jed remained silent. As a prosecutor, Erin was used to waiting out a pigheaded witness, so she remained quietly seated, determined to get

343

the outcome she wanted.

She wasn't sure how much time had passed when Jed finally turned to face her. "You're gonna wait me out, aren't you?" he asked.

Erin only grinned. She was damned sure planning to try, but sensing that Jed was beginning to consider her request, she pushed a little more. "It would mean a lot to me if you talked to him."

The older man eyed her, staring at her longer than she felt comfortable enduring.

"Son of a bitch. You're in love with him," Jed said at last.

Erin felt a hot blush cover her cheeks. "He's a good man. Why can't you see him for who he really is?" Since she had no intention of baring her soul, her reply was the best she could come up with.

And it turned the tables back on Jed, whose jaw worked back and forth as he clearly struggled for a reply. "I'll see him," he muttered, if somewhat reluctantly.

It wasn't an answer to the question Erin had asked, but it was the one she'd come here seeking to begin with. If Jed's condition weren't so serious, she'd have done a small dance of joy.

"Thank you," she said. Leaning over, she kissed his weathered cheek. "Good luck with the surgery, and I'll see you on the other side. You're going to be fine."

"I have to be if I want to see that baby you're carrying," he said gruffly, his voice raw. And even a little scared.

At the unexpected realization, Erin's throat grew tight.

She managed a nod at Jed. "I'll send Cole in."

As she headed back to the waiting room, Erin hoped her brief glimpse into Jed's soul, or at least into the frightened heart of the man in the hospital bed, would lead to some kind of détente between Jed and Cole. And as she told Cole his father would talk to him, she prayed that this wasn't the last chance either man would have to make things right between them.

Cole had approached mob bosses, murderers, and drug dealers with more ease than that with which he faced his father again. The weight of a lifetime — his lifetime — sat on Cole's shoulders. He knew the old man was disappointed in him, and that truth had permeated every part of Cole's life from the time he'd been old enough to understand what his father's constant anger meant. As an adult, he'd reached the point where he was more comfortable pretending to be someone else than he was being himself.

For a long time he'd blamed Jed for that, but his time back here in Serendipity made him look at things differently. He couldn't blame his father for who and what he was. But those deep thoughts, though raised because of his father's serious condition, didn't need to be dissected now.

He walked into the room, doing his best to ignore the beeping heart monitor, the IV drip in his dad's arm, and the way his larger-than-life father seemed to be shriveled up in the hospital bed.

"Hi," Cole said stiffly, coming up beside the bed rail.

"Hi, yourself," Jed muttered, unable, it seemed, to meet Cole's gaze.

"The doctor says they're taking you to the OR first thing in the morning."

Jed nodded. "At least it'll be before I have time to realize I'm hungry, since they're not feeding me beforehand."

Cole managed a laugh. "Says it could be a long surgery, but he does it all the time."

"I won't know it."

Same old gruff Jed, Cole thought. "I'll be here before they take you down even if you don't see me."

Jed hesitated before answering. He curled

his hands around the bars on the side of the bed, his knuckles white. "I appreciate that," he said at last.

Cole raised an eyebrow. He'd been expecting Jed to tell him not to bother. He wondered if Erin had read him the riot act on his behavior or whether genuine fear was behind those words. Like most things with his father, Cole suspected he'd never know.

"Erin's calling her folks. I'm sure they'll want to come by tonight and see you before surgery."

"I'm not going anywhere."

"They're good people. You're lucky to have them," he said, meaning it.

"I don't deserve them, you mean?"

Cole raised his hands up in front of him. "Whoa. I didn't say or imply that. And your doctor said we're not to go down that road," he reminded his father.

Jed groaned, laying his head back against the pillow. "Sorry. Old habits."

Sorry?! What alien had invaded his father's brain?

"They raised a good daughter," Jed continued before Cole could reply.

"Can't argue with that," Cole said, not surprised Erin was the one thing they agreed on.

"Son," Jed said, suddenly, meeting Cole's

gaze with a hard stare of his own.

Cole drew a deep breath. "What's up?" With serious heart surgery looming, Jed could say anything at this point and Cole wouldn't be surprised.

"Don't let the one good thing in your life slip through your fingers the way I did," Jed said.

Except that, Cole thought. The old man *had* taken him off guard. "Dad —"

"No. I don't want to have any serious discussions. We're just going to argue. That's been our way too long for it to change in the blink of an eye."

Which made Cole wonder if Jed meant he *wanted* it to change . . . eventually.

Jed reached for the paper cup filled with water and took a long sip. "But remember what I said. Just in case."

Cole exhaled a hard breath. No need to ask *just in case* what. "You're going to be fine," he told his father. He opted to focus on his father and not his obvious allusion to Jed's mother . . . or to Erin.

Jed didn't reply. He yawned, though, and Cole took that as his cue. "Get some sleep. I'll be here when you come out of surgery, and I'll see you as soon as they let me."

His father nodded, and an awkward silence ensued, no doubt thanks to the strain of their having been forced to get along for the last couple of minutes. But Cole had to admit, despite the discomfort between them, it'd been nice talking to Jed knowing no yelling was forthcoming.

He left the room, and for the first time that he could recall, he prayed — both for Jed to come through surgery and for the chance to rebuild some kind of connection with his father.

For years, Cole had rejected the idea that he needed anything from Jed Sanders. But faced with the prospect of losing his father, Cole was forced to admit he wanted a relationship with Jed. And he sensed, in a surreal way he didn't understand, that the key to who he could become lay with the man who'd shaped the person he'd been.

Cole and Erin drove back to Nick's house in comfortable silence. He didn't feel the need to discuss what went on in his father's hospital room, and Erin didn't ask. She knew from his somewhat calm demeanor that at least there had been no yelling or confrontation, and for that she was grateful.

She couldn't remember ever being more exhausted. At the top of the stairs, she turned toward the master bedroom, expecting Cole to head the other way to the room he'd been staying in for the last couple of days.

"Erin?"

She turned. "What's up?"

"I . . . Never mind."

Oh, there was something, she thought, studying him. Weariness was evident in his handsome face and she realized the strain of all they'd gone through, plus Jed, was wearing on them both.

"Talk to me." She walked up to where he stood, leaning on the railing.

He shook his head. "There was nothing specific. I just . . ."

Erin took a leap. "You don't want to be alone," she said, hoping she wasn't so far off base she'd be mortified when he said she was wrong.

He exhaled and nodded. Relief shot through her and she held out her hand. She didn't want to be alone either. As tired as she was, there was nothing sexual in her offer, and she didn't get the feeling he was looking to cross that line again either. But they shared the same concerns over her safety and over Victoria's craziness and potential next move, and now they both were worried about Jed. It made sense that they keep each other company while waiting for the morning . . . and for the surgery to come.

Cole didn't remember the last time he'd been hesitant in asking — or taking what he wanted. But he'd done too much to Erin in a short time to risk hurting her again, so no sooner had he called out her name, he'd rejected the idea of asking her to stay with him. He was relieved she'd either read him so well or merely wanted the same thing. He was too raw, too emotionally drained, to be alone.

By silent agreement, they went to her room, Erin disappearing into the bathroom to wash up. Cole stripped off his jeans and T-shirt and settled under the comforter. As soon as he lay back in Erin's bed, a sense of rightness and peace settled over him, one he didn't have the strength to think about or fight.

A few minutes later, she walked out of the bathroom wearing a black lace nightie that hit midthigh. It wasn't one he'd seen before — it was definitely meant for her new, growing figure. It covered enough to be considered decent, but her breasts were larger now, her cleavage enticing no matter what she wore. And no matter how tired he was, he couldn't deny the hardening of his groin, or the disappointment that rushed through him as he reminded himself tonight wasn't about *that.*

She paused by the bed and met his gaze.

"Get in. I won't bite."

She laughed and slipped in. She lay on her side, facing him, and he tried to ignore how much of her breasts were exposed in that moment.

"You okay?" she asked.

He shrugged. "I'm numb. So much has happened since this morning, I don't know what to feel. And we haven't dealt with the Victoria situation and we can't just forget she's out there. Waiting. Plotting."

Erin shivered and swallowed hard. "I know. But we can have Sam come to the hospital tomorrow and figure out another plan. If nothing else it'll be a good way to pass those hours of Jed's surgery."

He propped his head up with one hand. "Good idea."

She treated him to the sweet yet somehow intoxicating smile that was uniquely Erin.

She yawned then, and he was reaching over to shut the light when she squealed.

He jerked back around. Her hazel eyes were wide and glittered with an emotion he couldn't name. "Erin?"

"I think the baby kicked," she said in utter and complete awe.

He blinked. That was the last thing he'd expected her to say.

"Oh! I felt it again. It feels like little flutters from the inside."

Her face glowed with excitement, and he couldn't help but be drawn into the moment along with her. A slow burn of excitement unfurled inside him, as unexpected as it was sweet.

"Want to feel?"

The hesitancy in her voice touched him, and he nodded.

She took his hand and placed it over her stomach. Her skin was soft and smooth to the touch. Her gaze never left his as they waited in anxious silence for movement that never came. Just as he was about to remove his hand, Erin sucked in an excited breath.

"There! Feel it?" she asked.

He shook his head, the disappointment stronger than he would have expected.

She let out a sigh and frowned, an adorable pout, that had him aching to kiss her on those luscious lips. "I was worried about that. The books say sometimes the first kicks are only felt by the mom. It can take a few more weeks until you can feel it from the outside."

At which point, he might be long gone. The thought lingered unspoken between them, but Cole didn't want to ruin the closeness they were sharing. Nor could he tell her what was really going through his mind because he could hardly grasp the enormity of the thought himself. But if he had to be truthful, Cole couldn't begin to wrap his mind around picking up and leaving Erin or his child behind. Scarier still? Even if she weren't pregnant, even if he'd spent these weeks protecting just her, Cole knew he would still feel the same way.

This woman, so capable and independent on the outside, so soft and genuine and giving on the inside, had carved out a place for herself in Cole's heart. And that was something he'd never believed possible. Given how he lived — not just his job, which kept him isolated from the real world, but his preference to remain that way even when off duty — the concept of love and sharing a life had never crossed his mind.

For Cole, sex had fulfilled a basic need. Until he caught sight of Erin in a light purple bridesmaid's dress in Joe's Bar. She'd forever altered the course of his life. He just didn't know what to do about his feelings for her and the only life he'd ever known.

She watched him, her eyes warm and focused on his face as they lay in comfortable silence. His hand remained on her belly and she didn't seem inclined to ask him to move it, instead pressing it against the small baby bump, practically willing him to feel the kicks.

"I guess you can turn off the light," she finally said in a low voice, sounding as disappointed as he was that he hadn't been able to feel their child.

He reached over, turned off the lamp, plunging the room into darkness.

"Are you okay?" she asked him.

He knew she meant about Jed, not the baby. "Normally I'm pretty accepting about whatever life throws at me, but Jed's heart attack caught me off guard." And knocked down every wall he'd erected to protect himself from his father.

"Hopefully he'll come through fine," Erin said. "Then maybe you two will have a chance to repair the relationship."

Cole groaned. "Don't hold your breath for that to happen." He wasn't. And he didn't want her to be hurt when her hope for reconciliation didn't work out.

She shifted, obviously trying to get comfortable. "Babies can work miracles," she said into the darkness. "Or so people say."

He didn't know about babies, but he was starting to believe in Erin. As the minutes

355

ticked by, he listened to her breathing even out. Knowing she was finally falling asleep, Cole ached to pull her into his arms and feel her soft, sleepy body curl into his. He missed her warmth, her smile, her happiness aimed at him.

It took everything in him to stay on his side of the bed, but he did. Because he'd promised himself he wouldn't send her mixed messages, and taking advantage of her being there when he needed her would be all kinds of wrong.

Although wanting to hold her didn't feel wrong, but instead felt all kinds of right.

Seventeen

Erin woke in Cole's arms, warm, comfortable, and safe, feeling as if she was exactly where she belonged, with the father of her baby and the man she loved. And that was the thought that had her slipping out of bed to shower before he awakened.

Last night had been a precious gift, one she hadn't expected, but would always appreciate. They hadn't had sex, yet they couldn't have been more intimate if he'd been inside her body. He'd touched her belly, tried to feel their baby kick, had been as invested in the moment as she'd been.

He hadn't made a move on her, but she had to admit that if he had, she wouldn't have resisted or turned him away. She'd have grabbed that one final moment with him, and probably regretted it later. Which was why she hadn't been the aggressor. Last night was about Cole, his pain and what he needed from her.

He'd given so much to her these past weeks, putting his life on hold to watch out for her, take care of her, and she was grateful for the chance to give back. She didn't blame him for not being able to offer more — he'd made no promises. She'd done what she needed to do, tried to see if *they* could be more, and had come to accept his limitations.

He might not realize what a special man he was, but Erin did. They'd bonded and that would help them do what was best for their child's future. But now, Erin had to rebuild her walls and prepare for the time when Cole walked away.

A couple hours later, Erin sat in the hospital waiting room, staring at the clock on the wall, unable to believe the time could pass so slowly. Even knowing ahead of time how long the wait would be, the seconds, minutes, and hours crawled by. An optimist by nature, Erin believed in her heart that Jed would be fine, and she'd keep believing unless and until the alternative broadsided her. In the meantime, she needed to keep Cole's mind occupied and off what was going on in that operating room.

Just when he appeared ready to climb the walls, her brother Sam strode into the room with a Victoria look-alike by his side. Having seen her stalker up close, Erin could definitely see the difference in the twins. There was something off in Victoria's eyes, while Nicole's were here and present.

"Thank you so much for coming," Erin said, rising from her chair.

"Any word?" Sam asked.

Cole's jaw was set tight.

"Not yet," Erin said. "But it's way too early to expect news. The doctor said it's a long surgery."

Sam nodded in understanding. "Erin, this is Nicole Farnsworth."

Erin approached warily. Cole stopped her by snagging her waist. Okay, so he wasn't any more sure of this woman either. "Nice to meet you," Erin said.

Nicole's smile was awkward, and Erin realized the other woman wasn't any more comfortable than she was. "I wish I could say the same, but if my sister weren't making your life miserable, neither of us would be here."

Erin admired her candor, and her smile for the other woman grew wider.

"I'm sorry about your father," Nicole said to Cole. "Officer Marsden told me why we have to meet here."

"Sam. You can call me Sam," Erin's brother said, sounding as if he was repeating a refrain.

"Thanks," Cole said to Nicole. "Any word? From your sister?"

She shook her head. "I'm sure the fact that I led you to Victoria's hideaway didn't sit well with her."

"She can't know you were the one who told us. It's not like she told you the location in the first place," Sam reassured her.

"I know." Nicole glanced away. "Look, I wanted to tell you all I'm sorry. I feel awful about everything my sister's done to you." She raised her hands toward them, then lowered them again.

"You aren't responsible for someone else's actions, Nicole." Erin echoed a sentiment she'd said to Cole many times before, and in case he'd forgotten, she stepped closer and slid her hand into his, squeezing him tight as a reminder.

She glanced up at his handsome face, but his expression remained neutral, his mind, she was sure, in the OR upstairs. And she didn't blame him.

"Thank you for that," Nicole said to Erin. She hesitated, rubbing her hands against her khaki pants. "The other thing I wanted to tell you is that I have to get back home soon. I took time off from my job to look for my sister. But I'm not getting anywhere and I haven't heard from her, and . . ." She trailed off.

"Erin has a job, responsibilities . . . and she hasn't been able to do any of them because your sister could jump out of a corner with a knife at any minute," Cole said, making Erin realize that his silence hadn't meant he wasn't focused on what was going on here. She should have known better.

Nicole winced and Sam stepped up beside her.

"Erin's right. None of that is Nicole's fault," he said, scowling at Cole.

Erin decided it was time to empty out the room. Cole needed time to focus on his father and himself. "Nicole, thank you for coming. I guess I'd hoped you would have some fresh ideas for us on how to lure out your sister, but . . ."

"I don't. I really wish I did. Helping you find her hideaway was about the best I could do." Regret shone in her eyes.

Erin touched the other woman's shoulder. "I believe you." She'd dealt with enough people through the years, questioned the guilty and the innocent, and her gut told her Nicole Farnsworth was nothing more — or less — than she seemed: a woman worried about her mentally ill sister.

Sam nodded to Cole and met Erin's gaze. "Let me know as soon as you have news about Jed."

She smiled, knowing her brother truly cared about Jed. And in her heart, she wanted to believe her brother had come to like Cole as a person, despite the fact that he wasn't thrilled about the one night that had changed the course of Erin's life.

Even if she was.

Erin blinked, startled at the realization that if she could go back, she wouldn't change that night or its outcome. Her hand came to rest on her stomach, on top of the life growing inside her.

Her baby. Cole's baby.

How could she ever regret that?

Cole wasn't sure how many hours had passed when he jolted awake. Could there be any place more uncomfortable than a hospital waiting room? His neck hurt from leaning the back of his head against the wall, and he realized Erin had stretched out, her legs along the row of chairs, her head in his lap. She hadn't left him through this whole nightmare, and not because she needed his protection. She could have gone to stay with either one of her brothers for that.

He smoothed her hair with his hand and

she shifted, moving her head around, making certain parts of his body even more aware of her.

"Hey," she murmured, yawning as she looked up at him.

"Hey, yourself." He smiled at her.

"Any news?" She pushed herself into a sitting position and he missed her warmth pressing intimately against him.

He shook his head. "No."

She sighed and shut her eyes. He stared down at her beautiful face, making him realize she might appear fragile, but she possessed an inner core of strength he admired.

Before he could speak, the swinging doors opened and the doctor strode through. "Mr. Sanders?"

Cole rose, and Erin stood too. "How's my father?" he asked.

"He came through the surgery and is in recovery."

Cole's entire body nearly collapsed in relief. He hadn't realized how much tension he'd been holding inside until the doctor had spoken. Erin eased beside him and shoved her smaller body beneath his arm, bolstering him physically as well as emotionally. Sensing his need, as usual.

He swallowed over the unexpected lump in his throat, a dual assault from the news of his father as well as Erin's unconditional support.

"Thank you," Cole said to the doctor.

The other man merely nodded. "He'll be out of it for a while. You should go home and get some rest. Come back in a couple of hours, and you can see him for fifteen minutes the first time."

Cole nodded.

"Make sure the nurses' station has your cell number and go on. Leave here for a bit," the doctor said, then strode off.

Erin turned to him, a huge smile on her face. "That's great news!" She threw herself into his arms, treating him to a full-body hug. Her cheek touched his, her breasts pressed into his chest, and her lower body settled into the cradle of his hips.

But the overwhelming sense he got from her was emotion and elation.

"I knew you'd get your second chance with him," she said.

Her words proved right. She was truly relieved Jed had survived the surgery, not just for Jed, but for him.

"It's over," she said softly, pushing herself off him. Without meeting his gaze, she brushed the wrinkles out of her clothes.

He felt a loss that was somehow more than

physical and he watched her carefully. "Erin?"

"Hmm?"

"Something wrong?" he asked, going with his gut that this Erin was different from the one who'd held him close before and during his father's surgery.

She shook her head. "Not a thing," she said too brightly. "Let's do what he said and go home for a little while. We can eat something, rest in a bed, and come back in a few hours."

"Sure. There's nothing more we can do here."

"Good." She picked up her purse and started for the door.

He called her name once more and she turned, her eyebrows raised.

He swallowed hard. "Thank you. For being here during all this." He didn't think he could have gotten through it without her.

She inclined her head. "You're welcome." Her tense smile did nothing to reassure him. "That's what friends do for each other, right?"

Friends. The word left a foul taste in his mouth, as once again, his gut proved on target. With his father out of imminent danger, Erin was pulling away.

■ ■ ■ ■

The sun still shone bright when Erin walked out of the hospital, Cole not far behind. She walked quickly, trying to outrun the emotional closeness of the last twenty-four hours. She felt too much and wanted way more than she'd ever get from Cole, and now that his father was out of surgery, it was time for a little self-protection to return.

She sprinted through the parking lot on another unseasonably cool day, trying to remember where they'd left the car so many hours before.

"Erin! Slow down," Cole called out to her.

Knowing she couldn't distance herself from the hurt or disappointment no matter how hard she tried, she slowed her steps and turned back to him just as the sound of a gunning car engine ripped through late-afternoon silence.

From the corner of her eye, she saw a dark sedan barreling toward her. Everything next happened in slow motion.

Cole shouted her name and sprinted forward. Acting on instinct, Erin dove between the nearest cars, hitting the pavement. Ignoring the jolt of pain shooting through her on impact, she immediately pulled her knees to her chest and curled into a tight ball, her only thought to protect the life inside her. Erin heard the deafening crunch of metal as the oncoming vehicle crashed into the cars surrounding her and felt the vibration of impact on the car next to her, while shards of glass sprayed around her.

She wasn't sure how much time passed before she allowed herself to become aware of her surroundings again. Cole was shouting her name and she pushed herself to her knees, gathering her breath. "I'm okay!" she called out to him.

She braced a hand on the car next to her, using it to push herself to her feet. She could walk through the other aisle and find Cole, she thought, ignoring the pain in her side.

She took one step forward when she was stopped by the sound of a woman's shriek.

"Liar!" Victoria stumbled into Erin's only way out.

"You said you and Cole weren't together, that you didn't want him!" the clearly unhinged woman screamed at her.

"We're not! I don't!" Erin swallowed over her fear, forcing the words out of her bone-dry mouth.

Suddenly Cole stepped behind Victoria.

Relieved, Erin let out a *whoosh* of air, though she didn't acknowledge him, knowing he needed the element of surprise.

"Liar! You're with him. You're always with him!" She ran a shaking hand through her disheveled hair. "You need to go away and leave us alone."

"She will," Cole said in a perfectly calm voice.

Startled, the other woman jerked around to face him. "Cole?" Her voice softened.

He nodded. "Let's talk," he said, gesturing for her to step closer.

"You slept with her. You got her pregnant," Victoria said, her voice full of betrayal and hurt.

Erin leaned harder against the car door, the knifelike pain in her side suddenly robbing her of breath.

Cole caught her gaze, his eyes widening at the realization something was wrong. Erin shook her head. He needed to focus on Victoria.

"It was a one-night stand. It meant nothing," he assured the other woman.

At this moment, Erin knew he'd say or do anything to calm Victoria and subdue her. She'd been prepared to hear the worst on that night at Joe's, but that hadn't happened. Now she was unraveling from the stress of the last twenty-four hours, oh hell, from everything. The last thing she needed was to listen to Cole dismiss her and everything they'd shared.

"But you moved in with her," Victoria said, her voice shaking.

"Because you left me no choice. You had her shot, right?"

"I told him to scare her, not to shoot her!"

Erin closed her eyes at the admission.

"But the more you did to Erin, the more I had no choice but to protect her, because that's my baby she's carrying. It was about the baby, not *her*." Cole's warm, imploring gaze settled on the crazy woman. He held out a hand to her. "Come here. Let me hold you and calm you down, okay?"

"You really don't want her?" Victoria shot a triumphant look over her shoulder at Erin before refocusing on the man who was her obsession.

"Not at all." He beckoned to her with a gesture and a look, and Erin's stomach curled with unwarranted and unreasonable jealousy.

"Come."

Victoria finally broke and flew into his arms. He whispered in her ear, while slipping his arms down until he finally grabbed her wrists, pinning her against the nearest automobile.

"What?!" Victoria realized she'd been had and began to struggle, hissing and cursing, but Cole held on.

Erin sought her bag, wanting her cell phone. Just as she caught sight of where it had flown in the commotion, the sound of police sirens echoed around them.

"Thank God." Knowing it was finally over, Erin's knees buckled and she let herself sink to the ground.

Too many things happened at once, preventing Cole from getting to Erin. Hospital personnel came running, and Erin was immediately taken into the emergency room.

Cara arrived and subdued Victoria, who continued to shriek, even as Cara read the hysterical woman her rights. Nicole's arrival didn't help matters, since Victoria blamed her sister for coming to Serendipity and ruining her chances with Cole. Not rational, but then, this was Victoria. Finally, the hospital staff had to step in and sedate her, which meant booking would have to wait, but at least she was cuffed to her bed and had an officer assigned to watch over her.

Victoria was no longer a threat to Erin. But were Erin and the baby still in danger?

Cole started to head back to the hospital,

only to have Cara stop him. "I need your statement," she called out.

"I need to check on Erin."

"Sam and Mike are with her by now." Cara gentled her voice. "But if you want me to be able to hold Victoria and make the charges stick, you need to talk to me now."

Cole stared at the woman in uniform, understanding she was doing her job, but not liking her timing. "Fine."

"Tell me what happened here today. You're the only witness."

He hated reliving the moment he'd seen the sedan aiming for Erin, but he managed to give Cara a play-by-play, including placing Victoria behind the wheel. "She aimed directly for Erin and deliberately hit the parked cars in an attempt to hurt her in some way. She followed her path directly."

Cara finished taking notes and looked at him. "You'll have to come by the station and sign the statement, but that's it for now. Thanks."

He nodded.

"How's your father?" she asked.

"In recovery," he bit out. Though he knew she meant well, Cole's mind was in one place only.

She nodded. "Go," she said, tipping her head toward the building.

A few minutes later, Cole talked his way past the front desk and navigated the same cubicle area as the last time Erin was here. He had to restrain himself from ripping the curtains open one by one to see where she was.

"Cole."

He turned at the sound of his name. "Sam. How is she?"

Erin's brother walked up to him. "So far so good. They want to keep her for observation, but the baby's heartbeat is strong."

If Cole were near a wall, he'd have collapsed against it in relief. "And Erin?"

"She's bruised in some places from where she hit the ground, but she's fine." Sam slapped him on the shoulder. "You've been here for too long. Why don't you go home and get some rest? I'll call you if anything changes."

Cole opened his mouth, then closed it again. "Excuse me? You expect me to leave? Without seeing her?"

Sam met his gaze. "She needs rest."

"Who's with her?" Because Cole knew her brother wouldn't have left her alone.

"Mike's in there."

Cole eyed the other man warily. "And you're out here . . . why? To make sure I don't bother her?"

"Look, I get that you're worried. We all are. But I was just going to call my parents and let them know she's okay."

Cole clenched his hands into tight fists. "So they can come see her, no doubt. Yet you're telling me to leave, which means —"

Sam blew out a deep breath. "Erin doesn't want to see you right now, man."

What the hell? "Why not? Is she blaming me for this all of a sudden?" Cole ran a hand through his hair, crazy at the thought of not being able to see for himself that she was okay.

He wanted to hear the *whoosh, whoosh* on the monitor and know the baby was fine.

Sam looked more uncomfortable than Cole had ever seen him. Given that he was the easier-going brother, Cole's nerves were strung even tighter.

"Just say it."

Sam eyed him with pity. "Look, Erin said now that Victoria isn't a threat, you don't need to watch over her."

Fuck.

"She's scared, she's upset, and she's been under more stress than she can handle. Just give her some time to calm down and see things more clearly," her brother said, steering Cole toward the door with a hand on his back.

373

Cole let him, only because he knew better than to cause a scene and upset Erin, never mind that his entire body had gone into shock. A cold sweat broke out on his forehead at the realization that Erin was ending things.

Doing exactly what he'd told her needed to happen. He'd said himself, when the threat to her was over, he'd be gone. Back to undercover work. Out of Serendipity and out of her life — except for the minute details of raising a child, something they'd never gotten around to hammering out.

Erin had been smart. First she'd tried to make him see they could have a real relationship, but he'd withdrawn or rebuffed her every time. From the moment she realized he couldn't give her what she wanted, she'd put her armor on. Which was why she'd pulled away the minute she knew his father was out of the woods.

She'd known this day was around the corner, and she was protecting herself. He didn't like it, hated it in fact, but he respected her decision because her instincts were right.

It was time for him to wrap things up here and return to his world. His job. The job he loved, Cole was forced to remind himself, even as his stomach clenched and rolled in denial.

"Cole?"

He realized Sam was trying to talk to him. "Yeah."

"You're good?"

He forced a nod. "I'm fine. Erin's right. Victoria's under guard. When she's stable she'll be booked. Your sister's safe. She doesn't need me anymore."

Erin lay in the hospital bed, hooked up to the fetal monitor, an IV in her arm . . . just in case. She hadn't asked in case of what. She didn't want to know.

All her thoughts and whatever energy she had were going toward positive thoughts, calming breaths, and keeping this baby inside her. That was the main reason she'd sent her brother out to the hall, to make sure he waylaid Cole before he was able to get through the red tape and come check on her. The other reason she'd sent Sam to intercept Cole was that she was a coward. She didn't want to face him and burst into tears. She needed time to get herself together, and to do that, she needed the baby to be okay. Then she'd put the pieces of her broken heart back together.

"Knock, knock!"

Erin recognized the voice. "Come in, Macy!"

The minute her best friend lowered herself next to Erin on the bed, she let the tears she'd been holding back run free. Macy knew exactly what Erin needed and sat while she cried, not questioning her, not asking which part of her completely screwed-up life she was crying over, just hugging her and running a hand over her hair until her tear ducts ran dry.

"Thank you." Erin wiped her eyes on a too-rough hospital tissue.

"Any time. Where is everyone?"

Erin sniffed. "Mike got an emergency call and Sam's out doing me a favor."

Macy nodded. "Okay, so what can I do for you?"

God, she loved her friend. "Can you head over to Nick's place where I was staying and pack up all my things? You have the spare key to my condo, right?"

Macy nodded.

"Just drop everything off there."

"Will do. Anything else?"

"Not at the moment."

Macy eyed her with concern. "When are they letting you out of here?"

Erin shrugged. "I'm not sure yet. As soon as it's safe for the baby, and I'm not pushing it." She protectively covered her stomach with her hands.

"Gotcha. I'll bring some of Aunt Lulu's cake for you too."

"You're the best."

Macy grinned. "I know." She rose to her feet. "Let me get started on that errand. If you aren't out of here today, I'll be back to see you tonight."

"Thank you." She paused. "Macy?"

Her friend tipped her head to the side, her long black hair falling over one shoulder. "What is it?"

"I haven't told anyone, but I've been thinking . . . about my current job and the baby and changes I need to make." A planner by nature, Erin's subconscious had been putting together lists and ideas even before they'd fully formed in her mind.

"I'm here for you. I'll give advice or just shut up and listen. Whatever you need."

Erin managed a smile. "I know."

"Can I ask . . . what about Cole?"

She shook her head. "Not yet. I can't talk about him. I can't see him, knowing it's over . . . but there are some practical things I need to take care of before he leaves."

Macy eased closer to the bed again. "Like what?"

Erin glanced down at the white, waffle-textured blanket. "I need to see a lawyer . . . to discuss how to handle visitation, child support —" She swallowed a sob, determined to remain strong.

"Isn't it too fast to think about all this? I mean, you've been through a huge trauma. Your stalker has just been arrested. You need time —"

"I don't have time," Erin cut her off. "You said it yourself. Victoria's not a threat anymore. I'm safe. That means Cole can leave town anytime and go back undercover. I need to make sure these things are ironed out quickly, before he goes."

Macy stepped close and touched her hand. "Okay. Whatever you need, we'll do. And afterward, I can stay over. We can eat cake and ice cream, and watch *South Park: The Movie* and laugh over the dirty parts." Macy waggled her eyebrows, causing Erin to chuckle. "Anything for you — as long as I'm that baby's godmother."

Erin rolled her eyes. "As if there'd be anyone else."

"Yay, me!" Macy squealed, clapping her hands in joy, her laughter ringing out in the small cubicle.

"You're incorrigible," Erin said with a grin.

"There it is," Macy said. "I want to see

that beautiful smile on your face more often."

Erin didn't reply. With the thoughts running through her mind and the plans she had to make, smiling was the last thing she'd feel like doing for a good, long while.

Eighteen

Cole checked in with the hospital and learned his father was sleeping soundly and his vitals were good, but that he couldn't visit until the morning. He drove back to Nick's borrowed home, in no mood to pack up his shit or to do more than kick back and forget his problems for a little while. Tomorrow he'd move himself out of this house and drop Erin's clothes off at her condo at some point during the day.

In the meantime, since Erin didn't want to see him, Cole was on his own for the first time in weeks. He poured himself a bourbon and settled into an oversized chair. Alone with only his thoughts for company, the quiet mocked him, though he'd always appreciated silence before.

He'd barely touched the glass to his lips when the doorbell rang. "What now?" he muttered, heading to see who was interrupting his surprisingly unwelcome peace and solitude.

He opened the door, took one look at Macy Donovan, and groaned.

"Hello to you too," she said brightly, pushing past him and walking inside.

"Make yourself at home," he muttered.

"No thanks. I'm just here to get Erin's things."

On that pronouncement, Cole slammed the door shut, and Macy jumped at the sound.

"How is she?" Cole asked Erin's best friend.

Macy eyed him warily. "Physically? She's fine. A little bruised but okay."

"And the baby?" He allowed himself a pass of bourbon before she answered.

"Also okay. They're both hanging in there," she assured him. "How are you?" she asked, surprising him.

He let out a harsh laugh.

"What was that for?" Macy narrowed her gaze.

"You're concerned about me?" He treated himself to another swallow of liquid fire.

Macy stepped forward and grabbed the drink, snatching it before he could react and slamming the glass on the nearest table. "My best friend loves you, you moron. Of course I'm concerned."

Cole choked and needed a minute to recover before facing her. "Erin said that?"

"Men are so dense," Macy muttered. "She didn't have to say it. It's obvious. And you have to know it too. Why else would you duck and run?"

He straightened his shoulders, offended by the comment. "I did no such thing! I've been there for her ever since I found out she was pregnant, not to mention in danger."

"In every way but the one that really matters to her!" Macy poked him in the chest hard.

"Ouch, dammit."

"Baby." Macy flounced over to the couch and settled in, glaring up at him from blue eyes that would drive some other man insane with need, and Cole pitied the unknown sucker.

He shook his head. "Macy, what the hell can I do? My job is dangerous, starting with the people I meet and inadvertently bring home with me, like Victoria. She ended up being a direct threat to Erin and the baby. Not to mention I don't know from one minute to the next if I'll get out alive. How can I subject Erin to that kind of existence?"

She stared at him with an expression of disbelief. "Are you for real? Do you think that just because you decide to spare her the joy of telling her you love her and want to share your life with her she'll suffer any less when you go undercover?" Macy raised her voice as she spoke. "She loves you! Whether you tell her you return those feelings or not, she's going to experience everything you're trying to spare her from." Her gaze bore into his, never once letting him turn away or blink.

"Shit," Cole said at last, staring at the pint-sized dynamo who'd put him in his place.

"Yeah, I make sense," Macy gloated, obviously pleased with herself.

Cole wasn't taking the bait; his mind was on Macy's words. She'd announced that he loved Erin and he hadn't gone into a state of panic, nor did he want to run for the hills — or back to Manhattan, as the case may be. He also hadn't argued the point.

How could he when Macy was right?

When Sam announced that Erin hadn't wanted to see him, he'd sucker punched Cole and ripped out his heart. Cole just hadn't put together why until Macy threw the reality in his face.

Men *were* dense. Cole in particular.

His head spun, and not from the little bit of alcohol he'd consumed.

Suddenly Macy hopped up from the couch. "I see I made you think, so my job here is done. I need to get my best friend's stuff."

Cole gestured to the front of the house. "Erin's things are upstairs in the master bedroom at the end of the hall, but I can bring them to her tomorrow."

Macy shook her head. "She asked me to get them, and she doesn't need the stress of things not going as she expects — which reminds me. She's got plans."

Cole narrowed his gaze. "What kind of plans?"

"I don't know specifically, and if I did, I couldn't tell you. But I will say you have a few days to get your head on straight before Erin's given the okay by her doctors to go about business as usual." Macy paused, undoubtedly for emphasis. "In other words, once she puts some balls in motion, you're going to have a tougher time getting through to her . . . emotionally or otherwise."

Cole swallowed hard. "Explain."

The other woman shrugged. "She's talking about seeing lawyers, about formalizing things between you two. I can't say more than that."

She didn't have to.

Cole understood now, on a gut level, that

his legal eagle was already strategizing to keep him not only at the emotional distance she'd already established, but at a legal one as well. She undoubtedly thought to relegate his role in her life to that of the baby daddy who'd make payments and see his kid on a court-dictated schedule.

Nausea swirled through him as he realized that was exactly what he'd thought he wanted. What he'd basically told her was exactly what she'd get from him. Enough money to provide for her and the baby while he went back to his undercover life.

A cold existence with no friends, no family, no ties or commitments. An existence he'd liked because it was all he knew and it had suited him. Until the night Erin danced her way into his arms and his bed. Until she invaded his life and pulled him kicking and screaming into hers, opening his mind and his heart to possibilities he thought he'd slammed the door shut on forever.

Time and again, he'd thrown those possibilities and Erin's unspoken love back in her face.

Cole ran a hand over his burning eyes. "Macy?" He looked for her but she'd disappeared, having obviously headed upstairs to pack up Erin's things while he'd been lost in thought.

A few days, she'd said. Not a lot of time to fix the situation and change a lifetime. But if he wanted Erin, and heaven knew he did, Cole had to try.

Hospital rules gave Cole fifteen minutes with Jed for this first post-surgery visit. Since he'd met with the doctor this morning, Cole thought he was prepared, but the sight of his father hooked up to so many tubes — breathing tube, stomach tube, IV, chest tube, and God knew what else — made Cole's breath catch in his throat. He reached out only to realize Erin wasn't there to steady him, and that, more than anything, cemented the decisions he'd made and the things he needed to do once this visit ended. All with no guarantees that he'd get what he wanted in the end.

Cole pulled up a chair to the edge of his father's bed, close to his head. Jed lay sleeping and Cole didn't wake him. He needed rest, and it was enough to know he was breathing, his heart was pumping, and there was a chance for them to try to come to terms with each other. For the sake of his child, if not for himself. Cole had long since stopped expecting anything from Jed, and that hadn't changed.

"Hey, Dad." Since he had his father's ear

if not his attention, Cole decided to talk to the man, regardless of whether or not he could hear. "Glad you came through the surgery. You look like hell, but you're strong enough to get through this."

Cole spoke low, wanting only to say what was on his mind, what had been in his head and his heart for all these years. "I know I was a pain in the ass growing up. I'm betting my own kid will give me a run for my money." Cole managed a smile at the thought, along with a solid kick of fear.

He drew a deep breath. "But I'm not sure why we could never find common ground. Even as adults." He hesitated before saying the next thing, but decided he had to get it out before the feelings poisoned him even more. "I'm not sure why you hate me so much or why what I do now is such a disappointment." Cole shook his head, the pain of all the years nearly choking him.

"I won't do that to my kid. At least I'll be aware of trying to do better." In reality, Cole had no idea how to handle a kid and wished the baby would come with an instruction manual. At least he had Erin to guide him. No matter the end result between them personally, he had faith they'd do their best to co-parent.

Cole wanted so much more than some

formal arrangement, but after pushing her away for so long and hurting her in ways he was sure even he didn't know about, he didn't know what she wanted from him anymore. She wasn't answering her phone, returning his calls, or replying to his texts to see how she was doing. Not a good sign.

He was forging ahead with his plan anyway, because no matter what Erin ultimately decided, leaving his job and starting a life here in Serendipity was the right thing to do, for Cole and for the child he wanted a relationship with.

"I'm going to try to do better than you or I've managed so far," he said to the man lying in the hospital bed.

To Cole's surprise, Jed opened his eyes, meeting Cole's gaze. He swallowed hard, wondering how much his father had heard. Wondering if anything he'd said could break through the hard shell that surrounded Jed Sanders.

The same shell that Cole had protected himself with . . . until he fell in love with Erin and learned how much she — and life — had to offer.

On doctor's orders, Erin was on bed rest for a week. If she had no more cramping, she could then start to move around slowly and work her way back to a normal routine. But Erin had already decided her normal had to change, and she had no desire to wait to start making modifications in her life. If she couldn't go to the people she wanted to see, she'd just have to ask them to come to her.

Erin held court from the couch in her family room. Her parents, brothers, and friends came by, Macy with a different slice of Aunt Lulu's cake each day. Although Cole had texted her and she saw missed calls and voice messages on her cell, she wasn't ready to talk to him. Not until she had finished getting herself and her life together. Then, when she could act like lawyer-Erin, not Erin-in-love, she'd face him and know she could let him go without falling apart after he left.

To that end, her newest visitor sat on the chair across from the couch that probably had a permanent indentation from Erin's behind plastered into it. "Hi, Kelly. I really appreciate you coming by."

Kelly Barron, Nash's wife, a pretty woman with brown hair with golden streaks, treated Erin to a warm smile. "My pleasure, believe me. It's an excuse to leave Nash home alone with the twins," she said, an almost-evil twinkle in her eye.

Erin laughed. "How old are they now?"

"The boys are thirteen months. I swear they're twin terrors." But the love in her voice and her eyes was evident.

"How do you find working with babies at home?" Kelly was a paralegal for Richard Kane, an outstanding lawyer in Serendipity.

In an odd twist of fate, when Kelly was new in town, she had met and fallen for Nash, not knowing he had once been married to Annie Kane, her new boss's daughter. She'd also befriended Annie, not knowing the connection to Nash. Apparently, both exes had moved on, and with Annie married to Joe now, there were no hard feelings. And to help Richard out, Nash's firm had recently merged with his. Sort of incestuous, yet not, and everyone got along.

"Hard," Kelly said bluntly.

Erin wouldn't have expected anything less than the hard truth. "I cut way back on my hours, and we had to hire help at home for when I'm working. And my sister, Tess, comes by a lot, especially now that she's driving, which I love and which helps a lot. Honestly, the only reason I'm still working is for my sanity." She brushed her long bangs out of her eyes. "I need those few hours to feel like a functioning, competent adult. Which I suspect you'll understand soon enough." Kelly laughed.

Erin blew out a long breath. "So I'm guessing being an assistant district attorney with night court and on-call hours while also being a single mom could get difficult." She bit down on her lower lip in thought.

"Well, you'd need help at odd hours, but I'm sure it's doable. Anything is if you want it badly enough."

And there was the question. The more time she had with this baby growing inside her, the more chances she had to think about being a mom, and what kind of job would best mesh with that and be right for her baby. "I'll have to figure out what I want."

Kelly leaned forward in her seat. "I'm not trying to poach on Evan's territory," she said of the district attorney. "Well, maybe I am. But with the recent merger of the two firms, we had some people leave, and we're always looking for solid lawyers who can bring business to the firm."

Erin's eyes opened wide at that. "Really?"

Kelly nodded. "I can tell you that we're very flexible with new moms, because I was one, and I made sure to have my husband rewrite any policies I didn't like." She grinned, letting Erin know she definitely had sway over the man.

She envied Kelly what she had — a husband she loved, who loved her back, and children they were raising together under one roof. She swallowed hard.

"So . . . want to meet with Nash and talk to him about coming on board? For selfish reasons, I'd love to have you around. Another mom to talk to, a friend I could get closer to . . . and you'd have a whole new challenge, interesting cases, variety. No night hours in the office unless you wanted them. We're big on videoconferencing and working from home —"

"Yes!" Erin didn't have to think twice. Not only had Kelly done a good selling job but Erin already knew she had to leave the district attorney's office. She felt like she'd taken advantage of her colleagues there, she hadn't pulled her weight lately, and they needed someone with more time than she'd be able to devote from here on in. She just hadn't figured out what she wanted to do next, and Kelly's suggestion was perfect.

"Great! I'll have Nash call you, and you two can take things from there."

Kelly's warm smile assured Erin she was doing the right thing.

"Have you lined up babysitting help for when you need to work?" she asked Erin.

Erin pushed herself into a more comfortable position on the couch. "My mom is going to help in the beginning, and the rest depends on what you and I are going to discuss now." Erin's stomach flipped at the reminder of her real reason for needing to see Kelly today.

The other woman raised an eyebrow, but didn't press Erin to explain.

She closed her eyes, pushing back the pain and focusing on the reality, forcing herself to meet Kelly's patient gaze. "I need to have papers drawn up to give to the baby's father. Of course I want sole custody, but I need to give him generous visitation when he's around, given the fact that his job won't let him have set weekly hours."

The other woman reached for her bag, pulled out a legal pad and a pen, and started taking notes. "What's his job?"

"Undercover work in Manhattan. Last time he said he was out of touch for a year." Her throat hurt from the effort of pushing back tears. "I don't think I'll be hearing from him while he's on a job. He said he wants to take responsibility, and since I will need to work, I'll need help paying for the babysitter."

Kelly eyed her with concern. "You'll need a lot more than babysitting money. Take it from me, you'll want him to pay his share, and if he's willing, it should be easy enough to take care of."

"I don't think he'll give me a hard time."

She just wished she didn't have to take anything from Cole, but Erin wasn't stupid enough to let her pride overrule her common sense. She was already giving up the career she'd planned for a situation they'd both created, while he would go back to life as usual. She didn't resent the baby or the sacrifice. In fact, she was excited now and couldn't wait. But that didn't mean she would try to do it on her own.

If all Cole could offer was cash, she'd accept only what she needed to make ends meet. "This isn't about punishment or anger," she told Kelly. "I just want enough to let me care for my baby and be home with him or her when I can." It was bad enough this baby would basically have one full-time parent and one he or she barely knew.

Erin swiped at her eyes with her palm, and Kelly handed her a tissue in silence.

"Thank you." Erin appreciated the fact that Kelly didn't push her to explain her feelings. If she had, Erin knew she'd fall apart.

While she waited, Kelly jotted down a few more notes. "Erin?"

"Yes?"

Kelly looked up. "You know I'm close with Annie, Joe's wife, right?"

Erin narrowed her eyes and nodded.

"She mentioned to me that Joe has to look for a new tenant for the apartment over the bar. It's month to month, so when this one's over . . . Cole said he's moving out," she said gently. "Did you know?"

Erin shook her head, willing the tears not to fall. "But I haven't taken his calls, so for all I know, he would have told me."

"Is it okay with you if I give him a call? See if he has a lawyer he wants me to be in touch with over these things? Or did you want to talk to him yourself?"

Erin waved her hand through the air. "You do it," she said abruptly. "Please," she added, knowing it wasn't Kelly who she was angry with.

Rationally she wasn't angry with Cole either. Things were playing out exactly as he'd warned her they would. It was her fault, hoping for more. For something he'd expressly told her would never be.

Still, the less she had to do with Cole right now, the better off she'd be. She clutched at the blanket she'd draped over her stomach and legs, her head pounding and her heart breaking. Based on the easy flow of tears and the sharp pain slicing into her chest, obviously getting over Cole Sanders wouldn't be as easy as she'd hoped.

Kelly handling things would let Erin hang on to the one thing she had left of herself.

Her pride.

After visiting his father again, Cole spent the day in Manhattan, giving his boss the news in person. Rockford hadn't taken his resignation well, the man sputtering and turning beet red, but in the end he'd wished Cole well. And told him if things got boring, his old job would be waiting.

Cole might be a lot of things in Serendipity, but he knew bored with Erin wouldn't be one of them. He didn't know it in his gut; he knew it in his heart.

Enough avoiding. While in Manhattan, he called on his mother and stepdad and told them they were going to be grandparents. Afterward, he planned for the future. He put out feelers with old contacts, hoping to start up his own security firm, which would be based in Serendipity but would work with retired agents he knew who had spread out to various parts of the country. There'd be some traveling, but little danger, and the more guys on board whom he trusted, the less Cole himself would have to fly out and handle things in person. In the meantime, he had a huge nest egg from years of living minimally and frugally, he had jobs with Nick if he wanted time working with his hands, and most of all, he had a plan.

With that plan came hope. Though he cautioned himself against it, Erin's optimism had been contagious. But she was the last stop in his plan and he meant to tackle things in order, so he could show her that he meant what he said and had taken steps to prove it.

From the city, Cole headed back to the hospital in time for the last visiting hours of the day. He stopped to talk to the doctor, who'd just finished rounds. Jed had been moved out of the CICU and into his own room. They were already getting him up and moving, and Cole couldn't imagine the pain involved in such an endeavor — or the crap his father was giving the nurses.

He began walking toward the room and stopped right outside.

"Mr. Sanders, I need you to breathe into that tube. We can't have your lungs filling with fluid." An older woman stood beside the bed with a breathing apparatus in her hand.

Jed lay back against the pillows, refusing to look at her. "Go away."

Cole bit the inside of his cheek, debating whether or not to step in.

"Not until you blow. You don't scare me and I'm not leaving. I'm every bit as stubborn as you."

"Dang it, woman —"

"Ms. Reynolds. Lucy Reynolds. You can call me Lucy if and when you blow into this machine."

She stuck the equipment in front of Jed's face, and to Cole's amazement, his father let her help him sit up straighter and did his best to comply with her instructions. Jed groaned and winced and she finally eased him back against the bed.

"Good job, Jed!" the nurse said happily.

"That's Mr. Sanders to you, and you can call me that until you stop being a pain."

Ignoring him, she handed him a cup with a straw, from which he took a small sip.

Cole shook his head and walked into the room. "Still cheery as ever?" he asked his old man.

Jed's eyes widened as Cole stepped inside.

"He's doing well," the nurse, who was attractive and about his father's age, said to Cole.

"Well, I appreciate you putting up with him."

She glanced at Jed, her eyes warming with

amusement. "Anything he dishes out, I can handle."

His father muttered something under his breath, but his cheeks turned a ruddy color.

"I have other patients to check on, but I'll be back. Buzz me if you need me, Jed." She turned and walked out.

Cole pulled a chair up to his father's bedside. Silence surrounded them for a few minutes, before he finally spoke up. "Well, you made it through."

"Hurts like hell," the older man muttered.

"I'll bet."

Cole leaned an arm on the metal bed rail. "Listen, there's something you need to know."

Jed met his gaze. "What's that?"

Before Cole could reply, his cell phone rang. Unwilling to get sidetracked, he glanced down to see who was calling. Kelly Barron's name came up on the screen. He narrowed his gaze.

"Someone important?" Jed asked.

Kelly was a paralegal at her husband's law firm. The main firm in Serendipity. "Yeah, it's important." Legal documents, no doubt. But Cole planned to intercept Erin before dealing with those. "I'll take care of it when I leave here." Which had been his intention all along.

Turning back to his father, Cole gathered his courage. Though he'd prepped this speech, he knew it wouldn't be easy, and he could never anticipate his father's reaction. Especially after all he'd been through in the past couple of days.

"I'm staying in Serendipity. Permanently."

Jed blinked, the only indication he'd heard as the announcement settled between them. "Erin know?" he finally asked.

"Not yet. I had some matters to take care of first."

Jed nodded, his gaze focused on the wall across the room. "What if she won't have you?" His voice sounded raspy from the tube, and weak.

But his words were blunt and very Jedlike. At least it hadn't been couched in an insult. "I'm staying anyway. I have a kid to raise. That's more important than any job."

"Don't screw it up like I did."

Cole stiffened, unsure he'd heard correctly. In fact, he was damned certain he hadn't. But he couldn't ask. "I plan to do my best."

"So did I. My mother, your grandmother, raised me by herself. She worked and pretty much ignored me, letting me run wild."

Cole sat in stunned silence. Jed never discussed his past. Never considered it

400

important. All Cole knew was that Jed's father hadn't stuck around, and his mother had died while Jed was in the army. Now his father was talking and Cole was afraid to interrupt and have him stop.

"I was just like you were. Just like it." He pointed to the can of ginger ale.

Cole copied what the nurse had done and lifted the straw to his father's mouth. Jed took a few sips and, wincing, relaxed back again.

"Got myself arrested too."

What the hell?

"Yep. Just like you. But I didn't have a mother who'd bail me out or take me away. In fact, she wiped her hands of me. So the judge said I could do time in juvie till I hit eighteen, which was only a couple of months, and then he strongly suggested I join the army. Get myself some discipline before I ended up back in front of him again. If I enlisted, he'd expunge my record. I didn't see any better options, so I did."

Cole's mouth grew dry. At least Jed didn't seem to expect a reply, just kept talking.

"I met a colonel who took me under his wing," Jed said into the silence. "A hard son of a bitch who decided he'd make a man out of me. It worked. The discipline and routine suited me. Straightened me right up, and I knew if I'd had him around grow-ing up, I'd never have ended up in jail in the first place."

Cole blew out a long breath, finally able to gather his thoughts. "Why the hell didn't you tell me all this?" Knowing he'd been like Jed would have formed a bond, let him see his father was human and not a cold machine.

"Didn't see how it mattered." Jed's hands worked the blanket on the bed, crunching into his palms.

Anger washed through Cole but he wasn't going to pick an argument with a sick man. "Go on."

"I thought if I treated you with the same hard hand as soon as you started getting out of control, I'd reel you back in. Instead you rebelled harder. That only pissed me off and made me more determined to get through to you on my terms."

Cole opened his mouth but Jed continued to speak. "They were the only terms I knew. If they worked on me, I didn't see how it wouldn't work on you."

Cole shook his head in disbelief. "You didn't hate me." Shit, he'd said that out loud. Cole ran a hand through his hair.

"No, I saw myself reflected in you, and didn't like what I saw."

Cole forced himself to breathe before he got dizzy and managed to pull himself together. He hadn't expected a heart-to-heart with his old man — now or ever. And he wasn't sure what to do with the information Jed was giving him now. Cole supposed it provided understanding. Forgiveness wouldn't come overnight, though. The emotional scars Jed had embedded were too deep. How his father treated him equaled how he felt about him, at least in Cole's mind. And that had permeated every aspect of his life, including his time with Erin.

"I'm sorry I disappointed you," Cole finally said.

Jed sighed out loud. "It wasn't that. I just didn't know how to adapt when things didn't work. And then your mother and me and all that constant arguing, it wore on me."

Cole set his jaw. "It wore on her too."

"Which was why she left, but by that time, I couldn't see it. I could only blame you."

He shook his head. "Well, you did a damn fine job of that," Cole muttered.

"Yeah, well, I'm sorry," Jed spat.

Cole jerked in his seat. Jed was sorry. He hadn't said it nicely, but he'd said it. And Cole knew better than to make a production out of it either.

"What happened when I grew up? You couldn't let it go then?" Cole couldn't help but ask.

"Your mother left and almost immediately fell for someone else. *You* idolized that son of a bitch she married. That soft, good guy. And he turned you around. I resented that too." His father stared at the ceiling, his voice harsher, lower, and his obvious exhaustion leaching the color from his face.

"Dad, get some rest. We can pick this up tomorrow."

"Finishing it now. Then I don't want to talk about it again."

Cole raised an eyebrow. "What made you discuss it in the first place?" He couldn't contain his curiosity.

"Erin."

Her name caught him off guard. "How does Erin have anything to do with this?"

For the first time, Jed turned his head and met Cole's gaze. Cole stared into his father's dark eyes, eyes that looked so much like his own, unsure of what he was really thinking. Another thing he vowed to do differently: Let his child know there was someone who cared looking back at him.

"She's a good woman," Jed said of Erin.

"That she is."

"And she sees something good and decent

in you. Hell, she'd kick my ass if I wasn't already kicking it myself. Anyway, if someone like her can look at you the way she does, and face off against me on your behalf . . . oh, hell. Between Erin, the things you said to me after surgery, and lying in this bed facing my own mortality, I had to take a long look at myself." Jed drew a tired breath. "At us."

Cole didn't know what to say or how to react. He didn't even know what this all meant, other than that Jed had had some self-awareness lessons.

"I'm willing to meet you halfway." Cole put himself out there not for Jed, but for the child Erin was carrying.

Jed's expression softened. Just a little. "I'm too old to change completely."

Cole raised an eyebrow. That wasn't enough for him. But he waited Jed out.

"But I want to try. And I want to know that baby."

Cole inclined his head, letting out a slow breath of air. "Then you will." With Cole there watching and making sure that kid was protected from the way Cole had grown up.

He rose from his seat. If he was feeling worn out from this whole ordeal, he couldn't imagine how overwhelmed and exhausted his father must be.

Cole glanced back at the bed only to discover Jed was already asleep. He stepped out of the room and leaned against the nearest wall. It would take a long time to process this talk with Jed. Even longer to discover whether the tentative truce would last.

With Jed taken care of, Cole turned his attention to Erin. He was ready to head over and see what remained of the feelings she had for him, if he'd done enough work on himself and his life to be worthy of her. Or whether Erin was so set on not being hurt that she'd shut him out of her life completely — no matter what he had to say.

NINETEEN

Her doorbell rang and Erin walked over, looked out because she'd grown so much more cautious recently, and let Evan in.

"Hi," he said, clasping her hand. "You're looking well."

She smiled. "Thank you. I appreciate you coming straight from work. I know it's been a long day."

He loosened his tie and followed her inside. "Seeing you isn't an inconvenience."

"I'm sure you're wondering why I asked you to come over." She gestured for him to follow and she headed for the kitchen, where she'd left her tea.

"Yes, but I've been meaning to talk to you as well." Evan stepped up beside her.

She was still supposed to be resting, but she was allowed to get up for short periods of time, and Evan was one guest she didn't want to face lying down. "Can I get you a drink?" she asked.

"No, thank you. Erin —"

"Evan —"

They laughed. "You first," she said.

"Okay, I was a jerk that night at Joe's," he said. "Your private life is none of my business and I reacted from a . . . jealous place. I'd like to put it behind us. We don't need this affecting our work or relationship at the office."

She wrapped her hands around her mug of tea. "I agree. That's sort of what I needed to talk to you about too."

"So I'm forgiven?" he asked, looking boyishly charming.

She shook her head and laughed. "Yes, you are."

"Good." He braced his hands on her shoulders in thanks, then released her. "So what did you want to discuss?"

She wasn't ready to quit the district attorney's office until she'd spoken to Nash and was certain the job, salary, and benefits worked for her. But she did want to discuss a current case with Evan, and given how they'd left things between them, she'd known they had to talk in person.

"It's about Victoria Maroni."

"Aah." He nodded. "Something else I'm sorry for. I shouldn't have left you alone in that hallway where she could get to you."

He appeared contrite, embarrassed.

"I was never your responsibility."

"But I knew you were in danger, that you had a bodyguard —"

She shook her head. "And my brother and his wife, both police officers, were mere feet away. Forget it, please?"

He inclined his head. "Thank you. Again."

"There is something you can do for me."

He cocked his head to one side. "What's that?"

"Make sure part of any deal you make for Victoria includes mental health help?"

He stared in disbelief. "She had you shot, she nearly ran you down, she stalked you, she shredded your clothes, and here you are making sure she gets psychiatric help?"

Erin shrugged. "What can I say? No rational person would do anything like that, so clearly she needs help. Her sister said she suffers from bipolar disorder. Just call a doctor in to evaluate her. I'm not saying she shouldn't pay for what she did, but she needs to be medicated. Helped."

Evan studied her, his gaze warm, full of more admiration than anything else, and she wasn't uncomfortable. Maybe they could repair their friendship, after all.

"That man so does not deserve you," Evan said.

She stepped back and leaned against the counter. "Can we please not discuss Cole?" To her mortification, her voice cracked on his name.

"I told him if he hurt you, I'd kill him."

"He didn't hurt me. Not in the way you think. He never lied, led me on, or told me I could expect more. That's all on me."

Evan wrapped a friendly arm around her shoulder. "Come on. Let's go sit down."

She liked this side of Evan, she thought, as she walked with him to her family room.

"Well, this is unexpected."

Erin jumped at the sound of Cole's voice, and Evan stiffened.

"Ever hear of ringing the bell, Sanders?" Evan asked.

"The door was partially open." Cole shot a look at Erin that said she ought to know better.

Erin's breath lodged in her throat. So much for distance making it easier to deal with him. He looked delicious in a black T-shirt and jeans, and her heart swelled with happiness before she immediately reminded herself he didn't want a life with her — and sex wasn't enough.

"What are you doing here?"

She watched as he visibly blew out a long breath, then clenched and unclenched his fists in an obvious effort to control his temper over finding her with Evan. She didn't make it easy for him, instead waiting for an answer.

"I need to talk to you," he said at last.

Erin wondered if Kelly had been in touch with him already.

Evan stepped away from Erin. "Are we all finished?" he asked.

"Yes, I think we covered everything."

Evan nodded. "Then I'll go and let you two talk."

Cole's jaw worked back and forth but he said nothing.

A part of her had expected Evan to get into an argument with Cole, but surprisingly her boss didn't bait him.

"Take care of yourself. Don't come back until you're ready." He turned to Erin and kissed her cheek.

Cole growled but Erin ignored him. So much for Evan not provoking, she thought wryly.

"Thanks for being so understanding," she said, walking him to the door.

She waited until Evan had left before turning to face Cole. Hands behind her back, she leaned against the now-closed front door.

He stared back, his eyes warm, his lips

almost turning upward in a smile. Not Cole's normally deep, serious, unapproachable look. No, tonight it was Erin going for unapproachable, and she prayed she succeeded.

"Are we really going to do this awkward thing?" He gestured between them. "I mean, I can stand here and stare at you all night, but you're supposed to be resting."

She frowned. "How would you know?"

He raised an eyebrow. "I spoke to your lawyer on the way here." No hint of a smile this time.

"Oh." She swallowed hard. "Maybe sitting down is a good idea."

"Nervous?" he asked, following her back to the family room.

Erin settled into her normal place on the sofa. Cole didn't take the chair everyone else usually did. Instead he sat beside her. So close his thigh touched hers. She shut her eyes and forced air into her lungs. Big mistake, since his musky, masculine scent overwhelmed her, making her want to crawl into his arms, bury her face in his neck, and drink him in.

"I asked if you were nervous." He stretched his arm along the back of the sofa, too close to her neck. Her skin tingled at the whisper of sensation he effortlessly evoked.

"Why would I be?" Her voice sounded rough to her own ears.

"Your lawyer called me about custody agreements, visitation, and child support." The words rumbled out of him on a low growl.

"I thought we should finalize things quickly, before you go undercover again."

He nodded as if he understood, but those warm eyes of his were boring into hers, and now she was nervous.

"What makes you think I'm going back under? How would you know what I plan, when you won't take my calls? Answer my texts? When you wouldn't see me in the hospital after you were nearly killed?" he asked, the tension suddenly radiating from him in waves.

"Are you saying you're not?" she asked.

"I'm the one asking questions. How would you know what I'm doing? What I want?"

"I wouldn't." She swallowed hard. "But I thought I did. You told me when the threat was over, you were leaving. Well? The threat was over. I was just making a clean break." She folded her arms across her chest.

"What if that's not what I want?" He reached out, grasped her around the waist, and pulled her onto his lap.

She blinked, stunned. "This isn't a good idea."

"Hear me out."

"Not while I'm sitting on your lap."

"Trust me."

She opened her mouth, then closed it once more. "Talk, and make it quick." Before she started squirming against him.

"I'm not leaving you, our baby, or Serendipity." He pushed her hair off her shoulder, kissing the sensitive skin of her neck. She shivered but was determined to remain in control.

"You have a job."

"I quit."

She straightened her shoulders. "I . . . you . . . what?"

"I quit. Went to the city and did it in person."

Erin's eyes opened wide. "Why?"

"Isn't it obvious?"

She shook her head, afraid to think, to breathe, and lose the moment or find out she was dreaming. "Maybe it's obvious to you, but to me this has come out of left field."

He placed his hand beneath her chin and turned her face toward him. "I love you, Erin. It's that complicated . . . and that simple."

A wave of dizziness assaulted her. "You love me. Enough to quit your job and settle in Serendipity."

Cole nodded, but he knew a simple *yes* wasn't enough for this bright woman. "I love you, yes. I also love the fact that you fought for me. For us. That you opened my eyes to what I was missing, and to what I needed."

She expelled a breath of air, a small sigh escaping. He leaned in and kissed her parted lips. "What do you need?" she asked.

"You, sweetheart. I need you and everything that you bring with you. You gave me back my father, or at least a shot at having him; you showed me I could have a life, friends, a family. You make me feel like I matter, and I want to give you anything you want in return. Even if that's just a pancake breakfast."

"Oh, Cole. I love you too."

Her eyes sparkled with laughter and happiness, and the knot that had settled in Cole's chest since the shooting finally eased.

"Besides, I never did learn to cook," she said with a grin.

"Say yes to me and you'll never have to."

Erin leaned back to look him in the eyes. "Say yes to what?" she asked, more serious than he'd ever seen her.

He reached into his pocket for the other thing he'd taken care of in Manhattan and pulled out a small jewelry box. "You're already having my baby. Marry me —"

A huge smile lit her face. "Yes!"

A light airy feeling he didn't recognize suffused him and he realized what it was. Happiness, something he'd never before truly experienced. She'd given him that too.

"Are you sure?" he asked, teasing her. "You haven't even seen the ring."

"That's just icing on the cake. All I ever wanted was you." She ran her hand down his cheek. "But go ahead. Show me."

He snapped open the velvet box, revealing a solitary diamond in a white-gold band. Simple yet elegant, like the woman herself.

"How can you . . . I mean . . . it's — big!"

"I never had anyone to spend money on before." He slipped the ring onto her finger, knowing it would fit perfectly. He'd already asked her father for his blessing and her mother for Erin's ring size.

"Oh my God." She held out her hand, admiring the glittering diamond. "I love it because you gave it to me."

One more thing, he thought, drawing a deep breath. "I bought us Nick's spec house."

"What?!" she squealed in excitement. "Why?"

"You love it, for one thing. For another, we've already lived there together and you have to admit, it's a perfect fit for our family."

She wrapped her arms around his neck, pulling him close and kissing him hard. "I don't know what to say. You're right. It's perfect for us, our baby." She sighed softly. "Our *family*."

He held her close and nodded, groaning in satisfaction. "It's just more icing, honey."

She laughed. "Are you sure you won't miss the job?" she asked, sobering.

"I'm starting a business I know will work well. I'll explain it later, but it involves security and a lot of guys I used to work with over the years. I'll be fine. Want to know why?"

She nodded.

"Same answer every time. Because I have you. Everything else —"

"Is just icing," they said at the same time.

"I love you," she said, sliding her hand beneath his shirt.

"I love you too."

Erin snuggled into his lap, her arms around him, her head on his shoulder, and

Cole knew the icing was nice, but *she* was all he needed or would want. Ever.

EPILOGUE

"Are you sure the baby seat is strapped in right?" Cole asked, both hands on the steering wheel of the brand-new GMC Ford Yukon he'd bought to bring the baby home from the hospital. "Is she buckled in?"

"It's fine. She's fine." Erin stared at the bundle wrapped in pink, strapped into her car seat, blissfully unaware that her daddy was freaking out in the front seat.

Erin, sore from the experience of bringing their beautiful baby girl into the world, looked at her husband and managed a laugh. She'd opted to sit in the back with the baby while he drove them home from the hospital.

Not only did they have a new truck, fully loaded and very safe, according to Cole, but they had a new digital SLR camera with home movie capabilities, and the house had been wired with video cameras so they could watch the baby in any room. To say

Cole had lost his mind was an understatement.

But Erin loved every minute of his involvement, knowing what a change it was from the solitary, withdrawn, disinterested man he'd been when he came back to Serendipity.

"You okay?" he asked.

"Glad you remembered I had something to do with this too," she said, chuckling.

"Oh, I remember. Every last second of making her to you giving birth to her."

Erin tried her best not to blush. It might be natural, but it was still a mortifying moment, at least until the pain had wiped every last thought from her head.

But she was worth it, Erin thought, stroking her daughter's cheek, enthralled with her soft skin and tiny features. She wasn't paying attention, and it seemed like only seconds had passed when Cole pulled into the garage of the house, shutting the electric door behind them.

A few minutes later, he'd helped Erin out of the car and placed the baby in her arms. He let her go ahead, and she slowly made her way upstairs. Although the baby had her own room, they'd agreed to keep her in their bedroom, at least for a little while.

They settled her into the bassinet and Erin

eased herself onto the bed.

Cole joined her, stretching out beside her. "Your parents wanted to be here when you came home, but I talked them into waiting until this afternoon."

Erin grinned. "Good thinking." It would have been too much to have people here waiting for her, even if it was her mom and dad.

Ella and Simon had been at the hospital, so they hadn't been deprived of time with their granddaughter.

"I wanted my girls all to myself for a little while." His eyes were alight with joy, and Erin hoped she'd never again see the bleakness that had been there nine months ago.

"Say that again," she said, staring into his handsome face.

"What?"

"My girls." Erin would never get tired of hearing him refer to them that way.

"You are my girls. You were mine since the day I laid eyes on you at Joe's. I was just too stubborn to admit it."

She smiled. He was that. "I'm just glad we were able to pull off the wedding before she was born."

"I still wish you'd had a big wedding with all the trimmings. You deserve that."

Erin shook her head. "I deserve you."

They'd had a small wedding at the house on December 15, with Erin's family. Cole's mother and Brody had come — and to everyone's surprise, so had Jed, who had been on his best behavior. He hadn't stayed long, but he'd witnessed the ceremony, and they took what they could get from him.

"My dad gave me away and I walked down the aisle to you. The rest would have been icing." She loved that expression of his. "And you give me enough of that every day." She cupped his cheek in her hand. "I love you," she said, her voice catching. She shook her head. "Sorry. I'm still overly emotional."

He clasped her hand in his. "You think I'm not? Never, not once in my life, did I think I'd have . . . this." He swept his arm around for emphasis. "I didn't think I deserved it."

That truth never failed to upset and anger her. "You were so wrong."

"It's in the past." He brushed a kiss over her lips.

"Not far enough if you can still remember it," she muttered.

He grinned. "Did I ever tell you I love how protective you get of me?"

"You might have mentioned it once or twice." Each time she'd put Jed in his place, she thought, and it had been more than just once or twice.

"He's trying and you know it. What's that expression? You can't teach an old dog new tricks? But he's getting better. He catches his own slips now."

She frowned. She thought Cole was too forgiving of Jed's personality, but she supposed he had a point. The older man had stepped up, making an effort to be more of a father and to get rid of his bad attitude, but sometimes things *slipped.* That's when she couldn't help but step in and call him on his behavior.

Cole ran his fingers through her hair. She'd been letting it grow, and he liked to wrap the longer strands in his hand. "Jed's coming over with your folks later too."

"So are Mike and Cara, and Sam."

Cole met her gaze. "Umm, Nick and Kate asked if they could stop by too."

Erin burst out laughing. "For a man who didn't like to be surrounded by people, you sure have done a one-eighty."

"I do love our families, but I'd much rather be alone with you. Don't worry, I'll kick them out in due time."

She grinned. "I'll hold you to that."

A small squeaking noise sounded from the bassinet, and Cole shot to a sitting position before Erin could manage to roll over. *She is going to be one spoiled little girl,* Erin thought, smiling.

"Is my Angel hungry?" he asked, his face and voice softening when he talked to his tiny daughter.

The squeaks turned into a full-fledged wail. "I think she wants you," he said, laughing, as Erin unbuttoned her blouse.

He handed her to Erin. "Her name fits, you know." They'd named her Angela, but already Cole had taken to calling her Angel, and Erin knew the nickname would stick.

He nodded. "She's my Angel, just like you are."

Erin smiled up at him. "And that makes us both very lucky girls." Lucky in life, lucky in love.

Like Cole, she never dared to dream she could be this happy, or thought she deserved so much, but she'd do everything she could to appreciate her good fortune — and remind Cole every day of all the reasons he was worthy of it all too.

ABOUT THE AUTHOR

New York Times bestselling author **Carly Phillips** tossed away her legal briefs and a career as an attorney to become a stay-at-home mom. Within the year, she turned her love of reading into an obsession with writing. More than thirty published novels later, Carly writes sexy contemporary small-town romances, striking a balance between entertainment and emotion, and giving her readers the compelling stories they have come to expect and enjoy. She lives in Purchase, New York, with her husband, two daughters, and their dogs: Bailey, a soft-coated wheaten terrier, and Brady, a Havanese, who act like additional children. Visit the author at www.carlyphillips.com. Or catch up with her at facebook.com/CarlyPhillipsfanpage or twitter.com/CarlyPhillips.